Bad Intentions

NANNETTE SANDY

BAD INTENTIONS

Nannette Sandy

ISBN (Print Edition): 979-8-35097-711-0

ISBN (eBook Edition): 979-8-35097-712-7

© 2024. All rights reserved. No part of this publication may be reproduced, distributed, or transmitted in any form or by any means, including photocopying, recording, or other electronic or mechanical methods, without the prior written permission of the publisher, except in the case of brief quotations embodied in critical reviews and certain other noncommercial uses permitted by copyright law.

CONTENTS

CHAPTER 1. *Who I Was* — 1

CHAPTER 2. *The Plan* — 16

CHAPTER 3. *Deebo's Fate* — 29

CHAPTER 4. *Revenge for Deebo* — 38

CHAPTER 5. *Living Life* — 53

CHAPTER 6. *Helping Others* — 74

CHAPTER 7. *New Problems* — 88

CHAPTER 8. *Exposed* — 106

CHAPTER 9. *Free* — 120

CHAPTER 10. *Murder She Committed* — 142

CHAPTER 11. *To Catch a Killer* — 162

CHAPTER 12. *Make a Choice* — 182

CHAPTER 13. *Liar, Liar* — 201

CHAPTER 14. *Catch Me If You Can* — 221

CHAPTER 1.
WHO I WAS

I was in a deep, sleep or at least I thought I was, until I heard loud yelling and screaming outside my room door. I closed my eyes, but the sounds became louder and louder. I tossed and turned but eventually got out of bed to see what the commotion was. I put on my fluffy slippers and slightly opened my door. The crowded scene was like watching a fight on pay-per-view. People were chanting all kinds of nasty things. I could not see clearly. I rubbed my eyes to confirm that I was not dreaming. When my eyes cleared, I could see bodies wrapped around one another. One of the girls grabbed the other girl by her hair and dragged her to a metal chest that was up against the wall. The crowd thickened and my heart thumped watching everyone just stand looking at these girls trying to kill themselves. One of the girls' heads had blood coming out of it. She was used as a punching bag. Then her body dropped. The other girl started kicking her while she was on the floor. I looked around and saw faces with scary grins and fingers like swords. I wanted to help the poor girl who was bleeding. Her body lay lifeless on the floor.

"Can we get some help here? This girl is dead," I yelled. Then there was this sick silence that filled the room. The energy flipped on me. I began to walk backward slowly.

"You need to mind your business, bitch."

To whom was she talking? I do not know this girl; she is looking in my direction. I trembled.

"Yes, you. Do you want me to kick your ass now?"

I became the center of attention and realized she was talking to me. I turned around and started to walk back to my room. When I got to my door, something hard hit my head. I fell. I closed my eyes. I lay there on the floor for a few seconds. My ears rang from the yelling and screaming. The heavy breath of people swarm over me. I got up slowly and opened my eyes. A blurry figure came into view. It looked like a colorful cloud. Then extended arms pointed in my direction.

The next thing I know someone pulls me up. Did someone help me? I was not sure. Then my eyes see the mean girl.

"Now what? Are you going to fight?" She was a bully. I had never seen her before, but it was nothing new. These are the things you see and go through when living in a shelter for runaways and homeless teens.

"If you hit me one more time, I promise you I will kill you," I grunt.

All eyes were on me when I made that statement. Something came over me, and it was the fact that I had some warm substance running down my forehead. I knew I had to do something to let the fire go out. They say if you act tough, the message will get across that you are serious. The girl bumped into me and walked off. I sighed. I was relieved that I was going to live another day.

"You should go to the nurse. Your head is bleeding."

I touched my head and felt the watery substance. "Ouch! Is she crazy or something?" I grabbed the bottom of my shirt to wipe my face. This girl started talking to me.

"She is the new bully on this floor."

"When did you get here?" This brunette was tall and slim. She was pretty in an intellectual way.

"I moved in like a month ago."

"Well, my name is Kelly." Her hand extended.

"Nice to meet you. I am Kayla."

She gave me a look like she wanted to know what my nationality was. It is the look that all biracial kids get.

"Nice."

"I like your curly black hair. You must meet our crew—Deebo, Danny, and Faye. Do you want to go somewhere with me tomorrow?"

My head felt like resistant bands were on it. The movements were like drums. Kelly was demanding a first meet and greet. I started to walk in the hallway to the nurse's office. One was coming my way.

"Come with me. I will see to that wound."

Kelly got in front of the nurse's way.

"Hey, nice meeting you. I will knock on your door around ten." She pointed.

"What? Okay."

I just met this chick and already she has forced me to have a play date. I followed the nurse. The next morning, I was uncomfortable. My surroundings were unfamiliar. I was in bed. I do not remember who put me there. I raised my head. I immediately put it back down. My head rocked like it was dancing to music.

"You had an unbelievably bad wound. Why were you fighting? Fighting is not tolerated here, and you could get kicked out," said the nurse.

The throbbing continued. What is she talking about? I got attacked for no reason by this maniac girl that I do not even know. I did not start this mess.

"You must stay here another night to make sure that you do not have a concussion. I will be back to check on you in an hour. Stay out of trouble." She rests a tray down by my bedside.

"I did not start the fight." I raised my head. The nurse replaced my IV and walked out. She ignored me and my side of the story. Smoke came out of my nose.

Who does she think she is? Assuming that I am the troublemaker. I just got here. I was alone in the room. I was talking to myself. It would not be the first time.

The next morning, I woke up with Kelly's face close to mine. "Hi, I'm here to pick you up," she said with a happy breath.

"Um, I don't think I can go right now." I am in the nurse's station for a reason, I thought to myself.

"Are you in pain?" I felt fine.

"No, but I think I have to stay in bed."

She picked up my slippers and placed them in front of the area where I stepped down.

"If you are feeling fine, you can come with me. We must visit my friend Faye. She was the one who got beat up yesterday." *That is her friend—why do I have to go visit her?* I thought. I wanted to ask more questions about the brawl, but I did not want a full conversation with her. I did what I was told. I followed Kelly.

We walked in the hallway, and I saw one guy sitting on the floor in his room. His sheets were pressed and creased. It looked like housekeepers made it.

"His room is the best one in the whole building," she said with her hand out like she was Vanna White on the wheels. Some of them looked like weird people waiting for the nurse to drug them. I had to tell myself that I would get out of here soon.

Kelly walked into a room. A girl was lying down on her bed. Her blonde hair was dirty, and she had blue eyes surrounded by black and blue rings. I was guessing she got those from the fight. Her walls were pink, and she had posters of different musical artists on her wall. Two bookcases leaned against each corner of her room that looked like a small library. I dug it. I walked over to the case and pulled out a book.

"Do you like to read?" she asked.

"Not really. I like your setup here." My fingers brushed the books.

"Yeah, I think I have a little more decorating to do before I am completely satisfied."

These people are weird. This is not my home. I am not decorating anything. I am getting out of here as soon as I can. I glanced at the room.

"So now that you met Kayla, we will see you around dinner time. I am taking her to meet Danny and Deebo." The Faye girl waves. Kelly walks out of the room, and I follow her like I am under her spell. We walked to the elevator, and she pressed the number two. She walked out. She walked into the first room that was on the right.

"This is Kayla."

No regards. She did not care if they were busy doing something. She just barged into their rooms.

"This is Danny."

He was my height, with dark hair. A few ink marks on his arm. He reminded me of Dezi Arnaz. A younger version of him, of course.

"Hola senora," I smirked.

Then she sighed. "This hottie is Deebo." She displayed him like a piece of art. His back was facing us. He was not interested in meeting me. I had enough anyway. I turned to the doorway, to leave.

"Hey, what is up?"

I turned back around. My eyes widened. I saw muscles. Lots of it. He looked like a model. His skin is caramel with curly black hair and hazel eyes. His body blinded me. His carved art was everywhere. *He is hot*, I thought to myself. My body shivered.

"You don't speak." I closed my eyes and opened them back up.

"What is up?" I clenched my teeth. Why did I repeat the question?

"Yes, he has that effect on girls." I sounded like a dork when I responded to him. I walked out of the boy's room. "We will see you for dinner," she yelled out.

I kept walking. I got back to my room. I kicked my door to close it. I jumped on my bed. I watched the ceiling as if it were going to calm my heart down. I thought of this Deebo guy. My eyes created images of us together. He was here in my room on my bed. We were kissing. He tore into my body. He entered me and I moaned. I went to another world. The best vision I had in weeks. My fingers are warm and squishy. I opened my eyes. I am pathetic. I rubbed my hands on my sheets. He looks like a player anyway.

It must have been dinnertime because animals raced to the cowbell. That is what it sounded like when I opened my door. My nose got a whiff of chicken and mashed potatoes. I followed the scent. I walked into the cafeteria. I glanced at the food table. Three ladies stood behind the table. Each one held huge serving spoons like they were going into battle. I walked over to them and picked up my tray.

"Hey Kayla, we're over here."

Who knows my name? Great. She saw me. I should have known. I turned around to see. The girl who got beat up waved her hand. I smirked and walked to her.

"Hi. How are you feeling?" I asked.

"Oh, we fight all the time. It is the way of life here. How is your head?

"I am fine, thanks." I twirled my fork in the mashed potatoes. The noise got intense. "Is it always noisy in here?"

Faye was putting chicken inside her mouth. "Dinnertime is when we let it all out. You will get used to it." I put the water bottle in my mouth.

"I am getting out of here. I do not want to get used to anything; this is a freaking shelter," I mumbled.

"Faye thinks we should be on our best behavior to stay on the list. I agree with you. We must get out of here. We must find out how," Kelly says.

I pushed my tray away from me. Then Deebo reached in and stabbed my chicken. "Since you don't want it." I looked at him.

"I did not give you permission to take my food," I commented.

He started eating like he did not get fed daily. "He works out every day. I wish I had his appetite. When are you leaving?" Kelly asked.

"I do not know—as soon as I can. I am looking for work. I want to get my own place."

She slammed her fork down. "It is settled. We will look for work and get our place. We will live together."

I turned my head. I never said that. I do not know them very well. I just met them. *Why would they want to live with me anyway?* I thought. I did not belong here. I used to be rich. I had everything. I still remember what happened and how I got here. While I was still living at home, I had a friend come over one day to hang out. We watched movies and ate junk food in my room. Weeks after she left, I found some pills in one of my drawers. I could not remember who it belonged to at the time. A few days later I remembered my friend Asia was the last person in my room. She used to do drugs from time to time at school. I figured one day she would come back to pick them up.

Our housekeeper found the pills while she was cleaning. I thought I hid them. She thought they belonged to me, and somehow it got back to my parents. When I explained to them that the drugs were not mine, my parents freaked out. They felt I was dishonest. I got up the next morning and saw my things at the front door with a few boxes. I remember carrying all my things, looking homeless. Can you believe that? Who kicks their girl child to the streets without giving her money? At least they could have left me money to book a room at the Ritz.

It was rough. I can still see myself on the couch of a different friend's house, week after week. I never had a good sleep at someone else's house. I would sneak into the kitchen and look for food in the pantry, prying my fingers for candy, like a squirrel. I would look at pictures on my phone hoping my parents would call me. I used to sit near the window imagining that they sent a car for me. I was depressed. I was glad that it was me and not my younger sister.

My sister loves her life. Genoveve is a teen who has whatever she wants. I miss washing her hair and putting curls in it. Now that I am not at home, I know she needs me more than ever, especially since she is always home alone. I was not aware that it would have taken me a year to get to my place and leave the shelter. I did everything I could to look for a job, but I was not getting any callbacks.

My luck struck one day when I was going to the store for one of the counselors at the shelter and I bumped into this old lady. She was carrying groceries, and all her tomatoes and onions fell out of the bag. I helped her pick them up and carried them to her house. She thanked me with a warm smile. She told me her name was Tilda. She asked me a lot of questions about my life and where I lived. I guessed that she did not like my current situation, so she offered me a place to stay.

My friends Deebo, Danny, Kelly, and Faye live with me now at Miss Tilda's house. I did not want them to live with me in the beginning. We had each other's back when we got into fights at the shelter. Miss Tilda was kind enough to allow us to live in the basement of her house. I would have never thought that I would be living in such a small space. I had my room, but the others shared rooms. I was the only one that had a bathroom in mine.

We made the best of it. Even when we lived in a shelter, we attended school like normal teens. We went to Forney High in Forney, Texas. Not a lot happens here, and I had never seen the crew until I ran into them one day at school.

After school, we worked at a nightclub job that Miss Tilda got for us. I remember my first day when she took me to meet the bartender. We walked inside, and this man was wiping down the counter. He was not impressed with my presence. I watched him go to a room in the back and then come back to the front. I looked back at Miss Tilda, and she glanced at a chair.

"Do you want me to sit down or something?" I asked. What was going on? The strange man seemed like he wanted me to pay attention. "Umm, sir, I don't think I can work in the bar area due to my age."

He started mixing drinks. I looked at them both. I was only seventeen, and this had to be against the law for me to be inside the joint.

"What do you want me to do here?" I asked.

"Sweetheart, just follow. You will not be working the bar, but this is just in case we need you to."

"What? Miss Tilda, do you own this bar?"

"Now that is none of your business. We are all done here now, thank you," she said, waving to the strange man as she got up and walked toward the back door. I followed her like a lost puppy. On the way back home from the cocktail audition, Ms. Tilda did not speak a word. I kept my mouth shut. I slouched in the seat. I did not want to say the wrong thing, thinking that Miss Tilda was an old lady gangster or something.

"You need a job, and you will have to pay my rent every month, and the only way you can do that is to work at the club," she added.

"I am thankful for the gig, but I may be just too young to be working with alcohol." I played with my fingers.

"You and your friends will start tomorrow. When you get there, a gentleman will be waiting for you." That is when I knew that there was more to Ms. Tilda than meets the eye.

We still work our butts off during the weekends and after school at the nightclub. All the Forney High kids go for a night of fun. The building is old-looking, with a lighted star right above the door—the infamous star you always see in Texas. There is a front entrance and a back entry that no one knows about unless you work there.

The scene is always the same. Bright purple lights and teens everywhere with vapes and alcohol in their hands. How they sneak it in is surprising to me, but they do it and get away with it. Deebo was always the one that had girls lining up to speak with him. Danny was always with a girl in his arms no matter what. Me and the girls would just look for the cute guys to come through. We were single and the most boring girls you would ever want to meet. Every day was a freak show like the one we had last night.

I noticed a small crowd hovering over near the back area of the club. I got up and walked over to the small crowd. I could hear people gasping and whispering. I separated a few bodies with my hands to get inside the huddle. A young girl had overdosed right there on the floor. Her mouth oozed with foam, and her body freakishly spasmed. Her eyes rolled back up in her head. I quickly went into action.

"Call 911 now!" Everybody moves back. "Give us some air, please!" I yelled.

My eyes popped out of my head. I could not believe how people just stood there taking pictures of this poor young girl rather than trying to help her. The paramedics quickly made their way through the crowd, and they picked up the girl to put her on a stretcher. I watched them take her outside and put her in the van. I had enough at that moment and realized I needed to leave this disgusting place.

When we got home from work, I could not get the images out of my head from the events that happened. The apartment reminded me that we needed a bigger place. The beer cans and Cheetos all over the floor looked like they were a part of the carpet design. I got tired of looking at the mess. I kick the cans.

"You guys need to clean this shit up," I yelled. It was like I was talking to myself.

Everyone got up and left me in the living room. Deebo was the only one who stayed. He picked up the garbage bag and threw the cans in there. I went straight to my room and slammed the door shut.

I heard a knock right after. "What is up with you tonight?" Deebo's voice was on the other side of my door. I closed my eyes and then opened them back up. I walked over to my door and turned the doorknob.

"This whole scene is getting boring for me. We need a change," I mumbled.

He took off his shoes like he was in his room. I squinched.

"What kind of change are you talking about?" he asked.

"I don't know. This is not the life I dreamt about," I said.

"I thought you were happy that we all got together." He displayed a frown.

"Yes, I am happy that we are together, but something is missing," I continued.

I opened the drawer to get a T-shirt. I slowly walked into my bathroom. Deebo walks up behind me and takes my shirt from my hands.

"Let me help you with that," he says softly.

"Help me with what? I think I can dress myself."

He laughs and pushes me to the wall. I felt a soft blow on my neck.

"I can make you forget about tonight if you allow me to," he whispered.

His cologne was like an IV running through my veins. I pulled him close to me. He picked me up like a sack of potatoes and put me down on the bed. I unzipped his pants, and he helped me to take them off by sliding them down. He tossed my panties off the bed. I was not sure if I was going to stop this movie or let it continue to play.

He stared at me. I covered my breasts with my hands. He placed his body on top of mine. He did not say anything. He caressed my face. I inhaled and exhaled. I was praying he would kiss me to end the silence between us.

He finally kissed me. He caressed my body. He reached down to his pants that were on the floor. He pulled out a plastic object. I knew that Deebo was a pro because he had so many girls and he changed them like he changed his clothes. I was not mad at him for that because I was not sure what I wanted from him. I was not ready to be in a relationship, but I knew that I had feelings for him.

That night we became one. The crew was always nosey when Deebo was in my room, especially when he was in there the whole night. My heart fluttered.

"Are you okay?" he whispered.

I was still in shock that we were together in my room, naked.

"Yes, I am okay. Are you okay?"

"Hell, yes, I am in bed with you. This was what I always wanted," he confessed.

"I hope that I'm not one of those games that you just won now that you got what you wanted," I added.

"You are the one I always wanted, but every time I tried to make a move, you would always push me away." I did push him away. I did not trust him.

The next morning, I rolled over to look at Deebo. I caressed the space. I remained in bed, looked up at my ceiling, and reminisced about what occurred last night between us. I giggled. I was happy with my decision to have finally given him some. What does this mean? Are we together now or is this just a quick smash between friends? I did not know if this was what I wanted. I heard a knock on the door. I smiled ear to ear.

"Come in," I said with a melody.

"Damn, girl, you finally gave him some, huh?" Faye walks in with all her teeth showing. I quickly wiped the smirk off my face.

"Oh, wait you thought I was him. He must have put it on you. It was bound to happen. You two have been sweating each other since the shelter days."

"Is there something you need, Faye?" I grabbed the T-shirt that was on my bed and pulled it over my head.

"Okay, Miss, I was just checking on you, but I will leave you be. I guess I will see you at the club later tonight. Bye," Faye yelled out. She walked out of my room with a little dance.

I came out of my room to get breakfast. Everyone was in the living room. Danny stared at me.

"What's wrong, Danny?" I felt his piercing eyes. "Okay, spill it, how can I help you today?" I asked while I poured orange juice into my cup.

"I am trying to figure out how long we are going to live in this stupid place doing the same thing day after day." I turn around. I put my drink down.

"Do what every day?" I asked with my hands up.

"Not making real money and watching people that have it. Come on, you know what I am talking about. Oh, wait you do not have to worry about money because you have it already." I squinched my eyes at him.

"Are you freaking kidding me? If I do, please get it for me, because I have been busting my ass off at that stupid club night after night." Danny looks at me.

"Go ahead, say it. Why don't I ask my parents for money, right? So, we can get a mansion and chill out forever, right?" I picked up my glass and slammed it into the kitchen sink. I walked back to face him. I leaned in close to his face.

"Let me tell you something; get this in your head. I am not going to ask my parents for money, okay? Did you forget that they did not even care if I rotted out in the street? They kicked me out without any warning or anything. What kind of parents is that?"

Everybody looks around as if they can figure out how to solve the issues for Danny. Kelly looks over at Danny.

"We can rob a bank," Faye yells.

I was walking away but then turned back around to face Faye.

"What are you talking about?" My eyes stared at her.

"That is what I am talking about. I love the idea. Robbing a bank. Sounds so cool," Danny says softly while he sips on orange juice.

"We are not robbing a bank." I sat down on the couch with my feet up on the coffee table.

"Kayla is right. We cannot and we will not. Plus, we do not know the first thing about robbing a bank," Kelly joins in.

"I think we can do it," Danny says, standing up.

"I think we can do it," Faye adds.

"Yes, why not? Sure, let's do it. When you do, let me know so that I can spend the money," I responded. "I like that idea a lot. I mean we need to have a meeting after work to discuss the specifics. Hands up if you are in."

Danny raises his hand. Faye and Kelly put their hands up and there is a knock at the door.

"Wait a minute. You are down with this, Kelly? You are supposed to be the sane one out of this group." I pointed.

Kelly smirks and answers the door. It is my little sister Genoveve. She walks in and raises her hands.

"I'm down with whatever you're talking about."

"Are you sure?" Danny laughs.

CHAPTER 2.
THE PLAN

It is 4:00 a.m. and we just clocked out of work. Danny makes hand gestures for us to follow him. Faye, Kelly, and I walk over to the table near him. Deebo struts on after.

"What is this about?" I put my apron down on the table. Danny glances over at Kelly. She steps in like a TV host.

"I am speaking for all of us when I say we will be proceeding with what we talked about last night. We would like to step things up a little, and cash is the way to do so. Danny here is going to tell us how we can do this."

Kelly presents like a television host. Danny steps up like he is speaking in front of a large crowd.

"We can get a lot of cash—and I mean a lot of cash—from First C bank." He puts a corkboard with a white poster paper thumb-tacked in front of us. He draws an object. I started to laugh.

"I have a friend that can help us with all the specific details about this bank," Danny explains.

"Okay, so we are going to walk in there and they are going to give us the combination to the vault? Ha," I chuckled.

"Funny, ha, my boy is the guard for the vault room," he says confidently. My eyes light up. I was not interested in this activity, but I was curious to see how serious they were.

"I know how we can get automatic weapons for the job. My boy owes me a favor, and this sounds to me like the favor we need," Deebo chimes in.

"Wow, you think you can pull this off?" I asked, looking at them. "Okay, then you need to do a couple of things first."

"Okay, we are listening." Kelly puts her hand on the board to write.

"All right, get the layout from your friend the guard, and Faye, we need masks, and a getaway vehicle." I called out to Danny with my hands. "We're going to need some more information.

"Yeah, I got you whatever you need."

"Have your guy send you the layout of the bank—we need to see the exits, employee schedule for the day, managers' security codes, etc., and guards we're going to be dealing with."

"My idea is not so dumb anymore." His eyebrows raise.

"*Being smart* keeps us out of trouble, and here we are trying to get into some. It is a dumb idea."

"If we have a plan, we can pull this thing off, but we have to have everybody on deck." He storms out of the room.

I look at the poster board and touch it. *They want some action? Let's have some action*, I said to myself. I knew that we were going to get into something serious. I will have to be the one to get us out of it.

The next day it is early Monday morning in Forney, around 9:00 a.m. The sun is not out yet, but the sky is blue. The First Convenience Bank opens at 10:00 a.m. I got up to shower. I hoped that the crew would change their minds about robbing a bank.

When I got out of the shower, I heard the doorbell ring. I walked to my door and opened it just enough to peek. Deebo races behind me.

"Did you go to the bank on Friday?" Deebo asks his friend, who walks in like he lives here.

"Yo, Tommy, I'm talking to you, man, this is serious." Deebo pulls his arm.

"Yeah man, relax, I did. I cased the joint up and down. It's cool; we can be in and out if we pay attention to the exits that I outlined," he says as he sits down in the living room.

I put my shirt and jeans on quickly. I immediately walked into Deebo's room. Tommy faces me with sultry eyes.

"Dang, she is fine. Hey, little lady, how are you?" I stare the new guy up and down.

"Who is this?" My thumb points to this guy. "I do not remember us discussing bringing on another person on the job."

"Look, we need more than what we got—that's why I brought him," Deebo responds. Faye and Kelly rush into the room.

"We have to go to the bank right now," says Faye.

"I do not like the idea that we are bringing in someone we do not know. Okay, you asked for it. When we get pinched, get ready for my 'told you so' speech." I stormed out.

Moments later, we arrived at the bank. Kelly walks into the bank like a customer. She walks up to the teller. Faye, Deebo, and I enter the bank with masks on. Only a few customers were standing in line. Two employees behind the counter. One guard is at the front door, and one is inside the vault room.

"Everybody on the floor now. Push your bags and purses away from you." I became a different person. I was in control.

The customers lay on the floor and followed my command. The front guard pulls out his gun. Kelly bawls out a scream to play her part. The guard goes to her on the floor to calm her down. She puts her gun in front of the guard's head and motions him to lie back down as she gently removes his gun from his hands.

Deebo and Danny go to the back, and Faye and Kelly take care of the front entrance. A few minutes later, Deebo and Danny come running out. They stumble with stuffed bags, and Faye and Kelly rush to the front door like maniacs. Kelly takes the guard's gun and goes into the vault room. Danny's friend is hitting his face with his gun. He took his role a little too far. I took out a hammer from our carry-on bags and smashed all the computers. I even shot at the cameras that were in the ceilings. That one I got from a movie. I was proud of myself for that one.

After the bags were filled with the money, Danny and Deebo ran out of the bank. The employees did not have the time to activate the alarms. Our escape time was brilliant. We jumped into the getaway car that was waiting for us outside. Deebo's friend Tommy floored the pedal like he was driving a racecar. I screamed. They screamed. We just got away with our first bank robbery.

"I cannot believe we did it. Robbing this bank was like taking candy from a baby. When are we doing the next one?" Danny asks, breathing hard.

"We are not robbing another bank." I took the gloves and masks off. I stared at Danny with one eyebrow raised.

We walked away with around twenty thousand each. When we got home, I went straight to my bedroom. I closed my door. I threw the bag with the money on the floor. My head was all over the place. I used to spend that amount of money on a weekend shopping spree. I was not impressed by what we did. Someone could have gotten killed. A few minutes later, there was a knock at my door. I jumped up.

"Who is it?"

"It's me, your sister Genoveve."

"Come on in. How did you get here? Did Mom drop you off?"

She walked right into my room. She touched the bag.

"Get away from that bag right now," I ordered her.

She opened the bag.

"Did you hear me?!"

Her eyes widened. "Did Mom give in and send you your allowance?" She sticks her hand in.

"What do you think you are doing? Put the money back into my bag and leave it alone."

"Sheesh, sorry," she cried.

I snatched it from her and threw it in my closet.

"How did you get here?" I asked for the second time.

"Mom dropped me off. She had to go to some meeting, and Dad was nowhere to be found."

"I am not surprised at all. I remember living that life," I said.

"You do?" she asked. "When are you coming back home?"

I bit my lip. The veins throbbed in my temples.

"Do you think I just picked up and left for no reason?" I turned to my little sister to see her face.

"I do not know why you left. Mom and Dad never told me why."

Her face drooped. I realized they did not tell her the truth. I got close to her and put my arms around her.

"It was not my idea to leave you. I am taking care of myself. I want you to do the same."

She looked up at me. "Mom said she will pick me up later. Tell me what you got to eat. I'm hungry." She walked out of my room. I followed her to the kitchen. A few moments later, there was another knock at the door.

I swear, someone is always on the other end of that door, I thought.

"Miss Tilda! Oh, my goodness, I did not get a chance to get your groceries. I am so sorry."

"Oh no, that is all right, dear. I have all the food I need. I just wanted to make sure you were okay, because I have not seen you in a while."

"Yes, I know, Ms. Tilda. I have been terribly busy working and doing other stuff," I said kindly.

"Are they overworking you over at that club? Because you know, I can make a call."

"Oh no, my hours are fine. I do have a question though."

"What's that dear? What is your question?"

"You never told me your connection with the club." Ms. Tilda glides her hands on my furniture. She rubs her two fingers together.

"You know, dear, you may need a housekeeper or something. This place needs a little cleaning." My sister Genoveve chuckles.

"Yuck, your house is dirty."

"Shut up, Genoveve, and get your food," I ordered.

"Fine, I was just joking around. Forgive me. I'm going to my room, thank you very much."

It was a small room that Ms. Tilda used to do her sewing, but she just made it into a storage room. When I moved into the basement, I saw the room and asked Ms. Tilda if my little sister could have that room when she came to visit.

"In due time, sweetheart, there will be a time when I will tell you everything there is to know about me. But for now, I got to water my plants before they die on me like my last one."

"I'm sorry, Ms. Tilda, I forgot to water your plants last week. Please forgive me."

"Yes, dear, I know you have been busy; say hi to the rest of your friends for me." She walks out the door and Faye and Kelly stumble in looking like two high junkies.

"You ladies look like you need some assistance," said Ms. Tilda. Kelly and Faye wobbled.

"What the hell is wrong with you two?" I asked.

"Girl, we are feeling great right now. Yeah, Danny had some treats in his room. Do you want some? He has a whole bunch of these brownies," says Faye.

"No, I'm good, thank you, and keep the noise down." I clenched my teeth. Getting high, especially right in front of Ms. Tilda, was not something I wanted her to see. I had to remind myself that I am not a parent.

After the robbery, I begged my friends not to buy anything that would attract attention. If you watch enough crime shows, the one thing you learn is to never draw attention to yourself after you have committed a crime. If you do commit another crime, it needs to be something entirely different from the last one. So, after a few weeks, I got everybody together at the club after work to discuss the new gig.

I know I bit the crime bug. I walked to the back area of the club. I could see they were already sitting at the table in the back waiting for me to come. I wanted to treat this meeting like a professional. I wore a three-piece suit and carried a suitcase. My friends looked at me like I was some important person getting ready to save their life or something. I approached the table, put the briefcase down, turned my back on them, and was facing the poster board still up from the last meeting. Then I turned around with my hands in my pocket. I blind my friends with my lime-green plaid suit with a satin green collared shirt. Deebo looked around to see if anyone was concerned with my color choice.

"So, we have a very important event to go to tomorrow evening, and I want to make sure that you guys are ready to make some more money." I pace back and forth as speakers do.

"Remember, I'm the one that started all of this," Danny stands up and shouts.

"Yes, I know, and I have something else planned for us."

"Well, I'm down, what are we doing and what's the dress code?" Faye asks.

"Glad you asked that, because there will be a dress code."

"All right with the suspense! We are dying to know where we are going tomorrow," Faye demands.

"We will be working at a charity event tomorrow, where we will be dressed up in uniform." I brightened up like I was saving the world or something.

"What charity event? Please tell me what money we will get from an event like that, because it sounds whack," Danny proclaimed.

"Well, to answer your question, Danny, I will be training you on how to use the app to assist our rich folks." I was talking to them like I was a pro in the world of crime.

"You still have not answered my question."

"Yes, Danny, we will be working at an art charity event. My mom used to force me to go to these boring events where rich people paid ridiculous amounts of money to buy ugly artwork and paintings. I used to work these events, thanks to my mom, who would offer my time to these people without my consent," I added.

"Okay, how ridiculous are we talking here?" asked Faye.

"Like a hundred thousand a piece."

They grinned.

"Okay, so how does this work? Because I am dying to know how these rich people are going to allow us to take their money." Kelly raised her hand like she was in class.

"It is simple and easy. My mom knew the lady who hosted the event. They worked on a few charity events together. They do this every year, like this big party where people get fancy and spend their money to support all kinds of causes. Now I must show you how to work the app so you can help these people make an offer for a picture on these iPads." I pull out an iPad from my briefcase.

"Wait a minute, they give us iPads too?" Faye asks.

I started laughing. I knew I got their attention. "Yes, they are giving us iPads, but it is not ours to keep. We each get one to help potential buyers."

"Hell, no, I am taking these bad boys. You know how much I can get for these?" Danny holds his iPad up.

"No, you cannot take these, you idiot. We use them to work at the event." I shook my head with a smirk. "Now here is a video I want you to look at. It is thirty minutes long, and it will explain the company, what they do, and what we must do when we arrive at work tomorrow."

Kelly gets up and walks up to me. "You are a smart one, and I am looking forward to this workday. Do we get to eat dinner after the auction?" she asks.

"Yes, we do. I forgot to mention that we get to eat a meal from one of the finest chefs in Dallas. We cannot eat until after all the artwork is purchased. So, are we good guys and ready for our next exciting job opportunity?" I look at them. I handed out an iPad to everybody except Danny.

"Hey, where's mine?"

"I got another job for you at the event. You are going to be our lookout guy. We need a pair of eyes and ears to keep a look around the place to make sure nobody knows what we are up to." I put my arm around his neck.

It is three in the afternoon the next day. We arrive in our uniforms for the job. The event was in an upscale luxurious hotel in Dallas. The shiny gold posts held the place up, and paintings on easels were all around. There were waiters in black and white, with white gloves, and people in their expensive clothing, diamonds, and pearls. I looked for the host of the evening, and my friends were at their post waiting for the event to start.

"I am so glad you can help us out, Kayla. This is like old times when you were thirteen," said Ms. Kemp. She was the organizer of the charity event and she collaborated with my mom on a lot of other projects. "Your mother did not even tell me you were coming."

I was hesitant to respond, and I did not know how to answer since I had not been in communication with my parents for over a year now.

"Well, yeah, I did not tell my mom about me helping out; she's just used to me doing the work without bragging about it," I responded.

"Oh yes, I know how your mom can be. Is she still running around with her businesses?"

"You know her. She only has one thing in mind." I displayed a fake frown. There is no need to let everybody know my business. People started gathering in groups and I glanced to see if my friends were in place.

"I am happy to help anytime. We are all glad to be here."

Ms. Kemp looks around the ballroom. As the people continue to come into the fancy shindig, Ms. Kemp stops talking with me. She walks over to greet her guests. I walk over to Kelly, Faye, and Deebo and signal to them with my hands. Deebo was at a table full of beautiful older women. I just turned my head. Faye was beautiful in her white-collar shirt and khaki pants. She put her dirty blonde hair up in a bun. Her blue eyes were accented with blue eye shadow. I was not a fan of eye shadow. Kelly looked more professional. She had on a white shirt and khaki pants, with her brunette hair in a low ponytail. She wore eyeglasses that made her look like a smart person.

Then Ms. Kemp walks up to the front of the ballroom, stands behind a clear podium, and bends down the mic. She is in an all-white skirt suit and wearing extremely high heels. She looked like a human diamond with earrings as big as ice cubes, and her bracelet and heels were made of diamonds.

"Welcome to our annual Artsy Galleria for all the nonprofit organizations we support. You have been there for our children and supported our underprivileged communities with your generous donations and are here to do it again this year. Last year we raised five hundred thousand dollars, and this year we want to double it. We have incredibly talented artists. A lot of these paintings are in museums, and a few of them are hanging at the White House."

People nod their heads, smiling. I glanced at my friends. Kelly had her hands in one of the waiter's trays picking out grapes and cheese cubes. I waved my hand to signal not to do that.

"You will enjoy the fantastic dinner, finger food, and amazing desserts that are specially prepared for you by our well-known, highly requested great Chef Dior," she added. The waiters come around to the tables with gold water pitchers. One was carrying bread. The smoke from the pan of soft bread watered my mouth.

"When you see a piece you like, raise your hand and one of our associates will come to you with an iPad, where you will input your selection and payment information and hand it back to them," she explained.

An hour later the staff came out handing out plates with steak, lamb, and lobster. At that time, all the paintings were purchased by the buyers and ready for shipment. I signaled to the crew to start collecting the iPad from every attendee. At the end of the auction event, people rushed out of there like they were late for the train. The host walked up to us at a table.

"Thank you so much for your help today and for bringing your friends along with you," said Ms. Kemp.

"Oh no problem, it was fun working here after so long," I smiled.

"Now here comes the challenging work. Can you collect the payment information from our buyers and send it to me later? I will have someone come by your place to pick up the iPads when you have all the data."

"Sure, no problem, we are going to head out now so we can start tonight."

"Great. Once again, thank you for your help, guys, and have a great night."

We walked out of the building with the remaining crowd. The valet was already getting our car. I started stripping off the tie and jacket, and Deebo and Danny pulled out outfits from their knapsacks.

"You brought clothes. Wow, that was smart. I did not think about that," Kelly says.

"Yeah, well I got plans later tonight, and I wasn't going to miss a night with Crystal," said Deebo.

"Who the hell is Crystal?" asked Faye. "You know what? Never mind, one of your nasty hos."

When we got home Faye and Kelly worked on the iPad to get the payment information. I pulled out a credit card–looking device.

"Hold up, are we buying art too?" asked Faye.

"No, silly, that's the card that sucks out all of the numbers," says Kelly.

"Wow, I didn't know you knew about these kinds of devices," I said and rolled my eyes.

"There's a lot of things you don't know about me," she shot back.

"I see, but for now, let's get to work on these so we can get the info and then send the totals to Ms. Kemp. Remember, we are not going to touch the money until everything is entered into the system."

"How will the information be recorded and where did you learn this?" asks Faye.

I pick up the credit card–looking thing and demonstrate how to use the card to steal all the transactions. "This device steals the names, contacts, and credit card numbers. By the time these people figure out that something went wrong, they will assume the bank made an error."

"Wow, I forgot you know all about the rich folks. You miss that life, huh?" Faye looks at me.

"Nope, not at all. My parents were never home. I had idle time many nights to do crazy things, but I just hung out with the bad kids. That was the reason I started hanging out with the wrong crowd. I never did this stuff, but I watched them do it. I was always alone while my parents were traveling the world from country to country."

CHAPTER 3.

DEEBO'S FATE

A month later after the auction robbery, Ms. Kemp was calling me, but I would put my voicemail on. How long was I willing to dodge Ms. Kemp before she showed up at our place to ask what happened to the money from the charity? I set strict rules for my friends not to buy anything that could draw attention to themselves, and they obeyed my wishes.

When I was living at home, I remembered how easy it was to have money at my fingertips by just going to the ATM and withdrawing money and not worrying about account balances like everybody else. My parents were so cool with the bank manager that he would drop money off at our house. I just wanted my parents to be there and spend time with me and my little sister Genoveve. I wanted to do normal family things like family dinners, create fun TikTok videos, game night on Fridays, and eat pizza instead of worrying about destroying our healthy diets. Having money was nothing exciting for me, and I knew that it did not bring me happiness. I tried to explain that to Faye, Kelly, Danny, and Deebo.

It had been two months since the auction, and everything was cool until Deebo came home bleeding with scars and marks all over his face. I ran up to him at the door. His shirt was torn to shreds, and his pants had blood all over them. He stumbled and could barely talk.

"What happened to you?" My heart sank.

"It is nothing. I held my own."

"Who beat you up?" I started wiping the blood off his face, pulling on his clothes to look for cuts.

"They thought they could take me on, but I showed them."

"Do you even know who they are and what they want? How did they choose you to beat up on?" asked Kelly. She looked at him with worried eyes.

"I never seen them before, but I put a whip on them."

"Deebo, we have to know who did this to you." At that moment I was wondering if it was karma coming back to us for committing these crimes.

"Great, now you're telling me that people are going to start coming after us because of what we've been doing," Faye commented.

I paced around the living room. Deebo got up and went into the bathroom. "Are you thinking that somebody probably knows about the bank robbery?" asked Danny.

My eyes lit up like flashlights and I ran to Deebo in the bathroom. He was cleaning off the dripping blood from his face with tissue in the bathroom. "Hey Deebo, did they say anything to you or ask you if you had money?" He was quiet.

"Wait a minute, hold up." He checks the pockets of his leg pants. "The money is not in my pocket. They took it!" he yelled out.

"Great, so they stole from you and took your money. What makes you think that they will not be back for more at this point?" I could feel the smoke coming out of my nose. His face turned red, and his nostrils flared.

"It wouldn't surprise me if your friend Tommy, who you brought in with us for the bank robbery, set you up to rob you!" I said in anger.

"What are you talking about? I know Tommy, he is my boy he would not do that so stop with the detective crap."

Danny goes into his room and comes out with one of the guns we used in the robbery. He flips the latch and cocks it. "Looks like we're going to have to pay Tommy a visit," Danny says.

I faced Danny with raised eyebrows. "Are you kidding me? We do not even know who attacked him. We cannot just start shooting people for no reason."

"My man got his butt kicked, and we are not going to do something that is loco." Danny paces. Every time he gets upset; he starts yelling out Spanish words.

"Look everybody, just calm down and let us see if we can figure this out. We must see if we can find these guys and see who they are and what they want."

"So, we're not going to do anything to these dudes that jumped my boy?" asked Danny.

"I am not saying that. We must do some research, so we know what we are dealing with. Let's regroup tomorrow after work. Deebo, we will find the underlying cause of this. Please get some sleep. We must be extra careful now and watch our backs, because if it is your friend Tommy and he already knows about the money, then we can be sure he will be back."

After everyone went to bed, I sat back on the living room couch and rubbed my head. My mind was spiraling out of control due to the circumstances, and I did not want this to come back to us in the wrong way. I thought of the consequences of our actions, and I remember that I tried to explain to my friends that we were getting into something that would get us in trouble. No one listened.

Laying low seemed to be the right thing to do for us because we got away with a bank heist and stealing money from a charity event. The crew wanted to drive around to look for the guys that jumped Deebo. I thought it was a silly idea. It was strange that Deebo got attacked, because we never experienced any violence like that before.

The next day it was a quiet day at the club. Everything was normal, and we were working our shift. I noticed that the bar owner was not there, so I decided to take a break. Danny was just sitting down at one of the tables.

"Is it break time already?" I threw the cloth down that I used to wipe the bar top.

"Yes! I am the boss today, and I give everybody a break."

"Say no more; I got to call this girl I met last night anyway." Danny picked up a square bucket of dirty dishes and headed toward the back.

"See you later, Latin lover." Kelly walks over to us, waving to Danny. Deebo sees us and walks over to where we are.

"Where is the boss? I noticed he has been ghosting us these days," he asks.

"Something is going on with him. He has been moving funny," I responded.

"So, what does that have to do with us? We just work here, and it is none of our business to get into his." I raised and picked up my wet, smelly rags.

"We got everything to do with it. If our boss is hiding something or doing something criminal, we can all take the fall for it." Deebo leaned in closer to me, and I looked at him a little crazy and moved my head back.

"We do not need this piece of shit job anyway. I do not know why you want us to keep working. We got money. Remember?" He winked at me with his one eye like he was flirting with me.

"Ah, my friend, we need to keep up with appearances. We must keep the attention away from us and continue to do normal things, and that means working. It is going to look suspicious if we all just got up and quit."

"She is right," Kelly says.

"Whatever. I will be in the back slaving for no reason. Somebody, please hit me up when we get back to the fun place." He walked back to the kitchen area.

Kelly tapped me on the shoulder. "Hey, you think we are being watched by someone that knows what we did?"

"That is exactly what I think. Deebo gets attacked by a few guys conveniently after we rob a bank. Sounds like a setup to me. We need to get back to work before you-know-who sees us goofing off."

"Yeah, you're right, and I don't want to hear his mouth." I walk back to my work area and Kelly goes back to the kitchen.

The boss finally walked in very quickly. He passed me on his way to his office and did not say anything to anyone. I thought it was weird that he did not speak so I followed him slowly, tiptoeing like a cat burglar, and hid behind his office door when he went inside.

He closed his door slightly to where you can still see the inside of his office. The cracked view showed his messy desk with papers and old coffee cups with residue on it. He was pacing back and forth, shaking his hands. His face was red with sweat over his forehead. You could see the tension run through his body building up. *What got him shook?* I wondered.

He went toward his safe in his office. He looked up first to see if anyone was looking, and then he proceeded to open his safe by punching in the number code. I peeped my head in further and saw the numbers he was keying in. I closed my eyes. When he opened the safe, he stuck his hands in there and pulled out a black velvet pouch. He then opened the pouch, held the pouch in one hand, and wiggled the pouch into his other hand. I saw white clear diamonds fall out of the pouch, and he went through all of them with his fingers. He looked up to the ceiling and sighed with relief. After that, I ran to tell the others about the safe and the diamonds. A few minutes later the boss then walks back outside into the main area of the nightclub and calls for all the workers to meet him on the dance floor.

"I brought you all out here this evening because I must go somewhere for a few days, and I need everybody to continue working and running the club for me. I will appoint Kayla as the general manager until I get back. If there are any problems, you can let her know and she will let me know," he said.

I heard soft gasps and whispering. Everybody looked at me. Some of the staff were clapping to congratulate me. My body temperature rose to the highest degree. My friends looked surprised because I did not tell them of my newly announced promotion.

"Thank you for your hard work, and I will see you guys when I get back." He walked away and headed to the back door.

What was he talking about? I do not want to be the manager. He never discussed it with me. I ran up behind him.

"Hey, I don't know anything about running a club, and I don't like the fact that you would announce that I am the manager without letting me know about it," I yelled.

"What are you talking about? You are the best person for the job."

I kicked the box that was right in front of me. "I'm only seventeen and I'm not the best person to do anything around here, so you better get someone else to run this shit." I clenched my teeth. He grabbed his jacket and left through the back door. He then put his foot between the doors to prevent it from closing. He turned around with his squinched eyes.

"Watch your tone with me, young lady. To answer your question, I already did, and he will be coming next week to start, but until then you will run it. I have already promoted you to be the head bartender, so relax, I have no intention of making you my general manager. I chose you to do this because the staff listens to you, and you keep things organized for me. So, call me if you have any problems or need anything," he said.

He walked out of the club and slammed the door behind him. My head throbbed as I stomped my feet back to work. I knew he was up to something but just did not know what. I did not want to be the boss of anyone, and I wanted to stay low and out of trouble for a reason.

Later, it was close to 4:00 a.m. when the club shut down. The employees headed out one by one. I walked into the boss's office with my hands on my head. I could feel the pounding and I pulled one of the drawers open, wiggling around in the drawer for pills. When I found the pills, I sat down, placing my fingers on the lever on the side of the chair to adjust the height of the seat. Faye Kelly and Deebo staggered in.

"Well, look at you, I guess you're fitting in as the GM around here," Faye says with a grin. My lips remained sealed shut. Deebo started rearranging the messy desk.

"This man needs help. So boss, what do you need us to do?" he asks.

"Are you kidding me? It is just temporary. I did not ask for this. He said he hired a GM already. I am just filling in until the guy gets here next week."

"Okay, well, why do you look so bent out of shape? You are the boss until he returns. Have fun with it." Kelly parades her body around in the office.

"You do not think it is strange that he has been missing in action for weeks at a time, and that he comes in when no one is around? He is up to something. Danny walks in with half of his apron hanging off his body. I noticed a square iron box in the corner of the office.

"Is that a security safe?" Danny walks over to it and rubs it with his fingers.

"I saw him today when he came in. He walked in here. His whole arm was inside the safe. The next thing I know he is looking at diamonds."

"Diamonds!!! I say we get in that safe and take those diamonds. Who knows what else he has in there," said Danny. He wrapped both arms around it like it was his missing pet.

Deebo pushed in the office door to close it. "How are you going to get into it; don't you need the combination?" Kelly raised her eyebrows. I could feel the anxiety in the air. They wanted whatever was in that safe. I wanted it too.

"Wait a minute. I thought we were supposed to lay low, remember?" Kelly folded her arms.

"Right, we can't afford to get into something that we don't even know if we can manage," I replied.

"Do you have the number or not?" asked Danny. "If it is money, and we take it, we will have to be incredibly careful. We cannot let anyone know." He paced back and forth. I think Deebo had enough. He put on his jacket and walked out of the office. Faye twirls around behind the desk as if she were picturing herself as the GM. Kelly and Danny stared at the safe.

"Okay, I will do it." Danny stood up and raised his hand "I will open it. Just give me the numbers. I have the smoothest hands there are." He rubs his hands together.

"Okay, the number is 4-33-20-6-10... umm wait, 4-33-20-6-10-15 15!" I said nervously.

"Are you sure you got it right? Because you do not sound like it." He looked at me with one eyebrow up and one down.

"Will you put it in and stop playing around before someone comes in here?" I glanced at the office door.

Danny shook his head and pressed on the number pad. He closed his eyes. He inhaled slowly and turned the dial. The silence ruled the air. Kelly and Faye's eyes opened wide. Danny puts his ear close to the safe with his eyes closed. He turns the knob again and then he closes his eyes again and then stops turning. He smirks.

"Shhh." He puts his finger on his lips. We heard a click, and the safe door ejected. Kelly smiles, showing all her teeth, and Faye starts dancing around again.

"Okay, what's inside?" I started bobbing my head in excitement as if the music were on. Danny's hands were halfway in the safe. He felt a sealed envelope and pulled it out.

"This is it; this is the big secret you wanted us to find out." He smirked.

I looked at the envelope and then popped my head for a better look inside. "No, this can't be—he pulled out diamonds."

"There has to be something more than this stupid envelope," said Faye.

"Well, looks like it is nothing, Kayla. You were wrong about seeing diamonds."

"No, give me this envelope." I grabbed it from Danny. I tore at it to prove to my friends that the envelope was the golden key to whatever door we were trying to get into. I held the envelope over my head and a thin piece of paper with the number on it fell out. I read the name of a bank aloud that was underneath.

"Let me know what that stupid piece of paper is." Danny storms out of the office.

"Wait a minute—this might be a security box." I looked at the piece of paper in my hands.

"Is this what you saw when the boss opened up the safe?" Kelly put her hands on her head.

"I told you he pulled out some diamonds. He was counting it. I was not trying to get caught so I left right after that," I cried.

"Never mind, I will find out what is going on. I have a funny feeling that our boss is on the wrong side of the tracks." I sucked my teeth. "All right, well, let's call it a night." We put his papers and everything back the way we saw it on his desk. "We do not want him to know we were in his office, let alone in his safe searching his private stuff." I hit the light switch with my fist.

CHAPTER 4.
REVENGE FOR DEEBO

After yesterday's events with the security safe, I wanted to check some information about my boss. I started to become obsessed with his affairs. I was in my room putting on my clothes to go to the club. I heard a rush from outside of my room door. Deebo and Kelly barged into my room. I jumped up and gave out a yelp like I was in a horror movie.

"What happened to knocking? You scared me." The clothes in my hand fell on my carpet.

"Oh, sorry we just wanted to know if you want to grab some lunch. I am hungry and you know the big boy here is too." Kelly points to Deebo's stomach.

"Okay I guess I could eat something but then I must run and do something. Is everybody going?"

"Yea, I believe so. Danny and Faye are in the car" She glanced at the window.

"Okay, I am coming. I am looking for a shirt to put on. Let Danny know not to drive my car. Thank you very much." I yell. When I turned around Kelly and Deebo had already left the room and I realized I was talking to myself for those few seconds.

We arrived at the scrumptious burgers & pie shakes that were just up the street from where we lived. We sat down at a booth that seated us all. The server came over immediately. Her eyes stuck on Deebo. She acted like no one else was sitting at the table. Deebo smiled. I looked at the server and then glanced at Deebo. I kicked him under the table.

"Oww, what was that for?" He rubbed his leg under the table.

"Oh, sorry I thought you were the table." I grin with satisfaction. I could not let him know that I was jealous of the googly eyes coming from him and the server. We place our order to eat. I watched the server go to get the drinks. A group of loud boys came in laughing and throwing paper at each other causing a scene. We were laughing and joking around waiting for the food to come. Deebo screwed his face up when he noticed a few guys that looked familiar.

"I see the dudes that attacked me last week. They stole from me." He clenched his fists together. We glanced at the guys that walked in. "What are we waiting for? Let us get them, we can sneak up on them right now." Danny smacked his fist.

"No wait, I got a better idea. I need you girls to do that thing for me," He asked. Kelly and Faye looked at each other and then looked back at Deebo. "You mean *that* thing? Are you sure?" Faye blinked her eyes.

"Yea and do it now before they walk out of here" Deebo demanded.

We rush out of the booth and quickly walk out of the restaurant before anyone notices. Danny and I kept our identity hidden while Deebo followed the girls outside a few moments after. Faye and Kelly stood outside looking around the ground; to pretend they had lost something. Ten minutes later the three guys that attacked Deebo were outside and one of them walked over to Faye.

"Hey, you need some help" asked the guy. He pats his upper chest. He goes into his pocket and pulls out a cigarette. Then inserts it in his mouth.

"Yes, I dropped my earrings somewhere here. What are you up to?" she asks.

"Me and my boys are heading back to the house, do you want to come over? We are about to have a little party. We got some weed and beer to go with these burgers." he boasts. He held up the brown paper bag with food in it. Kelly danced.

"Ooh yes, and you said you got weed. I have not had weed for a minute." Kelly smiles showing her teeth. She never did weed in her life. She was lying.

"Do you live far because if your house is not close, we are not coming" Kelly says.

"Nah, my boy lives right by Gateway Parks." said the guy who pointed.

"Oh, cool that's not far from us either." Kelly responds. The two girls followed the guys into their cars. Faye receives a text from Deebo and it reads "As soon as you get to their house, text me the address and we will be right behind you."

When the boys from the restaurant got to their house with the girls, Faye quickly texted Deebo the address. I leave a half-eaten burger and a few fries with dried-up ketchup on the plates. We also left-half-drunken cups on the table. I slipped the tip under the tray and walked behind Deebo. Moments later, Faye and Kelly were in the guys' bathroom pretending to freshen up while they waited for Deebo, Danny, and me to crash the weed party. "You ladies, okay? You are going to miss the action we got going on out here," one of the guys said. He took off his shoes. "We will be right out just making sure you are ready," Kelly says as she puts her index finger on her lips. Faye nods with a smile. The boys quickly took off their clothes, leaving their boxers on.

"Hey man, I did not know they were trying to get it popping right away. I was thinking I would have to drag their stupid asses," said one of the guys, wiggling substance in a couple of drinks from a clear pouch.

"Yeah, they stupid all right. Didn't their fathers tell them not to go into strangers' cars? It is two of them and three of us. It is not going to be a fair game," said the other guy. Kelly and Faye opened the bathroom door and three individuals busted through the front door with masks and guns.

"Get the fuck down on the floor right now, everybody, including you two." Deebo pointed to Faye and Kelly to make it look real. Faye and Kelly had to play their part. It was something that they did when they were in trouble or needed a way out: "The thing."

The guys lay on the floor, and I stood by the door holding a gun. Deebo walked over to where the televisions were and smashed them with a hammer. Danny started smashing the game sets and consoles. The broken televisions, computers, and game systems were spread all over the floor. "Man, just take what you want; don't break my stuff." said one of the guys.

"Shut the hell up and be quiet before I break your face. We are taking these girls with us too. I am sure you do not have a problem with that," said Danny. "Take those dumb chicks; we do not care about them. Stop breaking our shit," the guy said.

Danny grabbed Faye and Kelly as they screamed, "Please don't hurt us." They had to go along with the performance.

"Shut the hell up and come on," said Danny. The apartment looked like a back alley after we trashed it. Danny grabs the girls and Deebo walks out of the apartment. I followed him, pointing my gun in the direction of the guys. We drove off quickly, and Danny kept looking in the rear-view mirror just in case the guys wanted to follow us.

"Do you think they noticed anything?" Faye asks. She plays with her hair to put it in a top knot.

"Notice what? They got their butts kicked like they did me. Payback is a bitch," Deebo commented.

"I'm pretty sure they will not mess with anybody again for a while," Faye says.

"They will be back on the streets trying to rob someone else," I proclaimed.

"You think they will know we set them up?" asked Faye, looking my way...

"No, I do not think that, but those guys are not into anything good. This is all they do, and they are not going to stop hurting people."

"We got our revenge for Deebo." Faye folds her hands. We hugged and shook each other's hands like it was a sign of togetherness. "Yeah, I got my money back," Deebo says. He raises his hands with the money in it. He pulls out his chain and looks at it like he just bought it.

The day after the setup, we went back to work at the club like it was a normal day. The bar owner finally returns to work. He brought another man with him, who wore a dark pinstriped suit. His blond hair was neat and slicked down. His skin had a nice tan, like he was on vacation. Everybody looked at him like he was some celebrity or something.

"If I can just have you all in the front here, I have an announcement to make." He raised his hands. Everybody slowly walked over to the main area to hear what the boss had to say.

"Sorry for my absence. I heard that you guys did well these few days. We even had an increase in revenue. I am afraid of that," he said with a smirk. "This guy right here will be my new GM for the club." He put his arm around the gentleman. "Mr. Tim Wright was a friend of mine for a long time and a club owner of his establishments for years before he sold his clubs. He is a cool guy and not into formalities, so feel free to call him Tim." he said.

"Why did you sell your clubs to manage one that is not yours?" I asked. I thought it was stupid for him to do that. I did not care what was going on with the club. I figured I would ask the question anyway.

"Ahh good question; well it's a long story, but when I got the business proposition it was an offer I could not refuse," he said with his tongue pushed to one side inside his mouth like in the movie *The Godfather*. I knew the answer was some bull. I walked away. The staff staggered to the kitchen. "We're going back to work, boss, we have a big event tonight." I waved my apron in the air.

Later that day, the young partygoers were pouring in the doors like it was Black Friday. As we got off work, we headed into our favorite spot at the back corner of the club. The music was loud, and the crowd got thick with people dancing and drinking. I saw the boss walking with the two guys from the meeting earlier. The new guy was walking close to the boss, and the other guy had a hand on him. They pushed through the crowd urgently. I followed them to his office. I hid behind a wall when they took him inside the office. Deebo looked over to where the gentlemen were going. He walked over to where I was hiding.

"What's wrong?" He shoved his shirt in his pants as if he were getting ready to fight someone.

"He looks like he is in a lot of trouble. Did you see the way they were holding him?" I pointed out. "Well, standing at this wall not knowing is not going to give us the answers. We need to go back there to see what is going on," he instructed. I nodded my head. I crept softly and noticed the office door was slightly closed and the men were arguing. I put my ears to the door. Deebo stood closely behind me.

"I am not going to ask you again. Where are my diamonds? I better not hear the excuse that you do not have it," said Mr. Tim, the general manager. I pushed the door a little to get a peek. He held a gun to the boss's face, and the other guy stood by the door to guard. "Look, I told you that when I went to get it nothing was in there. Somebody must have taken it out of the safe. I have a lot of workers here; it could have been anyone," he said. He was pale and had sweat all over his face. He looked like a frightened little boy.

"Now that is a lie because news got back to me that you took a visit to a jeweler last week," said Mr. Tim.

"How do you know I went to see a jeweler? Whoever told you that lie fed you some bull because I did not go anywhere. I took a few days off to oversee some business," he responded.

Then suddenly Mr. Tim moved his hand from the bar owner's head, walked toward the door, and turned around. I heard a loud sound. He shot the bar owner in the head. I jumped. I ran from the office toward the door leading to the main club floor. My body trembled and my heart thumped and was coming out of my chest. I thought I was about to die.

Deebo must have heard the loud noise. He hustled right behind me. I had never in my life seen somebody get killed up close like this, and I wanted to leave immediately. I walked slowly back to the table with fear in my body.

"What happened? We heard a pop," asked Danny.

"We have to go; let's get out of here."

"What happened, Kayla?" asked Kelly.

"We must get out of here right now," said Deebo. He waved his hands to get us toward the door. We walked out of the club and crossed the streets toward the parked cars. One of the employees who worked with us at the club came running outside.

"Hey, where are you going? We got to clean up after the club closes," he yelled.

"We'll come back after school tomorrow," Kelly yelled back. The guy shook his head and went back in. Deebo got in the car and slammed the doors.

I could not believe what happened. I was right about him all along. I knew he was into funny business. When we got back to the house, we went into the house and sat down in the living room.

"Now what are we going to do? The boss is dead, and Mr. Tim will be taking over as the head boss," Kelly said, standing up. She threw her purse on the couch.

"Plus, he's the killer," said Danny.

"He murdered a guy at the club. He's a mad man, and we can't work there anymore." Kelly wore sweat on her forehead. She tried to keep her eyes from tearing up.

"I am with Kelly on that. Why would I want to collaborate with a murderer?" Faye added. "Danny is right, we must continue to act like everything is normal. If we start moving differently, it will look suspicious. We must hold on for a few weeks until the smoke clears, and then we can figure out our options." I looked at everybody's faces.

"Someone knows about us robbing the bank. Deebo did not get jumped and robbed for nothing," Kelly says.

"What are you implying? The new guy does not know anything about us. He just got here. All he knows is that we work at the club after school. He will fire us." I raised both of my eyebrows.

"What do you mean, fire us? I do not know about that." Kelly tilted her head down.

"Look, no sense in trying to figure anything out; now let's get some sleep. We cannot do anything at this moment."

"We are now working for a killer," Deebo said. He stood up with stern eyes. He walked into his room. I watched Kelly, Faye, and Danny go into their rooms. I felt a shiver when Deebo made that comment.

Early the next day we met up after school in the parking lot. "Hey, I couldn't even concentrate today, how about you guys?" Faye had on sunglasses.

"Nah, I couldn't either," said Danny. I headed to our meeting spot. I felt a buzz in my pocket. I was wondering who was calling me. I stepped away to answer my phone. After the call, I came back to the group. My face showed it all.

"We're out of a job, right?" asked Faye.

"Yup, Mr. Tim said our services are no longer needed at the club. We can expect our last check in the mail next week." I looked at my phone, shaking my head.

"Oh no! Now what are we going to do? We did the little bank robbery thing, and we stole money from those bougie people at that charity place. If we do not work, it is going to look suspicious that we can pay rent without a job," said Deebo.

Students were passing by and getting into their cars. We remained in the same spot for an hour discussing our options. A cheerleader walked over to Deebo, and her eyes and mouth salivated. The girl looked at Deebo like he was a piece of meat. She turned her head when she passed him to get one last look.

"Wow, I'm surprised you're not going after her," I said softly.

"I don't care about her; we need to figure out what we're going to do right now," he said.

"I know exactly what our next move is going to be. Remember my aunt who lived in Rockwall?" I asked as I walked to our cars. They followed me. I thought about moving for a long time, and this was a perfect time to do it.

"I saw Mr. Tim kill our boss. He is not going to let us go just like that." Kelly skipped behind me to catch.

"Do you think he knows you saw what he did?"

"I don't know if he knows I know, but I don't think we should take the chance of staying where we are. The new guy at the club just fired us. He did not give us a reason or anything. I find that very strange. I think it would be in our best interest if we just disappear," I commented.

When we got back to the house I went straight into my room. I went into my closet looking for my big suitcase. I found it sticking out from the back of my closet. It was a turquoise suitcase with a big stain on the top of it. I remember the last time I used it, I spilled coffee on it on purpose. I wanted to get a designer one. Unfortunately, my mom never bought one. I pulled it out and opened it. I started throwing my clothes in the suitcase. An hour later my eyes drooped, my body was telling me I needed to sleep. The next morning, I found myself on the floor of my bedroom.

It was a new week, and we all met up after school at the cafe. We were the only ones who would meet up at the café, because we had friends who worked there after school. If students spent time together at the café, it was usually because a new coffee flavor was introduced.

Deebo and I were already sitting in the corner of the cafe. I looked up a few minutes later and saw Kelly, Danny, and Faye walking into the café.

"Hey guys, what's the new flavor today?" Faye asked as she slammed her bookbag down on the table.

"Oh, it is always vanilla and chocolate. I do not discriminate." Deebo smiled and pumped fists at Danny. I rolled my eyes. He always had to change the conversation around talking about girls.

Suddenly he moved closer to me in the seat. I rolled my eyes and shook my head. "I do not understand why you always get mad at me when I say things like that. I told you I want you, but you are the one that rejected me," he whispered in my ear. I looked at him again and then I got up to get my coffee from the counter.

"First of all, I was not talking about your little hos; I was talking about the coffee flavors," Faye explained as she pointed to the menu on the wall.

"People, we have more important things to talk about than Deebo's girls," Kelly proclaimed.

"I do not know why you two won't sleep together and get it over with. Everybody knows you both have the hots for one another," Danny yelled out.

"Dude, it is not me; it is her." Deebo points in my direction. Danny turns around to look at me like I am supposed to confess my love to Deebo right there in the cafe, for the world to see.

"They already smashed so it's not a big deal anymore," Faye yells out.

"When was this? Wow, you finally got some from the beautiful Kayla. How was it?" asks Danny.

"Look guys, we have to talk about the club, and for whatever reason, we need to know about those diamonds and how we can get our hands on them," said Kelly. As I walked back over with my coffee, everybody started to huddle. "Yeah, Kelly is right; we looked everywhere in that office and could not find anything," Deebo says.

"I think I might know where it is." Danny's eyes popped out of his head. Everybody looked at Danny to see what else was coming out of his mouth.

"What do you mean, you think you know? When we were at the club looking, why didn't you say something then?" asked Faye.

"Because I was not sure, but I am now. I saw the boss go to the basement. He had something in his hand. At first, I did not think anything of it. When he came back upstairs, his hands were empty. The diamonds had to be down there, and they were in the safe when Kayla saw him go in there. He just moved it out because he knew that Tim guy was coming for it."

Danny sounded like a true detective. We turned our heads and smiled at him. Faye leaned over and kissed Danny on his face.

"You are a genius," she said.

"You are right! That day, when I followed him to his office, he pulled something out of it, but I did not hang around to see what else he was up to. That piece of paper I found in that envelope had the name of a bank on it with a number, so it might be in a deposit box," I shouted.

"I say after work let's head in that basement and see if it's there, and if it's not there, we go to the bank," said Deebo.

We completed our meeting at the café. I was trying not to get into trouble, but we did so many sad things up to this point that it was too late to stop now. I was the one from a rich family. I had to be understanding to those who did not live my life or have any clue what it was like to have money and not worry about the next day.

That night we got ready to go to the club as real partygoers. Kelly and Faye were all dressed up as if we were going to a real party. I had on a white, slinky dress. I wore silver stilettos and carried a matching clutch. I wore my curly black hair slicked down into a flawless bun. Kelly wore a silver sequin dress, and Faye wore a tight black dress. I guess she did not get the memo.

All eyes were on us. We were no longer employees, so this time we could blend in with the crowd. We pulled up to the building and entered the club through the back door. Mr. Tim did not know about the back door access because he would have made sure to lock that entrance. If you did not want to pay to get in, you would enter from there.

After we got in, me and the girls pushed our way into the dancing crowd. I went after the guys. Danny and Deebo headed to the basement where Danny thought the diamonds would be. Danny led the way into the long dark hallway toward the basement. Danny opened the door, and Deebo followed him inside.

"I hope those three get what we came for because I don't think my feet can take these damn heels." Faye moved like a zombie ready to attack. Kelly looked over at Faye's feet with a grin. "What's so funny?" asked Faye.

"Girl, your feet are crying—not barking, but crying." Kelly put her hand over her mouth. Faye wobbled over to the table to sit down. A guy was watching them from the side and walked over to where the girls went to sit.

"Hey, what are you guys doing here?"

"What do you mean? We used to work here. Is it a crime now?" Kelly responded.

"I don't think it's a smart idea to be here since you got fired."

"When did it become a law that people cannot go to public places, you idiot?" Kelly snapped. "Do you mind? And get away from us!" She waved her hand like she was getting rid of mosquitos. He remained there looking at them.

"Look, mind your business and leave us alone. You do your thing, and we will do ours. Let's move to the other side. He's pissing me off just standing here." The ladies walked over to the other side. She looked back at the guy, but he disappeared. "Good."

Downstairs I turned papers around and moved boxes looking for the diamonds. Then I heard Deebo and Danny slap hands. "We got it! We got it!" I jumped up. "Omg, you got it!"

I felt a vibration in my purse. I opened it and saw Kelly's face on my screen. "You need to get out of there right now. I think one of Tim's snoop boys is heading your way. He was being nosy; I thought it was weird," Kelly said frantically.

"Okay, no worries—we are coming up right now; we got the diamonds. We will meet you and Faye outside, so head out there right now," I directed.

As soon as Kelly hung up, Tim's snoop boys and security came running into the main club floor like men in black. They pushed through the crowd looking for Faye and Kelly.

The security guard with two other men started running toward us, and we started pushing and knocking down everyone to get away from them. Deebo and Danny picked up two big sticks from behind a wall near the bathroom. Deebo hid behind a wall and then snuck up behind the two guys. He raised the stick and swung. Me and the girls ran outside. We ran onto the pavement and got in the car. Deebo and Danny jumped into the car after us. Deebo stuck the key in the ignition and started the car. The noise of our car sounded like we drove away like our lives depended on it. We could not understand why Mr. Tim was chasing us for no reason, but I was starting to think I had an idea why.

A few minutes later, we got to the house safely. I could hear everybody breathing. I could not believe we were being chased by Mr. Tim and his goons. "Quick question, please tell me why those men were chasing us?" Faye inhaled and exhaled like she needed a glass of water. We all turned to look at her.

"What? I have never been in a chase for my life before. I need to catch my breath. That man thinks we know something. There is no other reason that explains it. I'm going to bed. I am exhausted from running," I said. I went into my room. Kelly waved her hand, and Danny and Deebo went their separate ways.

The next morning, it was a Saturday, and I thought about Mr. Tim. I got up looking at the ceiling. I was in bed trying to figure out how much danger we might be in since we stole some diamonds from a killer who wanted them back.

I got up out of my bed. I walked out of my room and sat in the living room looking at the black velvet pouch. Deebo came out of his room and sat next to me. He took the pouch from me and poured the diamonds into his palm.

"Damn, I have never seen ice up close and personal like this before." He examined it like he was impressed. "You think it's real?" he asked.

"Yes, it's real, our boss was killed for this. Anyway, who gets killed for fake diamonds? That just doesn't happen."

I took them from him and put them back in the pouch. "I know these are real. My parents had diamonds lying around the house all the time. My dad bought diamonds for my mom for everyday occasions," I explained.

"Wow, I forgot you're the rich one in the group." I aimed my piercing eyes at him.

"If I were rich, we would not be stealing, remember? My parents cut me off financially, but with these diamonds, we are going to be okay. I know a place where we can get cash for it. I have an uncle that can help us with that kind of transaction." I tapped my feet as if I had just found a solution to our problems. "My aunt has this big empty house. It used to be my mother's house, but she told her sister she could have it. Now we are going to live in it." I folded my hands with reassurance.

"Let me get my bags packed because I am dying to get out of here—no offense, Ms. Tilda," Deebo says.

"Things are going to be better for us from now on. I am going to miss Ms. Tilda; she is so sweet to us, and I want to leave her a little something too. She kept us safe, and we owe it to her because she allowed us to stay at her house," I preached.

"You act like she let us stay here for free. We were paying rent for that mug. I am going back to bed. Are you coming?" Deebo looked over at me for a response.

"Maybe another time. I got somewhere I need to be," I replied.

"Can't say I didn't ask," he frowned. I just shook my head and smiled and waved to him. This was my second rejection. I knew that I had to make it up to him soon.

CHAPTER 5.
LIVING LIFE

Some days passed after the club mess. We headed to my aunt's house in the Rockwall/Heath area, a nice quiet city near Forney.

I used to love going to my aunt's house because she hosted these big fancy parties, and you had to be someone to be invited. When I got cut off from my family's fortune, my aunt begged me to come live with her, but I refused and demanded that I do it on my own. She was the only one in the family that cared about me and wanted me to live with her. Although I am not rich anymore, I love my life living with my friends. Most kids like me would kill to be in my past life.

When we got to the house, it resembled an open house. When I talk you can hear my voice to the other side of the room. No life displayed that someone lived here because my aunt moved to Dallas. She did not want the house anymore, so it just sat. Luckily for me, I had the keys.

A few days later, I was most excited about my friends moving because none of them had ever come close to living in a house this size before. In their eyes, the house is from a fairytale story as the driveway had a detailed brick way like *The Wizard of Oz*. There are six-car garages and a bridge that connects to the guest house and pool. The house had five bedrooms and five bathrooms, with a gym and theater room. A couple of offices are near the library. I know Kelly would love to use it. Danny and Deebo will live in the gym. The diamonds we stole from Mr. Tim will give us everything we ever dreamed of, but at what cost? After Danny and Deebo brought in the last box with our stuff, I called each of their names for us to meet in one of the big kitchens.

My only regret is that I did not get to say good-bye to Ms. Tilda as I wanted to. She was not home when we left the house.

I wanted to move quickly and quietly. Everything that was in the apartment belonged to Ms. Tilda. All we had was our clothes and shoes in plastic garbage bags that we carried with us from the shelter days to this house. She is going to miss us.

"What about Ms. Tilda?" Faye asked.

"We can say good-bye to her tomorrow if you want." I smiled at Faye.

"I left a box in my room."

"Faye, I told you to pack all your belongings. We cannot take any chances with Mr. Tim. The first place he will come looking is our home."

"I promise I am just going to get it. No one will ever notice I was there," said Faye.

"We hug Ms. Tilda grab your box and go."

"So where is your aunt? You said she lives here, right?" Danny's eyes wandered around the place. He nodded his head while he walked around. I know he was impressed.

"No, she is in her other house now. She preferred to live in Dallas."

"So, you just have a big empty house waiting for you to move in?" Faye's eyes widened. I shrugged my shoulders. I could not help it if my family had choices.

The next morning, I got out of bed. I went into my bathroom to brush my teeth. I went into the kitchen to get some coffee and saw Faye had on a cute sundress ready to go. I just had on a shirt and shorts.

"Do I have time for coffee too?" she asked.

"Of course. Here take mine. I am going to start the car." I extend my arm holding a cup of mojo. She grabbed the coffee and took it to the car with her.

We drove to Ms. Tilda's house to get Faye's box she left in her room. When we got to the house, I called for Ms. Tilda, but the house was quiet. Ms. Tilda rarely went anywhere, and if she did it was to the grocery store and back. I walked through each of the rooms looking for any sign of her. Unfortunately, we did not see her.

"Faye, get your box and meet me back here. She might be in her bedroom or something."

"Do you have your box?

"Yup," she yelled back. Then I heard a blood-curdling scream. My body shivered. I went running up the stairs, curious and scared at the same time.

"I just saw her lying there on the floor. I thought she fell or something," Faye's eyes were filled with fright. Tears ran down her face. She was looking down at the floor. I was shaking to follow her eyes.

"No!" My heart pounded like a drum. My body stiffened as my eyes glanced over the body of Ms. Tilda. I placed my fingers on her neck. I examined her body like we were from the crime scene unit.

"It looks like someone broke her neck." Her neck had bruises on it. Faye's tears dropped down like faucets. I walked over and put my arm around Faye to comfort her. I felt her heart beating with mine.

"Come on, we have to call the ambulance; there's nothing we can do for her now."

Moments later, the sounds of sirens became faint and then louder. A knock on the door startled me. I opened the door, and the paramedics rushed in. They went up the stairs and a few moments later they each carried the end of a stretcher with Ms. Tilda in it. Faye and I watched them carry her into the van. One of them came back to the house.

"Do you know what happened to her?" asked the medic.

"No, we just came to get our stuff. We used to live here. We were hoping to say good-bye to her," I replied. My hands got sweaty, and my body slightly trembled.

"Well, looks like she was fighting for her life because her room was left in shambles," said the paramedic. "We called the cops; be sure to stay here because you have to answer some questions," the man said.

"What are you talking about?" I asked.

"It is just routine. You two were the first ones to see her, so naturally they will want to interrogate you two."

We went back to Ms. Tilda's room. Her things were thrown on top of the furniture. Clothes were tossed around, and papers were everywhere like the perpetrator was looking for something specific.

"I do not know who could have done this. Ms. Tilda did not have any enemies." My body ached with sadness.

"Leave it for law enforcement to figure it out."

First, my boss gets murdered at work, and now my landlord. What is going on in Forney? Who would want to kill Ms. Tilda? It did not make sense, and I was trying to figure it out.

"We must call Deebo. Will you be okay while I make the call?" I held Faye's hands. Faye wiped her eyes and nose. I wanted to make sure she was okay before leaving the room.

"I will be right here." Her voice cracked when she talked.

"Okay, I will be right back."

I walked out of the room and stood in the hallway. The tears forced their way down my cheeks. You would think that I was the older one in the group, but I was not. We are teens, dealing with situations and suffering from the consequences that we brought on ourselves. I pulled my phone out of my pocket to call Deebo. Before I could get off the phone, I heard a loud slam on the other side of the phone.

"Who could hurt Ms. Tilda? I do not understand," Kelly asks.

"I do not know, but there must be some kind of explanation for this. Something is just not right," said Danny. I could hear him pacing back and forth. "Where are Kayla and Faye now?" he asked.

"They are still at the house. They must wait for the police officers to answer questions," Deebo explained. "I will call you if I hear anything else." I hit the end button to get back to Faye.

Later that evening, we arrived back at the house, and we met everybody in the kitchen. If you were in the room with us, you would figure out that someone died.

"I always knew something was up with Miss Tilda, but I could not figure it out. She got us the jobs at the club, and that was weird. The people over there were afraid of her, but I did not think she participated in anything illegal." However, she did not deserve to be murdered like she was. Kelly's face was red and puffy. She got up and walked away.

"We still do not know what happened. Let us turn in for now and regroup in the morning."

The next morning, we got up one by one staggering into the kitchen, still shocked by the news of Ms. Tilda's death. I was in my bedroom, with my body plopped on the bed. Seconds later my cellphone rang. I did not look at it. But it would not stop ringing. I glanced at my desk where my phone sat. Eventually, I went over to my desk to answer it.

"Hello, is this Kayla?" asked the voice.

"Yes, this is her," I responded. Immediately I felt tight. "Who is this?"

"This is Detective Williams. I did some poking around at Ms. Tilda's house. I am working on this murder case. We understand someone called her cellphone right before she was killed. It came up as an unknown contact. I wanted to see if you knew the number by any chance," asked the detective.

"How did you get my number?

"Just answer the question." I searched my contacts on my phone for the number.

"Yeah, it is 972-432-1234. That number was the number to the club where we all worked." I could not move my body. The thought of the whole thing made the hairs on my skin stand on end.

"What does Miss Tilda have to do with the club?" the detective asked.

"I have no idea." My eyes lit up immediately. Ms. Tilda was the one who got me the job in the first place, but I never knew what her connection was with the bar.

The detective's breathing lingered on the phone. "Um, quick question—what was your reason for leaving the house?"

"My aunt is allowing me and my friends to stay rent-free until she gets tired of us," I responded.

"We'll be in touch." That was it. I am now involved in a murder case.

The death of Ms. Tilda had us all broken. The whole city was upset. Ms. Tilda was sweet and was always willing to help someone, even if she did not know them, just like she helped me and my friends. Ms. Tilda was an old lady with connections and was feared. I wanted to research why.

The next day, the sun beamed through the windows to let you know it was the start of summer. Bored and with nothing to do, the idea of spreading out in the pool seemed the best option. We were jobless. I wanted us to look normal by working. We still had the diamonds. I needed to get it to my uncle so that he could give us cash for it, but with Mr. Tim looking for us, I knew it would not be safe to get caught with his diamonds.

Faye was sipping a cocktail with a mini green umbrella inside. Her body shimmered in the sun while Deebo and Danny sat next to a few girls at the pool bar. I did not know he invited people over. I felt the need to have a talk with the crew without the company. I signaled the guys to meet me inside. Faye locked eyes with me and obeyed the assignment. Kelly rose and followed.

"Mr. Tim killed our old boss, and someone killed Ms. Tilda. I say we must come up with a plan." Kelly stood in front of us with her sunglasses and a drink in her hand.

"Yeah, you are right, two murders back-to-back and close to home. We must find out what is going on, because we may be next," I said frantically.

"When do you want to start this research, Kayla the sleuth?" said Kelly. Her grin disappeared when I looked at her.

"I am being serious, Kelly; we must solve these murders and find out where Mr. Tim is. I was not a fan of our boss, but he did not have the right to kill him, and if he participated in Ms. Tilda's death, we need proof so that we can tell the police."

Immediately, it was like a lightbulb that switched on in my head. *Mr. Tim may be tied to Ms. Tilda's death since the detective found the club number in Ms. Tilda's phone*, I thought to myself. We were inside too long, because one of Deebo's girls walked inside the pool house.

"What is going on in here?" She was a cute girl with blonde hair and blue eyes. The model type.

"Hey ladies, why don't we take you guys out for something to eat?" Deebo put his arms on her shoulder. He walked briskly back outside. I followed and jumped right into the pool.

"Come with me to the club. We need answers," I demanded. "We have to do something; we just can't sit around not doing anything."

I bit my lip nervously. Kelly was my partner in crime when it came to research. I looked at her and she nodded. Kelly and I got out of the pool. I went into my room to change. When Kelly and I got to the club, we did not expect to see what we saw. A yellow tape was across the front of the club like the ones in the movie. The building looked old and dusty. I wanted to get a closer look. I stepped on broken glass and pieces of paper, looking around. There was garbage everywhere.

"What happened here? This place is gross. Mr. Tim closed the place down after he fired us." Kelly frowned; she covered her nose with her hands as she walked through the mess.

"I do not know about that, but this place has been closed for days. But why? Why or who closed it down?" I looked at the debris like I was a detective. We walked toward the front door, and I heard walking behind us. A man in a suit appeared.

"What are you two doing here? This is a crime scene," said the man.

"Yeah, we used to work here; we're trying to figure out what happened, that's all." Kelly folded her hands.

"Well, there is no job here, as you can see. However, if you have information about this place . . ." I walked up to the man.

"Where are you going?"

"He said we must leave," she scolded.

"I have an idea, so wait in the car and I'll be right there."

Kelly shook her head and walked to the car.

"I do have information; what do you want to know?" I asked.

"Who is the owner of this place?"

"The owner is dead, and I know who killed him. It is a guy named Tim. Well, the owner called him Mr. Tim." I stood there with my hands on my hips.

The man in the suit looked at me. "What do you mean, you know who killed him.?" he scrunched his eyes and took out a pen and pad. "You better not be lying to me; this is not a game."

"I'm not lying; someone that I know heard the gun go off when he was shot at the club." The man in the suit got closer.

"Who is this friend?" I moved back.

"Was anyone hurt? And when did this happen? Why didn't that person go to the police with that information?"

This man did not give me a chance to answer his questions. His face freaked me out. His nostrils got red and flared. I did not kill my boss. I was the one who was there when my boss got shot in his office, but I did not want the detective to know that. Every time you tell the police too much, you get in deeper with the case. I did not want to go through that.

"I mean if you were only seventeen, and you saw your boss get murdered at work, would you say anything?" The detective turned away and then looked back at me.

"Where is this friend of yours anyway? I will need to talk to him or her." He started walking away. I ran up behind him.

"I do not know where that person is, and I do not want someone hunting me down just because I am talking to you."

"I understand. I appreciate your help. I need you to come down to the office to make a statement. Your information is safe with me. Is there anything else?" When he got to his car, he opened his car door on the driver's side and threw his mini pad and pen on the car seat. I began to hesitate to answer, but I felt the need to tell him about my suspicions about Ms. Tilda's death.

"Yes. Ms. Tilda knew the club owner, but I do not know how. I tried asking her, but she would shrug me off," I said nervously.

"How do you know that?"

"Ms. Tilda was the one that got me the job at the club. To be honest with you, my friend and I were trying to find out what was going on because Ms. Tilda was family to us. What is your name?" I finally asked.

"My name is Detective Shims. I am one of the investigators in the case." He extended his hand. "Here is my card. You will find the address of my office and my telephone number. If you know anything else, please give me a call; whatever you tell me will be confidential. I will need you to come to the office sometime next week."

I took the card and repeated the name to myself. "Detective Shims." I walked back to my car where Kelly was waiting, her face flushed with anxiety. Her arms were folded and she squinched her eyes and raised her head.

"What took you so long? I sat here for hours waiting for you. What were you talking about?" Kelly asked. She had sweat on her face.

"I told him what I know, and who killed our boss, and that Ms. Tilda knew our boss, but I just didn't know who did it."

"You did what?" Kelly's face turned purple. "Why did you tell him that? He is going to ask us a bunch of questions and get in our business."

"Trust me, if we give him the impression that we can help with this investigation he will keep us on speed dial." I threw his business card toward her in the car. She watched the card fly on her lap. "We need him on our side when things get complicated." I put my hand on her shoulder.

"Ah, did you forget that we robbed a bank and stole from a charity event?" She had a point.

"Trust me, we are fine. I will not put my foot in my mouth."

We pulled up to the house. I parked close to the waterfall in front. I walked inside and noticed Deebo and Danny were nowhere in sight. I called out to Faye. I looked in her room and saw she was laid out with her eyes closed on her bed.

The next day Ms. Tilda had several funeral events that her family managed. After attending one of them at the church, we drove to her house to be with her family and friends. People were in the living room sitting on the couch. Some of them were standing and with plates in their hands eating food. There was a tray of strawberries, pineapple, watermelon, and raspberries on the coffee table that no one touched. I glanced at the wall and saw pictures of Ms. Tilda when she was younger. For a minute it seemed like I was in a meeting for geriatrics. I saw coworkers there and the bartender who was fired when the bar owner promoted me.

"What are you doing here? How did you know Ms. Tilda?" I asked.

"Are you serious? Ms. Tilda was our boss's mom." My ears stopped working. Hearing the news that Ms. Tilda was the mother of our old boss was interesting because that would mean either Ms. Tilda knew that her son was up to no good.

I walked over to where Danny was, and he was sitting in one of the living rooms with his foot up. He spat out a cherry that was in his drink. That was disgusting to see.

"You're not going to believe this, but Ms. Tilda was our boss's mom." I sat down next to him.

"What!" He pulled my hand closer to his. Deebo walked over to where we were standing.

"What is going on?"

"Ms. Tilda was our boss's mom. That means that lady was doing some criminal things with her son," Danny says.

"Man, this shit is getting crazier and crazier by the minute."

"Wait, we don't know that for sure," I added, "Ms. Tilda could have been an innocent bystander to her son's doings. She could be innocent in all this."

"Did the person that killed her think she had the diamonds?" I was asking like I would get a clever answer.

"I don't know, but we have to be very careful now because we don't know what they might know," said Deebo.

"What man?" Danny looked at Deebo. "The fact that they came to the house and killed her rubs me the wrong way because we could have been there."

"Yeah, he's right; if we were there, it could have been a different situation." I nodded. "Look I say we leave this funeral gathering and go home; we can figure this out later."

We walked out one by one and headed to the car. A black car with tinted windows was parked right out front. The person never came out of the car or even entered the house. No one noticed it but me, but then again it could have been relatives of Ms. Tilda, but you never know. I was freaking out because murders were happening back-to-back, and it seemed like it was getting closer to us. Not knowing who killed Ms. Tilda drove me nuts. Whoever the killer is, we might very well be in danger.

The next morning after the funeral, I heard my cellphone ring, and I tossed and turned before I answered it. I rubbed my eyes until I could see clearly. I picked up after the tenth ring, with one eye open because the other eye was asleep.

"Hello, who is this?"

"Hello, it's Ms. Kemp, your mother's friend. You collaborated with me at the charity event a few months ago," she said. I immediately jumped up. Did she figure out that we robbed her? My hand shook as I held the phone.

"Hi, Ms. Kemp, how are you?"

"I am not doing well. I noticed that we had a substantial amount of money missing, and I wanted to ask you if you knew of anything. I would have called earlier, but I have been so busy handling other things and, well, you know I am a busy woman," she admitted.

"Umm yes, I mean no, I did see something that did not look right; I can check it out if you give me an hour."

"Oh good, take your time then. I must make sure the gallery gets their payments to continue doing business with them. Call me later when you find a solution."

I hit the end icon on my phone. My heart pounded. I had sweat on my face, and I rubbed my temples. How was I going to get her the money we had stolen from the charity event? Then the lightbulb switch popped into my head again. I walked over to the living room and called for everybody to meet me there. One by one they came staggering out.

"What in the hell is wrong with you? It is early." Deebo was the first one to bitch. He rubbed his eyes.

"Ms. Kemp just called me, and she knows about the missing money," I said. Silence filled the room.

"No worries; I got this—we are going to pay her back, and it will be like nothing happened."

"How are we going to pay her back? We spent the money on jewelry, clothes, bags, and . . . lots of bags," Faye confessed.

"We got the diamonds. It is more than enough to pay back Ms. Kemp and even pay back the bank we robbed."

"Okay, now I know you're still sleeping; I'm going back to bed," Danny said and walked off. He put his hoodie over his head.

"Why not? It makes sense. Those diamonds are worth millions. We can pay them both back. It is the moral thing to do." I strutted around the room to prove my point.

"News flash—you don't rob a bank to go ahead and return it afterwards," said Deebo in disagreement.

"No, but we can do the right thing and return it and still come out as the winner."

Later that day, I thought about my decision to pay back what we took from the charity event and from robbing the bank. Kelly and Faye agreed with me, but the guys did not. I decided to visit my uncle in Dallas. I went into my room and pulled out a T-shirt and a pair of jeans. I grabbed my keys to my car and headed out. When I got to the building garage, I parked my car. I walked into a luxurious tall silver building. A security guard stood in the lobby. As I approached the elevators, the security guard that was standing there stopped me.

"Excuse me, miss, you do not belong here."

"Yes, I do—now you better move, or else your next job will be delivering newspapers."

"Young lady, you better get out of here." He gripped his flashlight and grunted. I ignored him and kept going to the elevators; he stood before me and pulled out his phone.

"Uh sir, we have a situation downstairs in the lobby." I ran into the elevator quickly and pressed the button. The security guard ran toward the doors, but the doors slammed shut. "Sucker." I am too fast Mr. Guard.

I walked out of the fancy elevators on the twentieth floor. The hallways were wide and empty. I looked at my reflection in the silver chrome panels that were everywhere. I walked on the plush carpet down the hallway and then turned around to a corner office. I opened the door without knocking and walked into this large modern office, with tall windows. The view of skyscrapers is like a painting. My neat handsome uncle had his back turned toward the front of his office. He sat in a fancy white chair talking on the phone. He twirled around in his chair like a ride. I had not talked to him for a long time, and I did not like him very much.

"Something came up; I have to go." He tapped his phone with his pinky sticking up.

"My dear, what brings you here? I have not seen you in months or years." I always liked his office. It looked like the ones you see in architecture magazines. I was not here for the small talk. I sat right in one of the leather chairs that faced him.

"Uncle, I am not here to plan the Christmas dinner. I have some diamonds that I need you to take off my hands," I demanded.

"Diamonds?" His eyebrows raised. "Where did you get them from?"

"That is none of your business, Uncle. Can you help me?" He paused for a minute and looked at me for a second.

"Well, of course, for you anything, my dear. How much are we talking about?" I took out the black pouch and poured the diamonds all over his glass desk.

"I need whatever this amounts to in cash."

"Wow, well, you remind me of your mom coming in here with your demands. I still love you anyway. Give me a second. I will be right back with your money. I suppose you do not have anything to put the money in, right?"

"Of course not," I smirked.

He gathered the diamonds and stood up. I got up while he stepped out and walked over to the window. I was like a hundred flights up. Okay, not that high. The view of Dallas was so pretty, and it gave me a nostalgic feeling. My uncle returned to the office with two silver briefcases and handed them to me.

"Here you go, dear, do you need my driver to take you to where you need to go?"

I ignored him. "See you later."

"Not even a thank you at all. You know, I told your mother to let you come back to the house. There was no reason for her to kick you out like that. You can live with me. I do not know why you are such a stubborn child. Stop this slumming around and get back to your privileged life."

"That's the thing, Uncle, it's slumming to you, but it's fine for me." I walked out of my uncle's office and slammed his door.

"What a rude little bitch," he mumbled. I walked back to the elevator. When I got outside, there was a car that my uncle provided waiting in front of the building.

I got in the black car and told the driver to take me to the bank that we robbed two months ago. We pulled up to the bank, and I told the driver to wait for me as I entered the bank. I told the security guard who was standing inside to take one of the briefcases and ask for a gentleman named Gary. When I came out of the bank, I told the driver to go to another location and wait for me until I got back. I walked into another building, walked over to a kiosk, and started typing. When I was finished, I pulled out my cell.

"Hi, Ms. Kemp, I just wanted you to know that there was some kind of glitch, but everything is accounted for. You can check it now." I smiled because I was happy that I returned the money. I walked out of the building and jumped back into the car.

"Now you can take me to my car."

"Yes, Ms. Kayla."

Later that evening, when I arrived back home from my uncle, everybody was in the living room watching a movie when a special news report came across the screen.

"We have some amazing news today: the FC bank that was robbed a few months ago had money that was stolen returned today. The bank manager has no information as to who dropped it off or how it was returned, but everybody is fine, and no one was hurt. "All eyes were on me. I shrugged my shoulders and tilted my head.

"We had enough money to return it."

"If we knew you were going to return the money that we risked our lives to steal, I would not have stolen it," said Danny.

"Doing a good deed once in a while doesn't hurt."

"How much did we get for the diamonds anyway?" asked Faye.

"Let's just say we are good for a long time."

I laughed and they started throwing popcorn at me. I blocked them with the sofa pillows. After that, we tried to watch another movie. Danny and Deebo left to go to bed. I tried to convince the girls to stay up, but they left me. I stayed out in the living room thinking about how good it felt to do good for others. I thought about how returning the money to Ms. Kemp and returning the stolen money to the bank was an amazing feeling. Would this venture be like Denzel Washington in *The Equalizer*?

I would have to sell it to the guys. Danny and Deebo did not show appreciation for the return of the stolen items. Why should they care now? They live in a big house and have access to a lot of money whenever they need it. Truly and honestly, they are living the life that I used to live. I thought everyone should be happy because this is life; they complained about living in Ms. Tilda's basement. I realized that pleasing others is hard and keeping them happy is even harder.

When I lived with my parents, life was easy for me and my sister. We did not need or want anything. The money took care of everything for us. The downside of that was that my parents were not there for me and my sister. Then I got kicked out and ended up living with my friends. I thought that if I could let my friends see that, they could be of purpose. We can start helping others with their problems, and life will be better. I wanted to solve the murder of Ms. Tilda and her old boss. Nothing is going to stop me, and I knew I could get the guys on board. Eventually, they would see that not only helping others is therapeutic, but it will keep us out of trouble.

A few days later, I yearned for a normal life. I was getting bored hiding from criminals. We decided to go shopping at North Park. We spotted Mr. Tim, talking with another gentleman by a sneaker store.

"What? Look, it is the murderer!" said Faye. Faye's face twisted. We were shocked to see this man out in the open, especially when we knew he killed people.

"It's a damn shame—he needs to be behind bars," said Kelly. She shook her head.

"Yeah, well no one cares that he killed someone except for us," I said. I shook my head in disgust.

"We need to leave because we can't let him see us," said Faye. Her voice cracked.

"Let's get out of here, guys." I threw my cup of soda in the trash can I was standing by. The last thing we needed was for this killer to spot us and come after us.

As soon as we started walking away, Mr. Tim walked away from the gentlemen he was speaking to and looked over at us coming down the escalator. He walked up closer, and his eyes met us. Then I saw him charging in our direction. We ran to the parking lot as soon as we got off the escalator. Faye lost her grip. Her purse dropped.

"Hold up guys!" Faye ran back to pick up her purse. "Omg, Mr. Tim is behind us. We must run," she said.

"What?" Deebo turned around and saw Mr. Tim. We ran like we were part of a track team. Mr. Tim caught our attention, and he stopped pursuing us. He got on his phone and he stood there with his hand in his pants pocket. I felt spooked because I started thinking that he was calling for someone to either follow us or kill us.

When we got back to the house, my body could not stop shaking, but I did not feel afraid for some reason.

"Well, he knows that we know he killed our boss and his mother," Faye commented.

"We have to think fast now and figure out how to get him off our asses." I sat down on the couch with my head down. "Danny, see if you can get a hold of your tech friend and see if he can find some information on Mr. Tim."

"That's going to be hard to do if we don't know anything about him," he responded.

"Well, we need to figure out where he stays." I wondered how long Mr. Tim watched us and if he even knew where we live now. I knew at that moment I had to contact the detective that was managing Ms. Tilda's case.

"What are you going to do now to keep us from running into Mr. Tim and his goons?" asked Faye. "There is only one thing to do that will keep us safe and protected."

"Don't tell me you're calling that detective we met at the club?" asked Kelly.

"Yes, I might as well let him know that Tim was chasing us. He is trying to kill us, for all we know. At least we can have someone on our side for a change."

"You think he can help us?" Kelly's eyebrow raised.

"Well, it is a chance I am willing to take, especially since he is the man working on the case. I am going to call him now. We can find out where he stays or something and put a tail on him."

"Wow, you sound like a cop." Faye smiled and looked at me like I was some scientist.

"I think calling the detective is a clever idea. I am not trying to die right now, not when we are so close to becoming a senior in high school," said Faye. Me and Kelly looked at Faye.

"How can you even think about school with all that we are going through right now?" asked Kelly. Kelly shook her head. I got up and grabbed my keys. I walked to the door.

"Look, I will be right back. Please just stay in the house until I get back," I demanded.

"Don't you think you need to go wherever you're going with one of the guys at least in case Tim is out there?" Kelly is the sensible one and always thinks about the smart stuff.

"I'll be fine—just stay in the house, please."

"Where are you going? I thought you were calling the detective," asked Faye, holding his business card. I wondered how she got it since it was in my room on top of my dresser.

"I am going to go to his office instead. He said I can go there if I need to talk to him."

I walked out of the house and looked around before entering my car. I adjusted my rearview mirror. I noticed that the same black car that was parked across the street at the funeral was right outside the house. I did not think anything of it and ignored it.

"Where did Kayla go?" asked Deebo.

"She went to see some detective to let him know that we were being followed by the killer and his friends," said Faye.

"What??" He thrust his fist into the wall. "Why did you let her go by herself?" he asked.

"I told her to ask you or Danny, but she wouldn't listen, and she just took off," Kelly responded.

"Shit!" He snatched his keys off the table in the foyer. "I am going to see if I can catch up with her. Stay in the freaking house until I get back. No one leaves."

I got to the detective's office of Mr. Shims, and when I got out of the car, I looked around to make sure no one was watching me. It was a small, brown, brick building. It had only four floors. I noticed the black car that was at the house. I walked into the building and rubbed across the directory with my finger for the suite number of Detective Shims. I walked down a hallway. I knocked on the black wooden door with his name on it.

"Come on in," he said.

"Hello Detective Shims, it's Kayla—we met a few days ago at the club." I walked into the detective's office. I glanced at my phone and could see that Deebo was calling my cellphone. I hit the "decline" button and put my phone on silent.

CHAPTER 6.
HELPING OTHERS

I was with Detective Shims in his office discussing everything that was going on with Mr. Tim and how he was following me and my friends at the mall. My phone continued to buzz while I sat and talked to the detective. I did not answer. *I will see him when I come out*, I thought to myself.

"Is there anything else you can tell me about this Tim guy?" asked Detective Shims. I was sitting in one of his chairs. He stood up and leaned against his desk facing me. I moved slightly back.

"No, that is everything. Just promise that you will have our backs on this." I sounded like someone finalizing a crooked business deal.

"I told you if you are being honest with me about everything you will be safe. I advise you to go back home and stay out of sight since they may be looking for all of you," said the detective.

"I am heading back now. I will let you know when I get back home." I proceeded to walk out of the office and outside the building. I went outside, walking toward my car. I looked down and noticed my wristlet was gone. I realized I left it on the detective's chair. I headed back into the building, but Detective Shims met me halfway. He was holding my wristlet.

"Here, I noticed you forgot it on my chair," Detective Shims said.

"Oh, thanks." I grabbed it and headed to the front door once again. I headed back out of the building. I got outside and a guy was walking in my direction and bumped into me.

"Excuse me, sorry," the stranger said.

"No worries." I turned to go toward my car, and another gentleman came out of nowhere and grabbed me. It happened so fast that I did not see it coming. I could see the black car door open. The stranger tied my hands and threw me in it. I was lying on black leather seats. My body rolled back and forth. I could see Deebo from the back window looking at his phone. By the time Deebo knew what was happening, it was too late. I did not know where they were taking me or who they were. I was not afraid or scared. I wanted to call my friends to let them know what happened. I wrestle with my hands. When did they do that? I did not remember that happening. They must have knocked me out. I was thinking it had to be Mr. Tim and his gangster friends.

"How long has it been since you were out there?" asked Kelly. Her screwed-up face demonstrated how she felt.

"It's been like an hour or so," said Deebo.

"No, did you see anyone outside the building?" Her voice cracked when she talked.

"I had my eyes on her car and the building the whole time." Deebo slammed his hands on the steering wheel. He started to think about how he missed Kayla, from walking out to her car.

"Listen to me, Deebo, you're going to have to go in there and find out if she is still with Mr. Shims," said Kelly.

"Yeah, I'm on it—keep your eyes on your phone just in case she tries to text us." Deebo ran into the building. I could only imagine how he and the crew were feeling.

I started thinking that my car was still in the same place. Deebo will see it and think I never left. Deebo walked right up to Mr. Shim's wooden door and stormed through without knocking.

"Who are you?" asked Mr. Shims.

"A friend of mine came to talk to you earlier today and I was wondering if you know where she went."

Mr. Shims slammed Deebo against the wall. "Who are you and what do you want with Kayla?" asked Mr. Shims.

"Get off me. I was waiting outside for her, watching out," said Deebo as he pulled the man's hand from him.

"What do you mean? She left like an hour ago," said the detective. He rushed over to his phone.

"Did you call her phone at least? Did you see her come outside?" the detective asked.

"Hold on a minute. I am trying to talk. No, I did not see anything. I looked down at my phone, for one second, and the next thing an hour passed and she never came out."

"We cannot do anything until at least forty-eight hours," said the detective. Mr. Shims walked toward his desk. He turned on his computer.

"What do you mean, forty-eight hours? We can't wait that long; they might try to kill her." Deebo's face looked sick. He kept on walking back and forth.

"Who are they?" the detective asked.

"The guys that were chasing us at the mall. I do not know." Deebo placed his hands on his face.

"Listen to me—if you call in a missing person for her, the first thing they will ask you is how long has she been missing. If you say three hours ago, they will tell you to stay home and wait for her. Do you know how many teenagers run away from home for a couple of days and then turn up?" he informed. Deebo paced back and forth trying to listen to Mr. Shims.

"I will do everything I can to find her, but you must calm down. They will not kill her, because they do not think she is a threat. This guy is not stupid; he wants to find out how much she knows about the club business with your old boss."

"Yeah, but we do not know anything. Kayla heard the guy got shot in his office, but he never saw her because she was hiding behind his office door," said Deebo. "Kayla told me that someone told her that someone shot him, but she did not know who." The detective hit the desk.

"So, she lied to me. Nothing I can do about it now. I am going to search for her. Go home."

It was a sad day because I was missing, and I knew my friends were going crazy looking for me. I drove in a black car for a long time. I did not recognize the area. After two hours of driving, the car stopped. The men got out of the car. They opened the back passenger door and grabbed me. One of them led me to a dark room that looked like a storage unit with boxes everywhere and paint and concrete mix. I was cold, and my body shivered.

"Why is it so cold in here and what do they want with me?" I said to myself softly. I heard someone walking toward the room I was in from the outside. I looked for a stick or some kind of weapon and saw a pair of scissors. I put it in my clothes.

"You must be cold here. We must keep this room cold for a special reason, but that is none of your business," said Mr. Tim.

What? This was the same guy that shot and killed my old boss at the club. He threw a jacket at me, and I caught it. I was impressed with myself because my hands were tied but I was able to catch it. He walked over to me and cut the ties.

"This should keep you warm until we come back." I wanted to curse him out.

"Why are you keeping me here and who are we?" I rubbed both of my wrists.

"Nothing to worry about. Don't you have one of those social media things that you teens go on night and day? By the time you do that I will be back with your dinner," he said. Mr. Tim smiled at me and walked out of the room.

"Why are you keeping me here? And I do not want any dinner! I just want to go home!" I yelled. Mr. Tim walked back into another room and came back out with something in his hands.

"You're not hungry; I need to ask you a few questions. Do you know what happened to my diamonds that were at the club?" I swallowed my spit when I heard that question. Me and my crew stole them from the safe that was in my boss's office. I did not say that to him. How was I going to answer this one? I played it around in my head before I gave a response.

"Diamonds? If I knew or saw diamonds at the club, no disrespect, but I would have taken them and headed for the border," I said. I figured if I were realistic in my answer, he would believe me.

"The question is, are you telling me the truth," he asked.

"Look man, I don't know anything about diamonds, but I wish I did. You fired us without any explanation. Then we see you at the mall and you start chasing us. What are we supposed to think? Stop and say hi?" I said.

"You're right. I believe you."

"So, you're just going to let me go like that?"

"Well yes, you said you do not know anything about my diamonds. You said if you did you would have taken it. I can accept honesty. Do not get me wrong—if you are lying to me, you will be sorry." His eyes stared at me with vengeance. "I am not going to waste any more time with you."

I was not sure about this freedom Mr. Tim was giving me, so I got up slowly, took off his jacket and threw it on the floor, then walked slowly to the door. Mr. Tim pointed his finger at the back door to the exit. Once I got outside, I was so relieved, and a gentleman in a suit came outside and grabbed me again.

"Wow, I thought you were letting me go," I said.

"Shut up! Mr. Tim told me to drop you off at your car."

"Oh, okay yeah, thank you, I appreciate it." I fixed my clothes and stared at the other guy.

He took me to my car outside Detective Shim's office. The car drove off so fast that I was not able to get the plate number. I got in my car and locked the doors. I placed my two hands together to say a prayer. Then I started the car.

"Wait a second; it's Kayla calling," said Kelly.

"Hey, where are you? We have been looking for you all day and night scared straight." My ears started ringing.

"I know, I know, that fool let me go."

"What did they want with you and are you okay?"

"Yes, I am okay. They just wanted information about the diamonds. I told him I did not know anything, and he believed it. I am on the way home. See you in a minute and let everybody know that I am okay." I exhaled. My heart was jumping. I started smiling.

When I got home, I walked in the door and I was rushed with hugs from my friends except Deebo.

"Hey guys, I'm all right—they didn't do anything to me." The warm hugs felt like home.

"I'm glad they let you go; we would have been lost without you, girl," said Faye.

"No, we wouldn't," said Deebo. Deebo did not hug me. He stormed off to his room. I followed him. He had steam coming out of him.

"What's your issue?"

"The next time you want to go on a crusade without letting people know where you're going, say something before you do it," he commented.

"Why? Were you worried about me?" I chuckled. I knew why but I wanted to hear from him. He never let anyone know how he felt, and I was curious about how he felt about me.

"What do you think? It is not a game; we witnessed a guy get murdered. We have information that could get us killed if we let out what we know."

"I am sorry; you are right. I do not want to put us in danger. I promise to let you know where I am going from now on."

He turned to face me. "Thank you."

The next day after the kidnapping debacle, Detective Shims came over to deliver some news.

"First of all, I am glad you are okay and that they did not harm you. Because of you, we were able to track them down and arrest Mr. Tim and his associates for the murder of Ms. Tilda and her son. We found evidence that linked them to her and the connection to the club. They were running a money-laundering operation at the club. We recovered everything that they had except for the diamonds. None of the employees saw the diamonds, and the place was swept." I looked at the others.

"Well, this murder case is closed. Once again, thank you for all your help, guys; please stay out of trouble and avoid clubs until you're of age." When he walked out of the house, all I could hear was sighs from everyone.

"We are out of the club business for good," said Deebo. Danny walked up to shut the door.

"We are in the clear, and we got the diamonds."

"Shut up; he can hear you," Kelly said.

"No, he cannot; he just left."

"We were able to do some good with it and solve a murder," said Danny.

"Ahh, two murders," I said with a smile. We belted out laughs.

"I like being the good guy. It feels great knowing that we helped capture a wanted felon," said Faye.

"I still cannot believe you were kidnapped. That is so crazy," said Kelly.

"I went down memory lane being in that warehouse all tied up. I do not want any of my friends to experience that."

"I can agree with that one. We had a long day. I say we go over to Ellum and have some drinks," said Danny. We headed out to Deep Ellum to one of our favorite rooftop spots.

Two months later, it was back to school, and I could not believe that we were all going to be seniors. I looked forward to some normalcy. Deebo and Danny were talking about the girls they were going to meet with.

"Try and do some work this year, guys; we want to go to college together like we plan to remember," said Kelly. Kelly's glasses fell on her nose.

"We are going to do work and we will have some fun too. This is our last year at Forney High, and we are going to make it the year to remember. You hear me, Danny?" said Deebo.

Deebo had his arms out like he was confessing his love to someone. Danny was FaceTiming some chick and decided to ditch the group.

"I will see you later after school. I am on my way to pick up the new principal's daughter, Ella es una Chica Bonita," said Danny.

"Okay Latin lover, see if she has a sister," said Deebo. I know Deebo and I slept together but I was not ready for anything more between us now. We had drifted apart from working at the club and with the crazy things we were going through.

The first day of school was crazier than ever. I do not know if it was because there were more cars than last year in the parking lot. I wanted something from the cafe at school. Kelly followed me. Some kids were already in line for drinks. Me and Kelly got in the line. I noticed that one of our friends who is always there every morning was not there.

"I wonder where Diane is; she's usually the first one here." I glanced at the room to look for my friend.

"Maybe she's with some hot college freshman and he took her to breakfast," said Kelly. She blinked her eyes twice at me.

"I hope so too; because I don't know her to never be in here." Diane was always at the local cafe no matter whether it was rain or shine, and I was overly concerned. I was next to step up to the counter.

"Yes, what's your order, hon?" the lady asked.

"Cheese biscuit with home fries, please." I did not waste any time. "Have you seen Diane?"

"No, I was hoping she was coming in to work today. She is usually off during the summertime but always comes back the first week of school. I called her a dozen times and left voice messages. If you see her, tell her we could use her help," the lady said. I took my food and walked away slowly.

"Thank you."

"Hey what's got you spooked?" asked Kelly.

"Let me know if you see Diane at school, and text me the minute you see her." I walked away without saying bye to Kelly.

"Bye." She shook her head.

In the front office, there was a line of students who did not fill out the returning students' forms, so they were holding up everyone else. At lunch, me and Kelly waited for the boys and Faye was talking to some new guy.

"I spoke to all the teachers today and no one has seen or heard of Diane today. You know she is the school president, and she oversees the newsletter," I said like Kelly did not know that.

Danny sat down with his lunch tray. "What's up?"

"I was concerned that Diane did not come to school today."

"She is thinking something might have happened to her," Kelly added. She rubbed my back.

"Why are you worried about something that does not concern you? She took the day off and will be back tomorrow."

"I hope you're right."

A girl was sitting across the way and locked eyes with Deebo. She was pretty, and most of the guys were already eyeing her down.

"Yo dude, Jesse is trying to put a spell on you." Danny displayed his dimples. He danced in his seat.

"Who the hell is Jesse"? He looked around. Danny points to her.

"That is Jesse—that fine-ass bottle of wine right there." Kelly stared at the guys.

"Yeah, I see her, but she can come to me. I am done chasing these girls. I am on a new vibe." He straightened his shirt out.

"Shit if you do not want her, I will gladly talk with her. See ya." Danny grabbed his lunch and went over to Jesse. Deebo did not move. He sat there eating his lunch.

"Wow, I'm surprised you let that one go." My eyes rolled.

"What? I have seen prettier," said Deebo. He did not face me. He held onto his phone.

"Yeah, like who?"

"I'm talking to one right now."

"Of course, you are." I looked right at him and smirked. Deebo looked around and looked back at me.

"I was talking about you, the prettier one." Deebo smiled, picked up his tray, and walked away. He left me sitting there with my mouth slightly open. I sometimes fail to realize that Deebo likes me and that I might be the only girl he wants to get serious with.

"When are you going to realize that you are the one he has always wanted since the shelter days?" I looked at Kelly like it was the first time I had ever heard of this information.

"You think he likes me like that?" I put a grape in my mouth from my lunch tray.

"Ugh, yes he does, and why are you acting like you don't know this already?" She raised her hands up.

"I do not know. I always see him with other girls talking to them and making out with them," I explained.

"He does that, so he does not have to think about you all the time. He does not care about those other girls. He does not want to be with them in a serious manner."

"Well, I cannot think about him right now. I am still a little worried about Diane." A loud sound rang, and that meant that our lunch time was over. It was also the end of the school day for us. We met up with Danny and Deebo at the lockers. This was always the norm during breaks or after school.

"Hey, you ready? Let's get out of here. Class was extremely boring, and I had a corny behind history teacher." Danny stuffed his books in the locker.

"It sounds like Mr. Walter and his stinking breath; he's the worst," Deebo laughs. "Yo, where are the girls?"

"I think they are coming in a minute and if they don't, we are leaving them," Danny added.

Kelly and I walked up to where the boys were. Another guy walked right by us. His eyes locked mine. He was the new guy that everyone was talking about and wanted to sleep with. He was particularly good-looking.

"Wow, if looks could kill," said Faye smiling.

"He is fine, and I want his number," Kelly chimed in. She licked her lips like sugar was on them. Deebo looked at me to see if I was intrigued, which I was, but I quickly turned around like it was nothing.

"I didn't even notice," I said as I closed my locker door.

"Maybe because he was looking right at you. He is the new guy that all the girls have eyes on. He is a football star from Garland and got transferred here to make some miracles happen for the team." Faye felt the need to tell us his history.

"Well, they're going to need much more than that to make anything happen because the team here needs all the help they can get," Danny added.

I slowly looked back at the new guy as we walked outside the school building. The parking lot was filled with students and cars with music and loud muffled sounds. The next morning, Deebo and Danny left for school and the girls were running late. Kelly was still trying to put on her shirt, and me and Faye were still messing with our hair.

"Come on guys, the boys left because we took too long," Kelly yells.

"Who cares, they just wanted to rush to school to talk to girls anyway," I said in my no-care voice.

"I didn't know you cared."

"No, I don't. I'm just giving you a reason why they left." I frowned at Kelly.

We got to our biology class, and the teacher handed out a quiz. Some students slammed their pencils on the desk.

"Now, it is just one small quiz to see where you are with vocabulary and lab work. Trust me, it should be easy; just take your time and answer all the questions."

When the teacher handed in the last quiz sheet, someone knocked on the classroom door. A police officer and a woman in a dark pantsuit walked in and whispered into the teacher's ear. The teacher nodded in agreement.

"Listen, students, we need your attention for a minute."

"Thank you, and hello, my name is Ms. Williams. I worked with an organization that works closely with law enforcement to help locate and find missing young girls. I am going to every class today and I want to ask you all if you know this person," said the lady. The students quietly talked amongst themselves with confusion in their eyes. She held a picture of a girl. The teacher glanced at it.

"If anyone has seen this girl in this picture in the last day or anytime, let us know. I am going to pass this around," she said. The picture of the missing student got passed around from student to student. When it got to Kelly her face became pale, she inhaled and exhaled. She slowly passed it to me, and my eyes widened.

"Do you know the girl in the picture?" asked the lady. I couldn't move my body. It was my friend Diane. The one missing from the café and the one they were looking for.

"I am afraid the whole class does. Her name is Diane White. She worked here at the local cafe, and she was a student here. The last time I saw her was right before summer break," said the teacher.

"Okay, thank you everyone for your cooperation," said the lady. When the lady and the police officer walked out of the room, the students gasped. The bell rang afterward, and it was like a herd of animals running for food. Me and Kelly started to walk down the hallway. I turned to Kelly.

"Did you see that? I told you something happened to Diane. I told you and you all thought I was crazy." I raised my eyebrows.

"I cannot believe you were right. I was hoping that you were wrong and that she was somewhere safe like Deebo said," said Kelly.

CHAPTER 7.
NEW PROBLEMS

The news about Diane being missing made my stomach hurt. It started to affect me a great deal. I wanted to do something about it but did not know what. What can I do? I am only seventeen. I lay down looking up at the ceiling, in my bedroom, which is what I do a lot if you have not noticed by now. My eyes glanced over at the pictures on my wall. I had pictures of my parents, me, and my sister. We were incredibly happy as a family.

I started reminiscing about how easy my life was when I lived at home. I did not have these worries. What if these issues still existed when I did live at home? I just was not aware of it because I was in a different space. I started to think about what her mom could be going through to have a daughter missing. I prayed that nothing bad happened to her and that she would be safe and unharmed. I heard a little noise outside my room door. I had a feeling who it was.

"Hey, are you all right in there?" Deebo stuck his head into my doorway. "I heard about Diane. I am sorry I was not taking you seriously when you said you thought something might have happened to her," said Deebo. My eyes watched the closed door. I opened the door and laid back down.

"Thanks for opening. Everybody is a little out of it about what happened." His face frowned.

"Well yes, I mean we saw her right before school ended and now she is nowhere to be found." I rubbed my eyes until my vision was a pure blur.

"Well, we must let the police do their job at this point. There is nothing we can do right now." I rose and rolled my eyes at him.

"What do you mean, there is nothing we can do?" I balled my fist. "There is plenty we can do, and I am not going to just sit here and do nothing."

"You're not the police, Kayla!" He clapped his hand to get my attention. "You cannot just go on a crusade to solve everybody's problems."

"Oh no, well watch me." My eyes opened wide with his response. "Diane is my friend and if it were any of you, I would do the same."

"I am going to call Detective Shims and see if he can help. I am going to visit Diane's family to ask them some questions."

"Look, if you want to help the police, I will help you. I am sorry if I am being insensitive." He scratched the side of his head and rubbed his temples. "I feel like it is a lot for you to take on, but I am here to help. We all are."

He came closer and wrapped his arms around me. It felt like hours passed while I was in his arms. My heart thumped. His cologne aroused me. His fingers softly caressed my legs. One day we will confess our love for one another, but it was not on this day.

The next morning, it was a Saturday. Kelly, Faye, and Danny were making breakfast. The aroma had me going and I could smell it from my room upstairs. The kitchen smelled like the countryside with freshly made biscuits and scrumptious breakfast meats. Danny moved the sausages around in a skillet and Faye and Kelly cooked the eggs. The countertop had all the fixings ready like a buffet. Me and Deebo walked downstairs together, and all eyes stared.

"What did you two do last night?" Faye asked with a funny smirk.

"Not a thing. I held her in my arms. She was upset about Diane," Deebo responded.

"Okay, so what's the master plan?" asked Faye as she sipped on some coffee. I grabbed a cup and put it on the coffee machine. I turned around and all eyes shot at me for my response.

"I guess I will start by asking Detective Shims where they are with the whole investigation on Diane and see where we can help."

"Okay well, that is what we will do. Call the detective and set it up." Kelly stood up and slapped her hands on her lap. "In the meantime, I think we can start with her parents. We can ask her mom what she did and where she went before, she went missing." Kelly sounded like a police officer herself.

"Let's go," said Danny.

We solved the murder case with Ms. Tilda and her son, which was by accident because we did not set out to do so. I saw the man shoot our boss and I could not keep that quiet. Now here we are trying to find out who took Diane. Me and the girls went over to Diane's house after breakfast. Danny and Deebo accompanied us but sat in the car. I walked up the stairs and rang the doorbell. The girls follow behind me. This fragile-looking older woman opened the front door.

"Hello, Ms. White, I am a friend of Diane's from school. I hate to bother you during this tough time, but I wanted to let you know that we want to help with the investigation. If there is anything we can do, please let us know." Her mom's face was worn, and her eyelids drooped. Her shirt and pants were wrinkled, her hair tousled like she just got up from bed. She stepped to the side to invite us in without saying it.

"Please have a seat." Kelly walked in first and I followed behind her. Faye trips on her own feet walking in. I watched the floor until my eyes spotted the living room.

"On the first day back to school, she wanted to pick some girl up and take her to school. I never heard her speak about her before. So, I asked her who this girl she was picking up. She said she is a first-year student, and she met her on Instagram," said her mom. Her tears rolled down her cheek. Her bottom lip started to quiver.

"Do you mind if we look at her laptop?

"No, not at all, feel free to go to her room. It is right there on her desk." her mom pointed in the direction of Diane's room. Kelly and I walked over to Diane's room. Her room was across the hall. Faye stayed with Diane's mom.

"Can I do anything for you like bring you some coffee?" Faye asked.

"No, honey, I am fine. Thank you for all that you girls are doing. I appreciate it. I just hope we can find her in time." Kelly and I stalked her Instagram feeds. She was talking to someone that we did not know but claimed to be attending Forney High School. She had a picture of Jane Doe on her profile and her handle just said "Betsy."

"Who would just name their profile 'Betsy'?" asked Kelly.

"What do you mean?" I asked. I moved my head closer to the screen.

"I do not know; it just seems weird. There are only a few photos. The girl's profile was mostly blank."

"This Betsy girl is weird; she says she is attending Forney but there are no outfit pics for the first day or any excitement. Usually, you would take a picture of your first day or post it," I commented. Kelly and I lifted boxes that were under her bed. I touched all her papers that were on her desk. I opened her closet. I put my hands on the shelves.

"Let us get out of here." We were only teens; we did not know what to look for. We walked into the living room to meet Faye and Diane's mom.

"So, what did you find?" she asked standing up.

"Nothing," I shrugged my shoulders. Kelly's eyes squinted.

"As soon as we know more, we will let you know, Ms. White. Thank you for letting us come over to look at Diane's room."

"Sure, no problem, and you will let me know something, right?" She held out her hands to mine. I caressed her warm hands.

"Yes, ma'am." We slowly walked to the door. My heart sank for Diane's mom.

"What's wrong with you?" Kelly's eyes widened and her arms folded. "You told her mom that we did not find anything."

"Okay so.

"But that was a lie. We saw that girl Betsy and the conversation on Instagram."

"Kelly, I do not want to give Diane's mom any false hope. We do not have anything to tell her that is going to make her feel better. That girl Betsy is weird, but it still does not give us anything. We must find out if she even goes to our school. That could be a lie as well," Kelly nodded. We dropped off the guys at home and then took off because they had enough of my sleuths' activity. We drove to Detective Shims' office. I looked all around the area. I remembered how careless I was when I got kidnapped. I did not need any repeats. I walked up to Detective Shims' office wooden door.

"Stop bothering me, Gregg, I don't want to hear any of your corny stories," he yelled. I opened his door.

"Oh, hi I thought you were that fool across the way," he pointed.

"So, you kids refuse to stay out of grown folks' business."

"We just came from Diane's house, and we spoke to her mom," I said. Detective Shims slammed his hands on the desk.

"You did what! I do not remember you being a detective in any way." His spit landed on the tip of my nose. I quickly used my arm to get it off.

"Come on, Shims, you know I want to help find this girl, I told you this." Kelly touched his things in his office.

"I understand you want to help, but because you are only seventeen years old, you and your friend here can get hurt by putting your nose where it does not belong. Where are your parents? Why are they not telling you to keep out of it? You keep your hands to yourself," he growled at Kelly.

"I live alone with my friends, remember." He played with the papers on his desk.

"What did you find? I know you found something."

"Yes, we found this girl named Betsy she was talking to on Instagram. She was going to pick her up the first day of school and she was never heard from after that," I said unsurely. Detective Shims grabbed a pen and pad and threw it on his desk.

"Put down the Instagram name of this Betsy. Do you know this girl? Does she go to your school?"

We never heard of this girl, and we do not know what she looks like," Kelly added.

"What do you mean?" Shims asks.

"She does not have a picture on her Instagram, so she is a mystery. She told Diane she was a first-year student coming into Forney High," I responded. I jotted down the information on the pad and spun it back to Shims on his desk. He spun in his chair to position himself in front of his computer. He typed on his desktop.

"There are no pictures. Don't you young people stay on this thing all day posting your life away?" His fingerprints were smeared on the screen.

"Exactly, so we were thinking that if this Betsy person shows up at school come Monday, we will keep an eye on her," I added.

"Your work here was a waste of time. Keep me posted if you hear anything at school."

"I guess it's safe to say we're partners?" Kelly looks at Shims with a smirk.

"I would not get too comfortable with this setup. We do not even know if we are dealing with a girl. This could be a man posing as a teenager. Have you ever thought about that? Get out of here, and do not go back to the girl's house unless I tell you to do so." He stood up with the pencil in his mouth and escorted us to the door to let us out. When we walked out of his office, he slammed the door. Kelly jumped from the impact. I shook my head.

The next day at school, everything was back to normal after the first week. The front office simmered down, and there were fewer students.

At the end of the day after school, we met at the parking lot like we normally do. "So did you see the girl you were looking for?" asked Danny. He brushed his black hair, slicking it down like he always does.

"No, nothing, but I have a feeling this person will show up eventually. Well, we got basketball practice. We will link up with you ladies later," Deebo said.

We watched the boys drive off. Later that night you could hear a pin drop. Diane's Instagram did not move at all. After hours of nothing, I shut my iPad down. Her mom gave me her login and password so that I could keep track of her feeds. I went to the bathroom, picked up my toothbrush, and put toothpaste on it. My cellphone buzzed on my bed. I ran over with my wet hands.

"Why didn't I get a call from you?" Detective Shims rings my ear.

"There was nothing to tell you, Shims; when I have something, I promise I will let you know." I growled and hit the end button. I was not sure why he was looking for information so soon.

The next school day at lunchtime, Faye was with her boyfriend and a girl walked over to sit down next to them. Her tray fell. Apples, bread, and tuna fish spread all over the floor. Faye's boyfriend picked it up.

"Thank you; it is my first week here." She moved like a new student.

"It's going to be okay." Faye's boyfriend smiled. He looked up to speak with her, but the girl disappeared.

"What is wrong? To whom were you talking?" asked Faye.

"She was just here. She dropped her tray. Anyway, am I coming over tonight?" he asked.

"Of course, you better, I need you to help me study for this stupid test."

Lunch ended and the class was about to start. As Faye walked to class, she buried her hands in her bag to look for her book. She walked away to her locker to retrieve it. As she approached her locker, a girl walked up to her.

"Excuse me, can you help me?" she asked.

"Are you lost? First day, huh?" asked Faye. The girl dug in her bag.

"What class are you looking for?"

"Ahh, it says history room 709—I was in the right area, and I don't know how I made a wrong turn."

"Nope, you are right. It is this way. I am heading there too, and guess what?" asked Faye.

"What?"

"We're late," Faye chuckled. They walked in during a conversation with the teacher.

"Go sit down, ladies, and don't forget to take these." Faye walked to her seat that she normally sits in, which is right in the middle. The new girl stared at everyone and held her books tight as she sat down. She parked her body where Faye was sitting. Faye raised her eyebrows. The girl smiled and bit her lip.

After the quiz, the teacher asked the students to pass the papers up to the front. Faye picked up her quiz and grabbed the new girl's paper that was sitting next to her. The paper slipped through her hands and fell on the floor.

"I got it, no worries," said Faye. When Faye picked up the paper, she noticed the initials B.C. Could this be the mystery girl named Betsy? Faye's eyes opened wide.

"I hate taking quizzes or tests, how about you?"

"Oh, me too. I study for them, and I forget about it."

"Where are my manners? I am Faye." She extended her hand. The girl shuffled with her books.

"Nice to meet you."

"I got to run. I will catch you later." Faye walked up to the teacher's desk. She pushed the papers around.

"What do you need, Faye?" the teacher asked.

"Oh, I forgot to write something down on my paper."

"Okay, find it and put it back. I will grade them tonight." Faye went through the stack of papers and saw the one with the initials B.C. She turned it to the front and back.

"What the hell is this girl's name?" she mumbled.

Later that evening, we were scattered on the sectional in the living room. Danny and Deebo threw paper around like they were on the school grounds.

"Can you guys quiet it down a little? I am trying to do some homework here." Faye typed on her laptop with schoolbooks surrounding her.

"Hey Faye, you were telling me about some girl you met in history. What is the deal with that?" I asked.

"Oh yes, so I met this girl while I was late for history class. She was lost and I directed her in the right direction. Turns out she was in my class."

"Anything else?" I said, shrugging my shoulders.

"Ah yes, so we had to take a quiz. I do not know why we did that because..."

"Faye, the details please." I tapped her on her shoulder.

"Sorry. I was picking up the quizzes, putting them on the teacher's desk, and when I picked them up, I noticed it said 'B.C.' on it. I tried to find out what her first name was, but she did not have her full name anywhere on that paper." Danny, Deebo, and Kelly looked at Faye.

"What?"

"What does this chick look like?" Deebo asked.

"She is very pretty, and oh yes, she had a blonde streak in the front of her hair. Looks like a clip-on; I am not sure."

"She put on a clip-on of a colored hair weft." Kelly's eyes squinched up. Deebo and Danny made ugly faces.

"What the hell is so funny?" I asked.

"That girl had my cellphone when we were practicing, and I know for damn sure I had my phone in my bag," said Deebo.

"She stole your phone?"

"I do not know. I went to get my bag after practice, and she came over to me and Danny to give it to me." He shrugged.

"Did she say what her name was?"

"We never got that far; she just handed it to me, and we left," he said.

That night, I was gathering all the mystery girl's content and trying to piece it together like a puzzle but realized I did not have enough to go on. I wondered if that mystery girl was truly Betsy, the one that was hanging out with Diane.

"I'm going to have to dig more on this girl," I said to myself while I looked at her Instagram page.

"Holy shit," I yelled out.

"What is the noise for?" Kelly yawned walking into my room.

"This chick Betsy is having a party this Saturday," I said.

"I thought she was new. Why does she think she is going to have a good turnout?"

"I don't know, but we are going to go to find out what the hell she is up to with this shindig." I had one eyebrow raised.

"I am not going. Seems like a death trap to me." Deebo commented with a smirk.

"Ha, I am with him. You are asking to be killed or kidnapped," Danny pointed to me.

"That is the whole point. She is drawing some kind of attention to herself; this is where she does her thing," I said.

"What? Turn into a vampire?" Danny opened his mouth and displayed his teeth. "This is not the *Vampire Diaries*."

"Ha," laughed Faye. "Wow, this is getting interesting. It would not be funny though if she were one."

"We must see what she plans to do at the party she is hosting. Who is coming with me?"

"I will go," said Faye, raising her hand like she was in class.

"I will go with you too," said Kelly. The guys turned their heads. I stared at the boys and blinked my eyes.

"Okay, but if she is a vampire and she turns on us I'm going to bite you as soon as we get back to the house," I said.

"Please do, I'll be in my room waiting patiently," answered Deebo. I sent Deebo piercing eyes to display my lack of patience. I knew that they might be right about the party not being safe. However, I told Diane's mother that I wanted to help the detective find out what happened to her daughter. This is just something that I had to do, and I was not going to stop until I got the answers I was looking for.

The new week was like last week and the week before. Same old thing: teachers, students, and unnecessary noise. The party day of the mystery girl came quickly. It was time to get ready. Kelly was fixing her hair, and Faye buttoned up her blue blouse that she was going to wear for the party.

"I think we need Deebo and Danny there with us in case something pops off," said Faye.

"I think we need them too, but they refuse to go with us."

"They should know that we need them for protection. Why do we have to tell them everything?" Faye nodded.

"You got a point there. I asked my boyfriend to meet us there for backup. He volunteered to come with us."

"I like him already," Kelly said. Kelly put on makeup from the compact that was in my bathroom.

We pulled up at the party that Betsy the mystery girl was hosting at around 10:00. The house was huge. I raised my head up and saw three levels and balconies. The landscape had colorful flower beds everywhere and bright green grass. The garage was filled with luxury cars and big trucks. I was able to see a crowd of students from the glass front door inside. The music vibrated in the neighborhood. People oozed out of the house from the front and back. It looked like the whole school was there without the staff. We pushed through the crowd toward the front door. People jumped into the massive pool that was lit up in a blue color around the edge. The balcony seemed like a meeting spot, like one of those '90s teen films where the new girl throws the party with the hot guy that every girl wants. Betsy was invisible, but we marched over to the bar. Most of the students were falling all over the place. I saw one bent over the kitchen sink. It was a mess. Another one had a substance coming out of his mouth, and he stood over the trash can.

"So, when is she going to make herself known?" Kelly had both hands spread open like she wanted a hug. Minutes later, the crowd gasped, and the teens started clapping, cheering, and blowing whistles like they had just seen a celebrity.

"Looks like our host has finally made an appearance." I followed the crowd. Betsy stood in the middle of the living room floor. She was shining with glitter all over in burgundy.

"Should we go over to her now?" asked Kelly.

"No," I waved my hand for the girls to simmer down. "Let her come to us. Let us split up and mingle." I walked around bumping into people. I kept my eyes out for anything suspicious. People were still coming in, and it was starting to become difficult to track everyone. I found myself at times pushing through bodies of all types just to get through the party. Kelly went upstairs to look around. She opened the doors as if she hoped for a prize behind them. Some of the rooms she barged into had couples making out.

"Gross, that boy smells—what's wrong with her nose?" Faye stood in the front to look out for her boyfriend. She was not paying any attention to anything else. I kept bumping into people with alcohol in their red cups.

"Hey sorry, it's so crowded in here."

"Yes, it is. Do you go to Forney?" he asked.

"Yeah yes, I do. Do you know where the bathroom is?" I glanced around.

"There's one over there near the hallway."

"Cool, thanks." My eyes spotted a door in the corner. I pulled out my brush and started brushing my hair to get it back right. Having mixed hair is not always the move. With my mother being White and my father Black, I was sure to have one type or the other. After the bathroom, I saw Kelly still talking to some guy upstairs on the balcony, and she looked like she was in love. Faye was still outside looking for her boyfriend. Suddenly, I heard someone yelling. I turned around to see what the commotion was.

"Hey, sorry I was trying to get that silly boy to put down my mom's painting. Well, you are here, thank you for coming," said Betsy the mystery girl.

"Yeah, sure."

"Right, I remember you as well. I am glad the word got around that I was having this party. You know, I am the new girl." She put her quote fingers up. I looked down at my phone to see a text from Faye. I looked at my phone screen and looked around.

"Where are you now?" I texted Faye.

I am in the front area of the house. I am about to throw out this cup," she responded.

"Stay there; I'm coming to the front now," I texted back. Betsy stared at Faye and watched her throw out the cup in the kitchen. She pulled out her phone and looked like she was texting someone. I was still trying to get through the crowd when this guy pulled me to dance. Betsy looked up at the front of the door with a smirk on her face. Seconds later, a cute guy walked in the front door and had his eye on Faye. Betsy got her phone out again. Moments later a cute guy appeared. Faye's eyes stayed on him. The cute guy watched Faye like she was a piece of meat. She had an admirer. Meanwhile, I was fighting my way over to her.

"Wow, I look that bad, huh?" said the cute guy.

"Excuse me, oh no, I am waiting for my boyfriend. I did not mean it that way, sorry," said Faye. Her eyes closed.

"No, it's cool. I'm looking for someone myself."

"Are you looking for the host of the party? What is her name again?"

"Her name is Betsy." Faye's eyes widened. She pointed to an area. "Oh, yes, she is right over—well, she was standing right there." Faye walked over to meet Betsy. The cute guy followed her. Then his phone dropped. Faye turned around to pick it up. Quickly after, Betsy showed up out of nowhere and put a cloth around Faye's nose. Faye collapsed. The cute guy and Betsy carried Faye into a nearby room. After getting rid of the guy I danced with, I finally came around to the front of the house. I tiptoed my way around to look for

Faye. I pulled out my phone to text. Faye did not answer. My body shivered. This sick feeling comes over me. Faye's boyfriend walked into the house.

"Kayla!" I turned around to see who it was. It was Faye's boyfriend. I had never met him before, but I saw pictures.

"You're Faye's boyfriend, right?" I asked.

"I'm Drake. Faye told me to meet you guys here," he said.

"Hi Drake, Faye told me you were coming. Thank you for meeting us here. We wanted to have a guy with us tonight."

"Yes, I understand; that is why I am here. Where is she? She is not answering my calls or texts." His hands were shaking nervously.

"She is not answering any of my texts either. I am going to look around the house for her. You do the same," I said. Drake moved into the crowd, pushing people to the side. I went upstairs and got to the middle of the catwalk. I watch Kelly romancing the same guy.

"Hey Kayla, did you find the mystery girl, Betsy?" Kelly's eye met mine.

"We can't find Faye." Kelly's face went blank.

"What do you mean, you can't find her?" She walked away from the guy she was talking to.

"Her boyfriend is here. I just sent him to look for her. She is not answering our calls or texts."

"Are you serious? Where did you see her last?"

"She was at the front door, five minutes ago, waiting for Drake. I told her to wait. I got up there and she was gone. I texted her and got no answer," I said. I looked and saw Drake's face was flushed and his nostrils flared.

"Anything?" I asked.

"No, what is happening right now? Where is Faye?" he asked nervously.

"Are you fucking serious? We're trying to find her," said Kelly.

"I just met you, and I do not know what is going on." His eyes tried to back up his tears.

"Look, Drake, Faye is our sister. We live together. We are just as concerned as you. I am going to call Deebo and Danny," I said.

"Do you think that's a good idea since Deebo told us not to go?" Kelly said with a smirk. "She is in the bathroom or something; I do not know. We will find her." My hands trembled.

"We need to call the police; people don't just disappear like that," said Drake. "I know that."

"We cannot do it now. She has not been missing long enough for the police to care. Trust me, I know. Let us sweep the entire house, even the basement and every room here," I demanded. You would have thought I was some captain of a police force. I was thinking that Betsy and the cute guy did something to Faye. Somehow, they must have gotten her out of the house before anyone noticed. The next thing I know, Betsy appears back into the crowd of the party, as if nothing happened. This time my eyes followed her. I rushed over to where she was standing.

"Have you seen Faye? The one you met in history class." My face got fiery red.

"Yeah, I saw her out front. She went to throw out a cup. Why, is she missing?"

"Who said anything about missing?" My fists balled up. My body overheated. Betsy moved away.

"Okay, well I guess it's safe to say the party's over," she says.

"Wait a minute, you crazy bitch, who said anything about missing? I just asked you if you saw her." I found it strange that she would assume Faye was missing. She was guilty. Drake and Kelly came rushing back to where I was.

"Does she know where she is?" asked Drake. The poor guy looked pale and sweaty.

"I don't know what your problem is, but I am trying to help you find her," said Betsy. I raised my hand and slapped her lights out.

"Kayla!" shouted Kelly. "This is not the way to find her. Come on, let us continue to look for her." Kelly grabbed me.

"I know that bitch knows something, and if I find out if you had anything to do with her disappearance, I'm coming back for you." Kelly pushed me in the other direction. Three police officers wasted no time entering the front door.

"Oh, thank goodness, the police officers are here. We need to let them know what is going on," said Kelly. Kelly and I walked up to one of the officers.

"Officer, one of our friends is missing, and we think something happened to her at this party," I said.

"Who called us?" asked one of the police officers. Betsy runs up from the crowd.

"I noticed that one of my guests was missing and got concerned so I called you guys," she said.

"She is a liar," I pointed out. "She did something to my friend Faye. I am going to find out." My nostrils widened.

"You cannot just accuse people of doing things without any evidence. I need you to come with me. I have some questions about your missing friend," said the police officer. I walked behind the police officer outside. I know in my heart that Betsy was the one who kidnapped Faye with her cute accomplice. The cute guy was not around and was the one responsible for getting her body out unnoticed. The next hour, Danny and Deebo showed up. Danny wore a blank face. After the police officers were done with me, we walked back to the car with the boys. In the car, you could hear a pin drop. Kelly began to fidget.

"Now we have two of our friends missing without a trace," she said. Her hands held her face. My head stayed down. I could feel the smoke that was coming out of Danny and Deebo.

"I told you not to go to that party. You do not even know her like that. You went anyway. Now Faye is missing!" said Deebo. His face turned blue. Kelly looked at Deebo.

"Did you forget not long ago you were recently kidnapped? What part do you girls not understand? Stay out of people's business." He was right. We should not have gone to the party. But the only way we were going to find out if Betsy had something to do with Diane's disappearance was to attend the party. I was glad that I did. I will do everything I can to find both of my friends.

When we arrived back at the house, the atmosphere was like a ghost town. We did not speak to one another. Deebo stormed into his room. He slammed his room door. He had every right to be mad because he warned us about the new chick and her stupid party. We came home without Faye because something happened to her at the party, and it was my fault. My heart sank. I wanted to be left alone like everyone else.

CHAPTER 8.
EXPOSED

After a dreadful evening, the next morning, I got up and pulled my shirt from the drawer. I put on my pants. I brushed my teeth. Danny and Deebo refused to speak to me and Kelly. They would walk past us in the house like we were not there. I wanted to do something about it instead of just not doing anything. I was numb about Faye's disappearance. I went to visit the detective's office to see Mr. Shims.

Around Dallas, rumors were going around that Betsy knew something happened to Faye and failed to give the police officers the information they needed. She stayed ten minutes from the school, in a gated community. I heard that she was the only child in her family. People say her parents are never home and that they would come home at weird times of the day. I saw her a couple of times in the city with the cute guy. I know he helped her get rid of Faye. I only pray that she is still alive somewhere. The police did not have any evidence to arrest her for Faye's abduction.

"We must stay low now that the entire world is looking for this Faye girl." Betsy was on the phone with the cute guy from the party. "I need you to make sure the holding place is secure."

"I got it, girl. How many times are you going to tell me things I already know? Besides, you know we have been doing this for a year now. You owe me a little respect; don't you think?"

"First of all, I do not owe you anything, and second my dad hired you. Continue to do what I say or else you will end up like that guy at the club," said Betsy.

"You are in no position to boss me around when your stupid-ass dad got arrested, remember? But I will do what I am told for now. I will talk to you later."

The cute guy ended the call. Betsy shook her head. She got up from her bed and walked over to her desk full of papers on it. One of them had a news clip of Diane, who was missing from the Forney area. She smiled as she read on about the news announcement of the abduction. As she continued to admire the story, her phone buzzed and moved around on her desk. She picked up her phone and held it to her ear. She smirked.

"Betsy, I need you and your friend to go over to the warehouse and get those packages out of there right now. News is getting all over the place about these missing girls, and I need them out of there now," said Mr. Tim.

"How can I get them out of there? I cannot make them move, and I cannot do this by myself, Dad. I already sent my guy to take care of everything."

"Manage it and do whatever you need to do. I will send my men to help you get rid of them."

"Wait, are you going to kill them? You said you were not going to kill anybody else."

"I am in jail; I cannot harm anyone. Just do what I tell you to do. I will talk to you later." She hit the end call button.

Moments later, Betsy walked outside of her house to get into her car. An hour later she pulled up at a mysterious location and parked in the back of an old, run-down building. It had broken windows and graffiti on the exterior. Betsy stepped out of the car and walked into the warehouse. She went into each room. A faint noise was coming from the back area. She followed the noise. Faye sat with a towel in her mouth. Her hands were tied behind her back. Her eyes could see bars.

"Well, here you are. Nice to see you again. Sorry about the way this looks. Did you see my friend around here? You know, the cute one you saw at my party. He was digging you, but I told him not to get friendly with the merchandise." She smiled. She kept talking to Faye as if she were at an auction selling humans.

A few seconds later the cute guy came along with a plate in his hands. A perfectly seasoned medium-rare steak and freshly steamed asparagus. He placed the white plate in front of Faye to eat.

"Ah, it looks like it is lunchtime." Betsy walked over to the plate. Her nostrils opened. The aroma of the steak filled the air.

"He must like you because none of the others ever got steak. Am I right?" Betsy turned around to look at the cute guy from the party. She waltzes. Faye's face burns red. She turned her head at the food. The cute guy held a steak knife and a fork. He cut the steak into small pieces. He reached in between the bars to Faye's lips. She kept her lips gripped together.

"You're going to have to eat, because I know Mr. Tim is not going to allow me to spend money on you like this every day." Faye's face was pale, and her body sagged.

"Look, just leave her. We must move them to another location anyway, so we do not have time for her to eat right now. Dad wants us to get them out of here. I am waiting for help to come so we can take them to another location."

The cute guy rose from the cage area. He rested the plate on the table nearby. Betsy's phone rang, and she walked over to where her phone was. She picked it up to answer and headed to the door leading to the next room.

"Come on, Dad's guy is here to help us move the girls." The two captors walked out of the room. Faye just stared at them.

She rested her head on the wall and closed her eyes. There was a soft noise coming from the same area she was in. She opened her eyes and turned around. She closed her eyes again. She heard a movement in her cage. She rose and looked harder. A dark object rests in the corner of the cage. Her eyes squinched at the object. She crawled to the area. She nudged the object until the covers fell. A body balled up. The body rose. Diane glanced at Faye. Faye's eyes widened. She wiggled her body. Diane wiggled her hands free. She removed the cloth from Faye's mouth.

"What? How did you end up here?" Faye asked. "We have been looking for you for days. The whole school knows you are missing." Faye's face glowed.

"I was spending time together with Betsy at her house, and the next thing I knew I was here. Funny thing, I saw Kayla here too when they took me. She was in one of the other rooms. I tried to call out to her, but my mouth was gagged from a cloth they stuffed into my mouth. I was surprised that they let her go. Is she okay?" asked Diane. The two slid to each other.

"Yes, Kayla is okay, and yes it was stupid of them to let her go. I am glad they did. They thought she knew something at the time, but she did not know what they were up to," said Faye.

"Look, we must watch out for these weird people. This is a family affair. Betsy's father is a criminal. I overheard him say he killed some guy at a club. This whole thing is a setup. They have been watching me for some time now, and unfortunately, I was not aware. They sell girls like us to make a profit. It makes sense now why we always hear about missing girls in the Forney area. The police never could find them," said Diane.

"I cannot even wrap my head around what you are telling me. This whole time we knew that something was off with this girl, but we could not figure it out. I met her in class not too long ago and I thought she was a nice person, but this whole time she was checking me out to do the same thing to me that she did to you."

"How did she get you?" asked Diane.

"She had some stupid party at her house, and me and the girls went. Deebo and Danny told us not to go, but we went anyway. We figured we might find out something about you or about Betsy and what she was up to. I was waiting for Drake to meet me outside of her house," Faye explained.

"Who is Drake?" asked Diane.

"Oh, he is, my boyfriend. Anyway, he was taking forever to come and so this cute guy came up to me trying hard and I remember he dropped his phone, and then next thing I know I was in a car going somewhere."

"Shit, they got their fraud together. There is no telling how many girls have fallen for this nonsense. It must be a good amount by this time," said Diane.

"I know Kayla is looking for us right now. We will not be here for long."

"You do not understand—they have been doing this type of thing for a long time.

"How do you know this?"

"This chick had like three parties this year already. Each party has some ridiculous reason that she tells everybody when they ask her what the occasion is," said Diane.

"Are you serious?" cried Faye.

"I hope Kayla finds us quick and fast, because if this is a normal thing with them, we might as well be dead." A few men walked in with garbage bags and tape.

"Well, it looks like you reunited. Too bad we do not have time to talk about what you wore yesterday and such. Get these girls out of this cage and into the van. We have a long ride, and I do not want my dad to keep calling me asking me if you did your job right!" said Betsy.

The girls huddled together. Faye's body shivered. Diane was still. The men got into the cage, picked each girl up one by one, and carried them. Diane screamed. Faye followed. One of the men punched Diane in the mouth. Her body dropped like a sack.

"You better be quiet before you're next," he said. "I don't want to see your pretty face scuffed up, okay hon?" said Betsy. She stood by the doorway to watch.

"I swear you are going to pay for all of it. Do you think you are going to get away with this? You are stupid for thinking that," Faye proclaimed.

"Oh, honey, I have been paid a lot of money to do this stupid thing for a year. Umm, let me see. We are up to twenty-five girls now. Well, it does not matter, because I got my money for each one." Betsy bent her fingers to look at her nails.

"Go on, get them out of here; we don't have time to waste." They walked out of the building into a dark van that was parked outside.

I got up early. I went into the bathroom and brushed my teeth. I jumped in the shower. I did not want to eat breakfast. I wanted to see Detective Shims at his office. I got in my car to see him. I arrived at his office, and his door was wide open. He was closing his computer when his phone started to ring.

"This always happens when I am about to leave. What do you have for me?" he asked. He walked over to his desk to get his pad and pencil. I looked at Mr. Shims as he was jotting down notes. His face smirked.

"Come on, let me take you home. We got a lead that might help find your missing friend," he said.

"Which one?" I raised both of my hands.

"I don't know—maybe one, maybe both of them, but I'm dropping you off first because you are not coming with me."

"Come on, this is not my first rodeo," I said.

Mr. Shims frowned. He snatched his jacket, and the doorknob almost came off.

"Where are your other friends? I am going to get them to a secure location." I jumped up. "Come on if you're coming."

We got outside of his office building. He walked over to his car and opened the passenger door for me like a true gentleman. Then he got to the other side. I started to feel good about helping him find my missing friends, Diane and Faye.

At the warehouse, Faye and Diane sat in the van in the back lying down. Their mouths were gagged with a piece of cloth, and their hands were tied. Mr. Tim's goons were driving them to another location, and Betsy and her boy toy were on their way to meet her father's associates. In the van, the driver's cellphone started ringing. He looked at the phone and turned his head.

"This man is calling for you—better answer Tim's call. I do not want you messing with my money," said the guy in the passenger seat.

"All right, stop crying and get him back on the phone for me. I did not know you were his little bitch," said the driver.

"Shut up and drive this van like you know how to drive." The guy in the passenger seat became fidgety. His hands shook while he held a cigarette. He pulled out his phone from his back pocket. He handed his phone to the driver.

"Hey, what's up?" the man asked. A few moments later, the driver hung up and shook his head and then turned the van around.

"Hey man, what are you doing? You were supposed to drive them to the beach."

"I am not driving anybody for no eight hours. They need to pay me more for that," said the driver.

"Are you trying to get us killed? He said we need to take them to the beach to make the drop."

"Well, then you can go take them if you want to when I get back to the warehouse because I'm not doing that." While the driver drove, the van bounced up and down. Diane and Faye swayed back and forth to the movement of the van.

Mr. Shims and I picked up my friends Kelly, Deebo, and Danny. We arrived at the secure location that he promised. Kelly jumped out. The front of the house had an incredibly old exterior. The windows were old with wooden frames. The house resembled a run-down scary house.

"This place looks like someone died in it. Is this place safe to be in?" asked Deebo. He dusts off his shirt. Mr. Shim got the kids' bags and threw them on the lawn.

"Hey, I have expensive equipment in those bags." Danny pointed to the ground.

"You're not on vacation or at an Airbnb. You are in the middle of an investigation and need protection from these maniacs out here. You are going to stay here and be out of sight until we say so," said the detective.

"Why does Kayla get to go with you?" Deebo threw his bag on the floor.

"I do not want Kayla to go with me, but she knows what Mr. Tim looks like."

"I do too."

Deebo snatched up the bags. He walked inside the old house. Danny and Kelly follow.

"Please let us know the minute you locate our friends," said Kelly.

"I will do my best to find them, Kelly, and bring them home safely."

The men who took the girls in the van brought the girls back to the warehouse. The driver got out of the van and left. The guy that was in the passenger seat remained. In the back of the van, Diane and Faye sat there. Diane started moving her hands to get out of the ropes. She untied her feet. She moved over to Diane. She got behind her and removed her hands from the rope. Diane removed the rope from her feet.

"We stopped moving; where the hell are we?" asked Faye. She went over to the window.

"I do not know, but something is telling me that we did not go far."

"How do you know that?" Diane got herself up and stared out the window.

"I remember that tall building over there with a red flag on top. It was there when we got in this van, and now it is here again."

"Okay, I'm not following you—what does this mean?"

"It means that wherever we were before we turned around. We are back where we started from."

"Are you serious? We must try to get out of this van right now before they change their mind again and drive us somewhere again."

"Look around for something sharp like a pair of scissors or a knife."

Diane and Faye tore the van up looking for weapons. Two men were outside of the van talking amongst themselves.

"Listen, I do not know what was wrong with the man, but he just stopped driving and turned the van around and drove back to the warehouse. Tell me what you want me to do now," asked the man.

"Looks like they are trying to figure out what to do with us. Continue to look around and see if you find something. This may be our only time now to try to get out of here," said Diane.

"I do not see anything. Wait a minute, I think I will see something. It looks like a nail file."

"Yes!" Moments later, one of the men opened the door to the van.

"Listen up, ladies, we are moving you out of this van," said the man. Diane and Faye had their hands behind them. One of the men walked toward Faye. Then his phone started to ring.

"What does he want now? I cannot even try to do what I need to do." He slammed the van door shut.

"Hey, I was about to get the girls back inside. Is there a change in plans?"

"Listen, when he comes back in here, we need to act fast and cut him," said Diane.

"Wow, we were supposed to rescue you and here you are rescuing me," Faye added.

Diane stood up and peeked outside the van to see where the guy was. Faye stood up to see what Diane was looking at.

The man walked over to the van, again. He stuck his head in and did not see the girls at first. He then stepped up into the van to see where the girls were hiding.

"Listen up, I don't have time for this. We have to go. I have to bring you inside now," said the man.

Diane and Faye hid toward the back of the van. The man entered his body into the van, and Diane found a pipe. She hit the man on his head. The man fell forward on his face. Faye closed the door.

"What do we do with him now?"

Diane went into the man's pants pocket. She pulled out a set of keys and quickly went to the front of the van. She jumped into the driver's seat and started the van.

"Get in the seat—put your seat belt on right now. I need you to keep an eye on him in case he comes too," Diane commanded. Faye dropped the nail file she had in her hand. She walked slowly to the passenger seat. She pulled the seat belt. Her hands were shaking.

"Where are we going?" asked Faye. She glanced to the back where the man lay.

"We are going to the police. Grab his phone and call Kayla to let her know we escaped."

Diane drove fast and passed the red lights. Everything in the van swayed back and forth. She drove through the streets like a mad woman.

"The GPS has a police station near here. We should be there in five minutes," she said. Faye kept her eyes on the man in the back.

I was still with Detective Shims driving around. I looked down at my phone when it buzzed.

"Oh my God!! I screamed. Where are you?" I asked. Mr. Shims glanced over at me.

"Is that your friend?" He had one hand up.

"Stay there—do not go anywhere. Stay right there. We are on our way," I said and jumped up in the passenger seat.

"Are those the missing girls?" asked Detective Shims.

I smiled. "They are alive and well," I said happily.

"Who is?"

"Diane and Faye. They are safe—thank goodness they just got to the police department. It is near to here." I pointed to the phone's GPS. "I told them to wait there."

Mr. Shims drove to the police department to meet the girls. I got on the phone to call Kelly with the good news. An hour later, Mr. Shims got the report from Diane and Faye. Detective Shims got on his phone.

"I need you to go over and pick up the kids from a secure location." Later that day, Danny, Deebo, and Kelly met us at Detective Shim's office.

"You guys must be tired; I'll take you home."

"I am so glad we found you. I was willing to do anything to find you," I said.

"Thank you, Kayla, and all of you." I wrapped my arms around Diane and Kelly tightly.

"Mr. Shims told me what you did for me. Thank you for being there for my mom. I appreciate it," said Diane. Diane smiled at Kayla.

"Kayla is stubborn and would not take no for an answer. She wanted to help, and I had to put myself in her shoes," said Mr. Shims.

"Now hopefully you girls think twice about going to a party without us." Deebo raised one of his eyebrows. I gave a chuckle, glancing at Deebo and Danny.

"Kayla, thank you for your participation in this investigation. It looks like you might need to study law enforcement in college," the detective said.

"Nope, I am not doing that. I'm better off just staying in my lane." Kayla raised both of her hands.

"Which is what?" he asked.

"Being a teenager." The laughter filled the room with warmth.

I came through for my friends. We would not have found Diane if it were not for my persistence. Looking for Diane allowed us to find my roommate Faye. I was incredibly happy with myself. I stood my ground and never gave up when it was time to go looking for my friends. I love them. I would do it again if I had to.

It was a long night. A long year. A crazy experience living with my friends. We have been through a lot. I got into the shower thinking about everything that we had done up to this point. I thought about how we stole from Ms. Kemp, robbed a bank, and then returned what we took. I thought about being taken by the bad guys and then getting back home. I wondered why the men who took me did not kill me. I wondered about a lot of things at that moment. I got out of the shower. I heard a knock at my door.

"Who is it?" I asked. I held on to the towel that was wrapped around my body tight.

"It's me, Dee." I exhaled.

"I just got out of the shower, but you can come in."

"Are you sure?" he asked from outside the door.

"Sure. Come in." I grabbed one of my oversized tees and put it on.

"Hi. I was wrong about Diane, and I wanted you to know I was sorry. I did not take you seriously when you sensed that something was wrong." He stood tall, and his light skin tone glowed right in front of me.

"It is okay, Dee, sometimes I do go bizarre and act like I am some detective. I could have gotten myself killed during all my crazy adventures. I promise I will listen to you" I said.

"Are you sure this time?" I nodded.

He walked up to me. I felt his warm lips on mine. As he kissed me, he raised my tee over my head. I helped him by raising my hands. His hands caressed my body. I had butterflies floating in my chest. He lifted me to bed. He made love so passionately to me. I began to see the clouds. My room disappeared. There was a picture of a sky that filled my room, and feathers fell all over.

CHAPTER 9.
FREE

The next morning, I looked over to see if I was dreaming. I wanted to see if Deebo was sleeping next to me. It was not a dream. I watched his breathing. We slept together and I did not know what it meant. *He is so fine*, I thought to myself. This would be the third time that we had sex in my bedroom. Can I believe that Deebo loves me like he said? Or is it just a phase? My eyes roamed up to my ceiling. I lay on my arms. My face is in a happy state. I know I have feelings for him. I know he has a lot of girls that he plays around with. I knew I did not want to be one of them.

After the rescue of my friend Diane and Faye, Detective Shims cleared us to return to our normal lives. That meant going back to school. We can go back to being normal teens like everyone else. I look forward to fun school activities, like the school dance and the prom. It was the end of March, and Forney High always hosted a dance for the Juniors, with prom following afterward.

"So, what are we wearing for the dance? I do not want to hear that no one is going," asked Faye.

"I am not going to any dance and going to the prom," Danny proclaimed. His eyes were buried in his phone.

"Who said anything about the prom? I was asking about the dance, and besides, it is safe to say we are all going to the prom after the year we had so far." Her eyes made contact with all of us.

"Why are we going to the dance? We are seniors and the dance is for Juniors," asked Kelly.

"Guys, we said we were going to the dance so we can have those memories. We could not attend the last dance because we were running from criminals, remember?" I grabbed my bag for school and put it on my shoulder.

"Our lives are back to normal. We are not in witness protection. We can make Faye happy and go to the prom," I commented.

"With the amount of money we have, we can finally stay out of trouble," Deebo added.

"Come on, guys, let's get to school—we can talk about how free we are later." I walked out of the house, and my friends followed me like I was the leader of the pack.

We arrived at Forney High, driving separate cars of course. I heard that annoying sound coming from my phone. It was buzzing, and I could see my mom's number across the screen.

"Are you kidding me? What does she want?" My mood quickly switched. "Hello Mom, what can I do for you?" I have not heard from my mom since she kicked me out of the house. I never got a text or a call from her. I wondered why she was calling me.

"Kayla! I am so glad you answered your phone. I was afraid that you were going to ignore my calls."

"Yeah, I was, but I am heading into class. I can't talk right now." I walked slowly into the school building.

"I want you to come to the house, I need to talk to you." Her voice annoyed the heck out of me.

"We haven't spoken to each other in a year or so," I explained. My emotions played with me.

"I know, I know. It is about your father. There are a few things you need to know about him. I did not want you to hear it on the news before I got the chance to tell you first."

"Okay, whatever, I will come by after school. See you later, Mom." I pressed the end call button. How can I face my mom after all this time?

"Who was that?" asked Kelly.

"If you can believe it, it was my mom." I walked in the hallway like I did not belong.

"Something must be wrong for her to call you unexpected, right?" My friend Kelly's eyebrows raised with doubt. I shrugged my shoulders. I walked into my class and Kelly waited for an answer.

After school, I had to calm my nerves before I drove to Dallas to see my mom. It has been a year since I stepped into my mom's house. I was interested in seeing what the house looked like. I pulled up to the long driveway. I remembered the beautiful landscaping and attractive exterior. It looked the same. I parked inside the tall bridge that led to the eight-car garage. I was the only one that had access to the garage because of where my room was located. It was good for sneaking out as well.

The beautiful water fountain, in the middle of the driveway, is still there. It used to be our wishing well that my friends and I used to throw coins in. The guesthouse and a boat dock that we never used brought back so many memories of when my sister and I were little. We would run out here and watch the water and talk. I wondered why my parents felt the need to have that because neither one of us knew how to drive one.

I stayed in my car for a minute. I sighed and took a deep breath. My parents never apologized for kicking me out of the house, and I was not about to forget that because of an invite. I got out of the car and looked around as

I walked up to the front door. I see the huge, tall doors, with checkered glass panes. I rang the crystal doorbell and waited. I stood out there. I looked around at the roses and the magnolia trees we had in the front. I rang the doorbell again. I turn around.

Is she crazy? She asked me to come here, and she is not home. I turned around and started to head to my car when someone finally opened the door. A handsome-looking young guy who looked to be around twenty years old was in my view. He looked physically fit, tall, and had beautiful blond hair and brown eyes. You get the picture right? I pretended not to notice but caught myself looking at him in the corner of my eye.

"Hello." I looked at the guy as if he did not speak English.

"Are you here for someone?" he asked. I quickly snapped out of the fine-guy trance.

"I am Mrs. Jensen's daughter. Is she here?" I said with authority. Who does he think he is? This is my house. Are you here for someone? I did not ask him this, but I wanted to. The cute guy smiled and walked backward to get out of my way.

"I didn't know Mrs. Jensen had a daughter, and a very pretty one at that." I passed him and kept walking to the kitchen area. I used to live here so I know where I am going.

"Who are you, if you don't mind me asking?"

"I collaborate with your father, and sometimes I come to the house if they need me to work on something. I am interested in commercial real estate." I was not interested in anything he had to say. He realized the silence from me and walked ahead of me.

"I will let your mom know that you are here. Nice meeting you." I glanced back at the guy walking away and thought I was a little harsh.

"Well, I see you met Christian," my mom said, waltzing in like she was some fancy goddess, in an Asian silk robe with her hair and makeup done. Her nails were bright red.

"He collaborates with your father at the office, and I asked him to do a couple of things for me."

"What exactly does he do for dad?" I was curious.

She walked over to the wine room and pulled out a bottle of expensive wine. She took out a wine glass, opened the wine with the electric bottle opener, and poured herself some.

"Do you want some wine, dear?"

I smirked. "I'm underage, remember?"

"Oh, please do not act like you and your trashy friends do not drink. You do drugs, right?" The blood rushed through my veins.

"You called me here to talk about Dad. Is he okay? Is he dying?"

"Why would you think he is dying? I wanted to talk to you about him," she repeated. By this time, I was getting annoyed, because my patience had run out.

"You keep saying the same thing repeatedly, and you are not telling me what you need to tell me. You are like an annoying friend who is socially awkward and cannot communicate. What, Mom?" I slammed my keys down on the counter. I walked over to the cabinet, took out a wine glass, and poured myself some.

"I don't do drugs." I sat down and looked at her.

"I am going to ignore how you just disrespected me in my house." She continued with her wine. "Your father's business is not doing well, and he is stealing money from other businesses. I called you here because I am divorcing him, and I did not want you to hear about the divorce from anyone else."

I rubbed my temples like I was studying for a test. I poured another glass and looked around the kitchen. I glanced at my mom. I exploded.

"I have not heard from either one of you in over a year. You did not care if I was rotting in hell. I had no money because you closed all my accounts. All I had was the clothes that I grabbed. I did not do anything wrong to be treated like garbage."

"You could have told us that the drugs were not yours. We told you to call that girl so we could talk to her, but you refused to prove that it was hers and not yours. We had no way of knowing otherwise. We do not do drugs in this house, and you know the rules."

I got up slowly to put the wine glass in the sink. Tears fell on my face. I could see her breathing.

"My word should have been enough, Mom." I walked out of the kitchen. I saw the guy hiding behind a wall. "It was nice meeting you too."

A week went by after the terrible visit I had with my mom. I was in a good place and had forgotten all about my family issues and lack of a relationship with my parents. Finding out about my parents' divorce was not a shock to me because they were having problems before I left the house. I was confused when she called to let me know. She knew where I lived and where I worked when I moved out of the house, but never once picked up the phone to call or came by to visit. That bothered me a lot, and I wondered if my parents even loved me. A new school week approached. I slept in. I wanted to stay in bed curled up to forget all the drama. I grabbed my remote to watch television. The day went quickly, and it was like I did not even get rest.

"Hey sleepyhead, how was your day?" It's after school already. I do not know why Kelly felt the need to bother me. She rushed into my room and slammed her school bag on my desk, with no regard. Everybody else stayed downstairs, but not Kelly. She had to come straight up to my room like she wanted to catch me in the act. She talked about being bored and tired of coming home and not having any kind of fun. The money we now have should have made them feel better.

"I had a great day doing nothing and a bad day thinking about my mom and my dad." Kelly sat on the bed and took off her shoes like she was in her room.

"Ouch, that night when you told me what she said I felt sad for you. I know it was tough seeing her after all these months. My family sucks too, but at least my parents call me from time to time to make sure I am not in a dumpster somewhere," she boasted. I rolled around in my bed with the covers on my face. I did not feel comforted.

"I would not mind that at all, to be honest. Even if they did not believe me about the drugs, at least a call from them now and then would not be so bad."

Later that evening Deebo and Faye barged into my room to bother me about going out. "Okay you have been just sitting here all day, you need to get some fresh air. So, I say let us spend time together tonight." Faye clapped like it was supposed to get me up. It was annoying. Deebo walked over to my closet and started pulling out some clothes. Last I checked he was not a stylist.

"What are you doing in my closet?"

"I am just picking out stuff. I do not know what you girls wear, but here is a start."

"I would not wear any of those to a night out."

"Go in the shower and pick out what you would wear. I am waiting for you downstairs, and I want you to look hot and sexy. Is that okay with you?"

"Well, that is the sign for me to head on." Kelly put her hands over her ears. "He is right, do not take forever in the shower. See you downstairs."

Later that night we headed out to a couple of bars in Dallas. We ended up at one of our favorite ones to hang out at. We filled an area at the restaurant and waited for the waiter to come to the table. I danced to the music that was playing in my seat. My eyes met this cute guy's face. Faye talked to Kelly on the phone. I found myself staring at the cute guy's face again.

"Who are you looking at over there?" Faye gives me the evil eye. Deebo was sitting next to me, and I acted like it was nothing. Remember, Deebo and I had several intimate moments, and I was not about to mess with whatever we had going on.

"What are we drinking, guys?" I pick up the menu and stare at it like I have never seen it before.

"No, you see somebody over there—who is it? Is it a cute guy checking you out?" Faye looks over in that direction. I put my finger on my eyes, to give her a hint. She did not get it.

"Girl, will you quit it, and where is your man anyway? How come he is not here with us?" I ask. I wiggle around in my seat.

"Do not try to change the subject, but since you asked, he had to work tonight, but I get to see him tomorrow. You never look at the menu because we come here all the time."

Deebo ignored our conservation. I was glad that he was not aware of what was going on. The waiter asked for our drink orders. I looked over at Deebo, and he was still texting. *This is a wonderful time to get away*, I said to myself.

"I am heading to the bathroom."

"I will come with you. I left my lip gloss at home. I cannot find anything in this purse." Faye's hands were buried deep in her purse.

Deebo stared at us. We walked to the ladies' room. We passed a group of guys, and that familiar cute guy's eyes met mine again. In the bathroom, Faye found her lip gloss. I looked in the mirror. I did not need to use the bathroom. When we walked out of the bathroom, I felt piercing eyes. Right before we got to our table, this handsome guy reached out his hand to me right in front of my path.

"Hey, where did we meet? You look so familiar." His blond hair was perfectly in place. I stared into his brown eyes.

"That's a lame-ass line, but I forgive you since you're fine as hell," Faye confesses.

"Yeah, it is you. I work for your parents, remember? You came home last week, and I answered the door."

"Oh, yeah, hi," I said. Faye glanced at the guy and then looked at me. She blinked her eyes and then walked back to our table.

"Who the hell is that?" Deebo stared hard. Even though Deebo never talked about our current relationship status, we both know that we are together.

"I am doing okay. Listen, I wanted to apologize to you for last week," said the cute guy who works for my parents.

"For what?" I asked.

"I know you saw me eavesdropping, and that was not right. I should have been minding my business." In the distance I watched Faye talk to Deebo.

"Oh, it's cool. I am embarrassed you had to hear it. It was nice seeing you, but I must go. I am here with some friends."

"Yeah, sure. Can I get your number or see you again?" I received a chill sensation.

"How about I call my mom and get your number from her?"

"Yeah, cool. Have a good evening. Hold up, you did not ask for my name." I tried to stay calm. My mom already told me what it was. I asked anyway.

"What is your name?"

"I'm Chris—well, Christian, but I like Chris, and I know your name is Kayla, right?"

"Yup."

"Well, I'll let you go since you are in a rush. I look forward to your call," Chris responded. The cute guy was in a trance. He looked at me as if he were scared it would be the last time. I walked back to the table, with a straight face, so that I would not let on that I liked the guy.

"Where do you know him from?" Deebo did not waste any time. Faye's eyes popped out of her head.

"Oh him—he was at my parents' house when I went to see my mom. I am starving. Let's get some food. Are you good, babe?" I buried my head into the menu. He looked back at Chris and turned back around to look at me. I was saved by the server. Moments later, the waiter carried platters of wings, French fries, egg rolls, and mozzarella sticks.

After hanging out at the restaurant, we headed home. The guys wanted to finish the night with a game of pool. Deebo and Danny went into the game room at the house. After a couple of rounds, Danny left Deebo. A few seconds later, I heard a knock at my room door.

"Hey, can I come in?" Deebo's voice came through the door.

"Come on in. Did he beat you again?" I said sarcastically.

"No, he went chasing some girl or something—I don't know. I wanted to spend some time with you, if you do not mind." I was throwing all my dirty clothes in a basket.

"You don't have to clean up now; I already saw the mess."

"Screw you."

"Just joking. My room is worse than yours."

"Maybe you can come into my room and help me clean it."

"Why are you here? You look a little occupied, like you are trying to keep yourself busy or trying to avoid something." I swallowed a lump.

"I am still a little bothered about my mom and my dad. They are getting a divorce, and even though I do not care, it still bothers me."

He grabbed the clothes from my hand and pulled me to sit down on my bed. "I am sorry about the sad news. That is why I came in here to check on you."

Strands of my hair fell near my eye, and he brushed them aside. He was sexy with his mannerisms. At that moment he was kind and gentle. I am used to seeing him lust over other girls at school. It was surprising to see him be soft with me.

"Thank you for thinking about me." He removed his sneakers. "Are you getting comfortable in my room?"

"I am." He stood up and raised his muscled arms. I was blinded by his body of perfection. He removed his T-shirt. I pretended not to be bothered by his heartthrob looks. He walked over to the door. His finger turned the lock.

He walked back to me. I felt his lips on mine. They were warm and soft. His ab muscles formed a perfect six-pack. I wanted to jump all over him. I waited for him to make his move. He continued to kiss me. My blouse fell. Deebo always made me weak when he touched me. Each time I had sex with him, my feelings became increasingly intense. I wondered what would come out of this night. The best part of the whole evening was that he allowed me to forget about my parents and everything that was going wrong in my life.

The next day, Faye wanted us to get ready for the school dance for the juniors. We are seniors and we promised her we would attend. I did not remember why we said yes, but Faye always had a way of getting us to do what she wanted.

"I don't know why I even try to fix this hair of mine because it never does what I want it to do." Faye played with her hair like she was a life-size doll.

"Why don't you just do what I do and put it in a ponytail? It works every time," I commented.

"Well, not if it's dirty and needs a shampoo and conditioning. Oh my gosh, I am so done with this hair." She tousled her hair.

"Well, you are going to have to do something because we are late. Let's go, girls. I am starting the car right now," said Kelly. She rushed out of the house.

"I'm coming, I am coming! Wait for me! I just got to get my math book," I yelled.

It was lunchtime. I was the first one in the cafeteria. A few minutes later, my friends met me there. When I saw Deebo, our chemistry seemed to increase in heat. It was because of the night we had. I was feeling a little shy about the whole thing. We sat together. His arm hooked around my neck. All eyes were on us.

"Wait, are you guys finally official?" asked Danny. A French fry fell out of his mouth. I smiled.

"You're not shy to talk about it, right"? Faye darted their eyes at me.

"Even though it took her long enough, she finally came to her senses and saw that I was the man," Deebo confessed.

"'The man'?" asked Danny.

"No, *The Man*." He high-fives Danny. Laughter filled the air.

"Got it, got it," Danny nods as he eats. I was happy. For the first time in my life, I was genuinely happy. I hope that this feeling never goes away.

A couple of hours later school was over, and I was headed home. I glanced at my phone. My dad's number flashed across the screen. I was in shock because suddenly my parents wanted to talk to me now.

"Hello, Dad."

"Kayla, your mother is snooping around in my office. I want you to let me know if she gives you any of my things that do not belong to her." My brain went numb.

"Umm, sure okay," I responded.

"The reason I am telling you this is because my secretary came into my office and caught her by surprise. She was caught digging in my files that are confidential and have important financial information from my clients."

Why are they calling me suddenly? I was trying to figure it out. Should I get in it or stay the hell out of it? That was a question that remained in my head. I did not know how to manage the situation.

My mom was looking for something and I am guessing that it was documents that belonged to my father. Why was my mom digging for things she had access to? My mom was a business partner with my father, so it was a little strange. When my dad called me, he acted like my mom was no longer a partner. I decided that if I wanted to know the answers to my questions, I would have to go to my parents' house again.

Later that day I headed over to my parents' house. When I pulled up, this time the front door was open. I walked into my dad's office and saw my mom close one of the filing cabinets. She had papers spread all over the desk. I heard the doorbell ring.

"That's Chris. I called him to come over. I need his help with all these documents." The housekeeper let him in, and he walked right through the foyer without anyone telling him where to go.

"Oh, good, thank you for coming over on such short notice. I need you to help me find something." My mom greeted him like he was the solution to the problem. She walked quickly toward the kitchen, leaving Chris behind for him to catch up to her.

"Yeah, sure Mrs. Jensen. I came quickly from the campus, what are you trying to find?" He scratched his head.

"I need you to look through these spreadsheets and see if you see something fishy. Your boss is up to something, and I want to know firsthand so that I can let my attorney know."

"Why would he be hiding anything? I thought you both owned the business." I sat there observing. I was thinking the same thing as Chris was. My mom smirks. She looked at him without answering him.

"Why are you here? I thought you were too busy to come by." She looked in my direction.

"He is hiding something and that is not your business, young man. Your job is to do what I ask and look for any amount of money that was taken from one account and transferred to another." Chris went inside my dad's office like he was hypnotized to do so. He picked up a few papers. He paused. My mom looked at him. Her face frowned. What did he see?

"What is your issue? Why did you stop looking? I need to find out before he gets home." she demanded. His eyes squinched.

"Umm, Mrs. Jensen, I can't do this." He put the documents back down on the desk.

"Do what?" she asked.

"I cannot look through Mr. Jensen's papers like this. It is not right and probably illegal to look at private accounts without his consent. I do not want to get in trouble." His eyes were sincere.

"Are you stupid? just get out of my way." She brushed him as she walked toward the papers and grabbed them. "I do not know why you came here in the first place if you were not going to help me," she grunted.

She went through the papers while Chris watched. I thought about interrupting her, but it just did not seem like an enjoyable time. It did not take a scientist to see that she was ignoring my presence. Chris did as well. So, I grabbed my things and left the room.

I walked to the front door to go outside. I cannot figure her out. One minute she acts like she needs my help and then the next she is acting like I do not exist. My father asked me to talk to her and she ignored me. This is the main reason I choose not to make amends with my family. They are not interested in having me back at the house. When I was living at home, my sister and I did everything for ourselves. My parents just made sure we had access to the money. They kept a stash in one of my dad's drawers in case we needed it for anything. It was all coming back to me. One day I will have to warn my little sister that she will have to fend for herself.

After the craziness with my mom, Chris let himself out. I saw my dad in the distance pulling up to the front of the house. Chris looked fidgety. He was acting strange when my dad walked up to the front. I did not know why he was afraid of my father.

"I did not know we had an appointment today. Did I miss something, Chris?" My father loosened his tie.

"No not all. Mrs. Jensen wanted me to help her look for something. I was just on my way out. Good-bye, Mr. Jensen," he stuttered. "I do not want any trouble, Mr. Jensen. Please tell your wife I had to go." Chris hustled to his car.

"What trouble? Did you know that witch was at my office being nosy and looking around?" My dad yelled at Chris outside of the house.

"No sir, I will talk to you tomorrow. I got to study for an exam. Please tell your wife good-bye," Chris yelled out of his car window and drove off like he stole something. My dad did not even look at me once he passed me and went into the house. All I could do was shake my head and get into my car.

The next day at Forney High, I was tired. I floated through the hallways like I was on something. I wanted time to fly by. At the end of the day, I did not wait for Kelly, Faye, Danny, and Deebo. I got home and dropped my bags on the floor. I kicked them against the wall. I lay across my bed. My eyes saw clouds. I thought about all the things that have happened since I was living on my own.

Then it dawned on me, and I thought about the cute guy Chris. I thought about how cute he was and how I wanted to kiss his perfect lips. I remembered he wanted my number from my mom. I forgot to get his number when

I was at the house. I wanted to ask him a couple of questions, and I knew that if I wanted to talk to him, I would have to get his number from my mom. I glanced at my phone on my bed. I texted her. A few moments later I heard my doorknob rattle. Deebo walks into my room. He does this all the time. He waltzed in like I invited him.

"Hey, what are you doing?" I jumped up. My only frame of thought was why is he here?

"I am thinking about my mom. She was going through my dad's stuff, and I do not want to know why," I responded.

"Why are you dodging her?" He sat at my desk.

"It's a long story, but where are you going?" I asked.

"I was going to ask you if you want to go to our favorite spot so we can eat and have drinks and have dessert." He displayed a grin.

"Dessert? Now you know we do not eat dessert." I waited for a comeback. He stood up off the chair. He approached me. He grabbed my hands.

"Whoever said anything about dessert at the restaurant? I was talking about dessert right here with you and me as the final dish." I smiled. Our arms embraced. We engaged in a passionate kiss.

"Wait a second," I pulled away.

"What?"

"We can't go out tonight because tonight is the dance, remember, and we promised Faye we were all going to attend," I said.

"I forgot about that. Does she want to go to this thing?" He dropped his hands from my waist. He walked to the door.

"Yes, and we have to go because we said we would go together."

He glanced back at me. I smiled. About an hour later we were running up and down the house to get ready. Deebo and Danny were all dressed up ready to go to the Forney High School dance. Faye and Kelly were waiting for me. I took the longest to get ready. I was the last one to walk out of the house. We got a party bus to pick us up. Once we arrived at the school, the parking lot was crowded with other buses and luxury cars. All eyes were on us when we rolled in. The whole place became a spectacle.

"Well, Faye, you can't say we never did anything for you, girl." Kelly was fixing her eyelashes and looking at herself in her tiny mirror.

"Exactly, and I'm only staying for an hour or two because I already know this dance is going to be lame as heck," said Danny. I started to take selfies of me and Deebo in our outfits in the backseat.

"I am very thankful that you did this for me, and I promise you we will all have fun. We are seniors now, and it is time we take some time to make memories." Faye had her arms up like she wanted us to agree with her.

"Yes, seniors—that's why we should not be here since this is a juniors' dance, remember?" said Danny. He wore this dark suit like he was James Bond. Deebo was all in black and kept the tie off.

The dance was lit, as we would say, and everybody was having an enjoyable time. The chaperones were these cool substitute teachers, and they only had one principal there that we all liked. Mrs. Sara Shaffer. She was loved by everyone at the school because she was so cool, young, and hip, and she rarely gave out disciplinary action to students.

Students were coming in, and the gym started to look like a nightclub. The DJ started the music and the crowd went crazy. After we mingled, we sat at a table in the back where we could see everyone coming in, and I saw someone that I did not want to see. The cute guy, Chris! He was at the front with some girl. I could not tell if she was his date, but it was strange because he was not a high school student. I kept looking at him and I was freaking out. I wanted to know why he was here and who he was here with.

"Hey, me and Danny are leaving but we will be back to scoop you ladies up later on," Deebo whispered.

"Deebo, that is not part of the plan. We are all supposed to be staying here. I do not think it is fair for you and Danny to leave." Faye narrowed her eyes at the boys.

"Girl, you wanted me to come, and so I did. I could leave and not come back, but I said I would. Chill out." I sighed. I was glad to hear that Deebo was leaving. The cute guy Chris came in with this pretty young lady in his arms, and he took her over to some group of friends. He turned around a few times, but luckily, he did not see me. How in the hell am I going to hide from him all night at this dance? I panicked. I had mixed feelings about the whole thing. I did not want him to see me here, but I was also glad to see him.

An hour later my friends were taking selfies with people, but I decided to lay low and hide in the corner. People were going outside and coming back in. I looked around and I did not see Chris. I jumped up as if the DJ was playing my favorite song. I started to think that I was in the clear.

"Hey Kayla, wow, I didn't think I would spot you here at the dance," said Mrs. Schaffer, the principal.

"Oh hi, Mrs. Schaffer, yeah, I promised my friend Faye that I would go—so, ha, clubbing with the junior," I smirked.

"That is great because I am going to need a few of you to help with the cleanup committee afterward. Would that be a problem?"

I got quiet for a moment and thought to myself that I did not want to help clean up anything and that I wanted to get the hell out of there as quickly as possible before I ran into Chris. Then I thought that staying after the dance might be a wonderful way to not run into him.

"Yeah, sure, no problem. I will make sure all my guys stay and help since we are seniors crashing the party." I chuckled.

I glanced at my phone and saw that my mom called me several times. I am glad that I missed them all. I suspect my parents were still arguing nonstop because of my mom messing around with my dad's business documents.

It was clear to see why these two had their separate quarters and why they would be headed to divorce court. The thought of them breaking up was not upsetting to me; it was the fact that they expected me to get in between it and pick sides. I was hung up on the fact that they did not care if I was dead or alive.

Finally, the music stopped. The school dance ended. Kelly, Faye, and I looked for garbage bags to assist the cleanup party that the principal wanted us to help. Deebo and Danny were not back yet, and I was happy that I missed Chris, or so I thought.

I was picking up empty cups and throwing out garbage around the gym. Danny strolled on in with some chick. He was alone. No Deebo. Great! I was glad about that.

"Hey, I hope you guys are ready to go, because I did not come over here to pick you girls up if you're not ready."

"Where is Deebo? Wasn't he with you?" asked Faye.

"Deebo said he would meet me here in a few minutes. Please be ready when he comes so we can leave. I got this pretty lady I need to tend to." He smirked.

"Hi guys, thank you so much for your help tonight cleaning up. I just have one more favor for you. I need some assistance moving some cabinets back in place at the storage. Please come with me so I can show you." Mrs. Schaffer, the school principal, led the way. I quickly followed her so that I could be out of view.

Kelly, Faye, and I grabbed the filled garbage bags. Danny and his unknown girlfriend were locked in arms but picked up garbage bags and followed behind.

"Hey guys, I'm going to finish up and I'll meet you up front when I'm done," I said. I cleaned the area I was working in. Doing all this cleanup work made me have to use the bathroom. I came out of the back room to enter the bathroom and bumped into someone. It was Chris, the cute guy who collaborates with my parents. My heart thumped. I could feel the heat and sweat building up as I stood in front of him.

"What are you doing here?"

"We got to stop meeting like this. I mean for real; it is getting a little weird, don't you think?" I stared into his brown eyes. He stepped forward, right into my space. I remain quiet.

"I brought my little sister here to the dance and I was bribed by her principal to help out afterward with cleaning up."

"I see you got the memo as well. I am surprised to see you here too because I thought the dance was for juniors. Last I checked my sister did not skip a grade." he laughed softly.

"No, she did not. My friend Faye talked us into coming, and I now see it was a trap well planned."

"Hey, listen, the reason why I wanted you to call me is, well, two things, but the first was that your mom has been acting strangely lately and I wanted to let you know."

"What do you mean by acting strangely?" I sucked in a breath.

"Look, I do not want to start any problems, but your mom asked me to snoop around in your dad's office again. It looked like she was trying to find something incriminating on him, and I told her I was not down with that. I think you should find out what she is doing. I do not want her to get in trouble."

Smoke came out of my nose. My sweaty hands gripped the garbage bag. "No, thank you for telling me. I've been meaning to call her, but I just could not get myself ready to do it. What was the other thing? You said two things you had to tell me?" I uttered shyly.

"Oh, uh yeah, the other thing was that I wanted to maybe ask you out or something, but I don't want to sound pushy." My eyes brushed his body. He walked up closer to me. We were face to face and eye to eye.

"How do you feel about that?" My body starts to tremble. My face is blushing like a rose bush. I was into him. He looked good and smelled so good. I thought to myself.

"Um, yes, sure, I'm fine with that, yeah, I'm fine with that." I stuttered to get the words out and I sounded like a fool that has never talked to a boy before. I could not take my emotions.

"Can I get your number now?"

"Yeah sure, let me show it to you." I took my phone out. I held it up.

"Here you go," he said. He sent me a text.

"Did you think I gave you a fake number?" I asked.

"No, not at all, I texted you a question." I looked down to read the text. I started to sweat once again with my heart pounding out of my chest as I tried to stay calm. My eyes glanced at what it said: *Can I kiss you?*

"Umm, I mean, I do not see a problem with that. Do you mean right now? Or later?" I was stuttering again. He got closer and planted a soft kiss on me and it was slow, and it was dreamy, and while we held each other my fingers released the garbage bag I was holding. After the kiss, he looked at me and my eyes followed him. It felt like a mutually satisfied emotion shared between us two. Afterward, I started walking back to the storage room where everyone else was. Then Deebo appeared.

"Kayla!" I turned around and saw Chris looking at Deebo. The two guys gave each other the look of death.

"Hey, are you guys ready to go?" Deebo raised his hands for an answer. Chris stared at us and then he started picking up the decorations that he had before we bumped into each other.

"Kayla, I will call you later. Have a good night," said Chris. I closed my eyes when he said he would call me back. My eyebrows went in opposite directions. I was afraid that Deebo would hear what he said.

"Thank you everyone for your help this evening. The dance was a success, and now we will have to do it all over again for prom. I am glad that the prom is at a hotel, and I will not have to worry about cleaning up after that," said Mrs. Schaffer.

"Where were you? We thought you were going to help us in the storage room," Faye asked me suspiciously.

"Yeah, I know, I got caught up on the phone with my mom and then that guy Chris was here and he saw me so I couldn't ignore him." Faye's eyes widened. I looked at her to calm down.

"Please tell me what you guys are talking about." She sounded like a little sister being nosy.

"We talked about how mom was snooping around in my dad's office the other day and he thought it was very strange. He wanted me to know so we exchanged numbers and all that good stuff."

"What? You took each other's numbers? He wants you badly."

"Will you shut up? I do not want Deebo to know anything about me and Chris," I whispered back.

When we got home from the dance, Deebo walked into my room and rushed into my bathroom. I watched as he freely let himself into my personal space without asking. He closed the bathroom door. I grabbed my phone to see if Chris texted me. He did.

"I want to repeat the events that occurred this evening, but I want to know something, and we can talk about it another time. I know you got a lot going on right now, but please call me tomorrow, so I do not feel like I am coming on too strong with you," he texted. After I read the text, I knew exactly what Chris wanted to know, and it involved Deebo. The question is, will I tell him that we are a couple?

CHAPTER 10.
MURDER SHE COMMITTED

"Today a top-rated surgeon, now a real estate mogul, was found dead in his estate this morning. Mrs. Jensen found her husband nonresponsive and called the ambulance, where he was pronounced dead at the scene. Mr. Jensen is known in Texas as one of the most requested surgeons around town. He has donated millions to the Texas Health Foundation and BSW. No news as to what happened, and the investigation is ongoing," the anchor reported.

Me and Deebo were still in bed in my room, and my television was turned off. He turned to face me and put his lips on one of my cheeks. Not knowing anything about what happened to my father, I was still in la-la land with Deebo. Eventually we got up. I grabbed my clothes and I watched him put on his. After we got dressed, we went to the kitchen. I was coming down the stairs while Deebo's hand tickled my neck.

"Why is everybody so glum?"

The atmosphere displayed that something had gone wrong. The living room felt like a ghost town. Kelly walked over to me and put her arms on my shoulder with a hug. My stomach began to cramp. I looked at my friends and looked back at the television. I picked up the remote to turn it up. Deebo sat down slowly. His eyes stared at the television.

"What did they say? What did they say?" My voice starts to crack. Faye stood up as if she had an announcement to make. Her face frowned. I could see her body tremble.

"Your father was found dead this morning. Your mother found him, and she called the ambulance. Whatever you want us to do right now, just say the word, Kayla."

I sat down and I could feel the tears rolling down my face. I did not have a good relationship with my parents. I was hoping that we could patch things up and that eventually I would be able to visit them like a normal family. I felt hugs coming from all angles. When I got taken, I did not know if I would ever get back to my friends. They are the only family that I have. After I hugged everyone and told them what my experience was, I went to my bedroom to hide but my friends missed me. I played the sad news over and over in my head. I pretended that it was not true.

My room door was still open. Deebo walked in slowly. He closed my door. He sat down on my bed next to me. I felt Deebo's hands curled in mine. He did not speak but he comforted me in his own way. Kelly went to call my relatives to give them the sad news. My phone kept ringing off the hook. Every so often I would glance at my phone hoping that it was my dad. It would turn out to be relatives that I had not spoken to in years.

"Kayla is in her room not wanting to talk to anyone right now." Deebo talked through the door. "We must find out how he died and check on her mother." The doorbell rang. I could hear everyone rushing to the door to see who it is. I could not move.

"Oh, my goodness, I assume you heard what happened. Where is Kayla? I need to talk to her right now, please get her." I can hear my mom from my room. She charged into the house as if she owned it.

"We are sorry for your loss, Mrs. Jensen; we already called some of your relatives for Kayla, and if you need anything we are here to help. But feel free to go to her room," Kelly said as my mom stormed right past her without any acknowledgment. "She has been stuck there ever since this morning after we watched the news." Kelly watched my mother move like she did not just lose her husband.

"Thank you, darling, please pour me some wine as well for the both of us if you can, thanks." My mom knocked on my door.

"Kayla, hon, it's your mother, can I please come in?" I looked at the closed door and wondered if I should let her in. I realized that my mom needed me. My phone kept going off with text messages from everyone at school. Chris's text flashed across my screen. He was the only person that I wanted to speak to.

"Hey Kayla, I am so sorry about your dad. I want to be there for you so badly, but you have not answered my phone calls or text messages. I am on my way over to your house; your mom gave me the address. I hope you do not mind." Hearing from Chris made me feel so much better. Then I remembered my mom was waiting outside my door. I finally got up to let her in. Deebo exited.

"Well finally, thank you. How are you doing? I do not know where my head is right now. I have the business to tend to now and all the things that your dad was busy working on," she ranted. I tried to hug her, but she kept talking. I looked at my mom like she was weird, ranting about things when her husband was found dead.

"What are you talking about? Dad is dead. Do you even care?" I stood up, confronting her.

"What! Oh please, it is no surprise your father was parading around Dallas, with his whore on his hands, and now you are going to ask me if I cared. Kayla, grow the fuck up." My ears started ringing like a doorbell.

I turned around steaming like an iron at her reaction. "I am going to oversee funeral arrangements and have your aunt help me with it. If you want to be a part of the service, you know my number." She walked out of my room, and Kelly was right in front of the door with the two glasses of wine to give to us.

"You're too late dear; I'm leaving now, but next time you might want to move faster when you're asked to bring something for someone," she growled.

Kelly's eyes got red. I could not believe how rude she was after finding out that her husband died that day. It was like she had no emotion for him or anyone. Things were starting to be clear about my parents and their relationship. I wondered what she was up to and why she cared so much about the business she and Dad owned together.

About a couple of hours later, the doorbell rang. I had a feeling that Chris was out front. I was unable to prevent the sense of anticipation, which I knew would be obvious on my part. I was still in my room lying down. I kept thinking about my mom and her behavior. I must find out what is going on with her.

"Hello, can I help you?" asked Kelly. Faye was in the living room talking with Danny and she heard Kelly talking to someone. She came rushing to the front door.

"Oh, hey, hi—Chris, is it?" she interrupted. "I am Faye, Kayla's friend." Her hand extended. "You were at the school dance. Well, I know you are here for Kayla," she said, pushing her way through to be the one to deliver the cute guy to me.

"Let me bring you to her." Kelly's eyebrows raised. Deebo came down from upstairs and he watched Faye walk Chris to my room. He quickly walked over to Kelly.

"What the fuck is he doing here?" he asked with his finger pointed in the air.

"Look, Deebo, he is just a friend of Kayla's. His sister goes to Forney. Her family sent him over to give their sympathy," explained Kelly. She bit her lip, hoping he bought it.

"No! I keep seeing this fool everywhere we go. He likes her, and he is acting like he does not know that we are together." His hands were balled up.

"Well, I do not think he knows that. I mean, we all do not know what your status is relationship-wise," Kelly said softly.

"What do you mean?" I asked Kayla.

"All know that. I do not have to tell the entire world about it, and she knows it so that is all that matters."

Kelly sat down and put her hands on her head. Faye walked back out to the living room area where Deebo and Kelly were talking. Deebo walked over to Faye, steaming.

"Why is that dude over here?" He pointed in the direction of Kayla's room.

"Oh, he works for her parents. He was at the house when her parents were arguing or something," Faye explained. Deebo's eyes squinched. He began to pace back and forth.

"You said his sister goes to our school. Why didn't you mention he works for her parents?"

"I didn't know that, so stop acting like a jealous boyfriend," Kelly commented. She walked away to the next room.

I knew that Chris coming over to see me would make Deebo unhappy. He knows that Chris likes me. "Why can't they come out here and talk?" He continued to argue with the girls.

"Give Kayla space Deebo; she just lost her father," said Faye.

"Yeah yes, I am tripping. Let her know I am outside in the back if she needs me," he said calmly. Faye smiled at Deebo as he walked away.

In my room, Chris was sitting at the desk facing me. I was sitting on my bed with my back against the headboard.

"You should have seen how my mom was acting when she came here. She had no feelings for my dad. She acted like he was in an accident, and it was his fault. I feel so sick right now I could vomit," I ranted. Chris moved over to my bed.

"Why haven't you laid down yet? You are still in distress with everything that is happening right now. What can I bring you from the kitchen?"

"No, you don't have to do that, thank you," I responded.

"Well, at least lay down—here, let me set you up." He laid me down and put the covers on me. I could not help feeling warm and fuzzy.

Chris walked back over to the desk, where he was sitting, and he started fixing papers on the desk. "Wow, if I knew you like housekeeping, I would have hired you for myself."

"Ha, do not get used to this. Seriously, I would do anything for you for free. All you must do is ask." I turned around to face the other side of my bed to avoid facing him.

"What is the matter? You never had a guy be so blunt?"

"No, it's not that; I was wondering where you were like six months ago," I responded.

"I am here now with you. Ever since I saw you at your mom's house, I could not stop thinking about you. When I kissed you at the dance, I wanted to take you away." I turned back around to face him.

"Take me where?"

He walked back over to the bed to be closer to me. "I wanted to take you to my house and finish what I started."

"Wow, a little forward for a first meet-and-greet, don't you think?"

"I am not going to waste time with the things I want. I want you, Kayla, and I know you have some things tied up right now, and that is why you are stalling with me. I get it. I am not a high school kid who has a crush on you. I am a college guy that knows what I want," he explained. My heart started throbbing so much that I was afraid that I would stop breathing.

"What do you mean about tied up?" I asked.

"So you're going to act like you don't know what I mean by that." I looked downward and knew exactly what he was talking about.

"Okay, I will say it: that guy out there is in love with you." He pointed to my bedroom door. "I can see it. You have feelings for him too. But I wonder if you feel the way you do with me when you are with him."

He started playing around with one of the Post-it pads, waiting for me to respond. "Well, I cannot discuss this right now. You are right. When I am with you my heart beats so fast, I cannot even breathe. You make me feel alive. I do not feel like that when I am with Deebo," I confessed.

He walked back over to me and kissed me. I sat up as he was kissing me, and he laid me gently back down. He proceeded to gently place his body on top of me. We were caressing and kissing passionately. He kissed me softly on my neck and moved down to my breast. I started to breathe heavier and then I suddenly stopped the action that was going on.

"I'm sorry. I know it is too soon for you to be with me right now, and I understand that. Hopefully, you will tell your boy that you are in love with me."

"How do you know that I am in love with you"? I asked. He gave me that "come on, are you serious" look and then I gave him the look that proved he was right.

"I am going to go now before your boy goes crazy and tries to bust in here. If you need me, just text me and I will come running." He got up from the bed and walked to the door. Deebo was coming in from outside at the same time. His face screwed up.

"Are you still in my house?" asked Deebo. Chris just looked around the big house and smiled.

"You have a nice house. Thanks for allowing me to pay my respects." Chris smirked at Deebo.

"Yeah, you're not welcome, but I'm sure you know that."

"Kayla is just a friend," Chris shouted back. Deebo nodded in agreement. As Chris walked out the door he added, "for now anyway." He left Deebo with a little warning.

"In your dream, homie! Get out of here." Chris laughed and got into his car. Kelly and Faye came running into the living room.

"What the hell is going on out here?"

"I am telling you, that boy is evaluating me. He thinks I do not get down like that, but soon he will find out when I punch him in his mouth," Deebo proclaimed. Then he stormed into my room.

"What was that?" His thumb pointed to my bedroom door.

"What was what?"

"Allowing the blond-haired man to stay up in your room with the door closed for hours. You would not have allowed me to do that."

"He was not here for hours." My eyebrows raised.

"It seems like that to me. What is up?"

"Deebo, I cannot do this with you right now." I was avoiding the question.

"Do you like him or something?"

"If you want to argue, I suggest you find someone else. My father is dead, and I need peace right now." His eyes darted at me before he left my room. I knew in my heart that I was falling for Chris and that I had to think things out with my feelings for the two guys.

Later that day, my phone rang. I saw Detective Shims' number flash on my screen. I was afraid to answer because I knew that I could not bear any more sad news.

"Hello, Detective Shims, why are you calling me?" I asked frantically.

"I need you to come down to my office first thing tomorrow. We must talk. I found out that your father was murdered." I froze.

"Wait a minute—murdered, what do you mean? Like someone killed him on purpose?"

"Yes, that's what I said, and I'm sorry I had to be the messenger of bad news, but if you're not ready to talk I understand."

"No, yes, I will come down to the office. I will see you tomorrow." I ended the call.

Who wanted to murder my dad? It was the most bizarre thing I had heard all day. Now I know I must talk with my mom whether I want to or not. My dad was murdered. No—this cannot be happening. I thought that my situation with my parents was bad, but I never saw this happen. I felt embarrassed and wondered what people were saying about my family.

The next morning, I got up to get some coffee downstairs in the kitchen, and one by one my friends staggered in. Last night people were coming in and out to pay respects for the loss of my dad. I was still confused that my mom was not showing any emotion about Dad, and I could not believe that he was murdered. Then there is the cute college guy Chris. He was pressing the gas on me badly, and I was willing to go all the way with him last night with Deebo outside my room. There was just too much going on for me at the same time, and I was not sure how I was going to figure it out.

"Hey, how are you feeling?" Kelly faced me with sympathetic eyes.

"I am hanging in there. I must see Detective Shims. He says my dad was murdered," I explained.

"Are you serious? Who would want to murder your dad?"

"Probably everybody," Danny responded. The others came downstairs looking for breakfast.

"Didn't you say your dad was shady and doing people wrong?" Kayla looks at Danny.

"Not me, you kept saying that." He pointed his finger at my face.

"You should listen to your mom. She is tired of covering up for him or something. She was in his office looking for stuff the other day right before he died." Faye looks in my direction.

"Yeah, but she was looking for something that was going to incriminate him. I will fill you in when I find out more from the detective; I am meeting with him today." I gathered my car keys from the kitchen drawer.

"I am coming with you!" Deebo demanded. I turned around and paused for a quick second. Then I remembered what happened the last time I went on my crusade to work on a criminal case.

"Yes, I would very much like your company," I responded.

"Smart answer. Glad you learned your lesson."

"We think it's best too," said Kelly. Me and Deebo walked out the door. I inhaled and exhaled. I was happy to have company to visit the detective. Seconds later I looked for my phone in my purse and realized I did not have it.

"I forgot my phone. I will be right back."

"I will be right here waiting for you." Deebo pulled the car around to the front. I walked back into the house and headed for my bedroom.

"What did you forget?" asked Faye.

"My phone."

"OH, you do not want to forget that. You might get a text from someone you do not want to miss," she said with a grin on her face.

I looked back at Faye and smirked. I walked into my bedroom and did not see my phone right away until I looked under the cover of my bed and the phone was there. I unlocked it, looked at the messages, and saw Chris's text.

"I miss you. I need to see you right now, but I know you are busy. Call me so I can hear your voice," he wrote. I was turned on by Chris's text but maintained my composure when I got back outside in front of Deebo.

We pulled up to Detective Shims' office. We both watched our surroundings like we were sneaking to go somewhere private. The last time I got kidnapped right under Deebo's nose, and he did not want that to happen again. When we walked into Detective Shims' office, he was going through some photos of my father's body. I walked slowly toward Detective Shims' desk where all the pictures of my dad's body were scattered around.

Deebo picked up one of the pictures. His eyes popped open wide to see my dad in such a horrific state. He quickly walked up to me and hugged me. His face went blank, and I already felt bad on my own. Finding out that someone murdered my father was very scary to say the least, and I was starting to think that the killer wanted to kill me next.

"I need to ask you some questions about your dad, but if you can't do this now, let me know," said Detective Shims.

"No, I can talk. What do you want to know?" I asked.

"Okay, your mom said that she just found your dad on the floor unresponsive, but he was pronounced dead when the crime investigation unit arrived."

"So how did he die?"

"The medical examiner said he was poisoned."

"Poisoned?" Immediately I went dizzy like I was on an amazingly fast carousel.

"That just doesn't make any sense because it was just my dad and my mom at the house that night."

"We must find that out. Your father had a drink that was laced with something, but we will get more information later. Do you know anyone that wanted to hurt your father?"

"I would not know if he did. I left the house right when I turned sixteen."

"All right, then I am heading to your parents' house to talk to your mother. She might have left a few things out."

"What things?" The hairs on my skin rose.

"Someone was there at the house besides your parents," he commented.

"I am coming with you."

The detective was trying to say that if it was only my parents at the house on the day that my dad was murdered it had to be one obvious clue. I did not want to go there.

"Are you sure you want to come with me?" he asked to confirm.

"Yes."

"Well, I am going too. Kayla needs my support and protection," Deebo added.

"Okay, let's roll, take the lights off, and close my door."

"There's no sense in talking you out of it since it's your mother," he growled. Detective Shims shook his head and walked out of the building with a mean streak. I could tell he was not happy about us going with him.

So, Deebo, and Detective Shims headed over to my parents' house to speak to my mom to discuss the events that took place on the night my dad died. Meanwhile, back at the house with Faye, Danny, and Kelly, they were just home still trying to process everything that was going on with my family.

"I think that we should stay out of the public eye for a few days until the case is solved. The murder of Kayla's dad just does not sit well with me. What if this were to get back at us for helping the detective find the bad guys that took Diane and Faye?" Faye explained.

"Whoever killed my father did it for a reason. My parents were not doing anything bad or committing any crimes to my knowledge. Me and my friends were the ones that robbed a bank and stole from a charity event. We are the ones who blew the whistle on that Betsy girl and her kidnapping operation with her dad. We also helped find the people that participated in killing Miss Tilda, and her son."

"Yes, we must watch our backs now. It could be anybody. I am going out; this is too much for me." Danny wore a hopeless look.

"We are not to leave the house, remember. I think the detective would want us to stay here for the time being," Faye says, walking behind Danny.

"I will be back, don't worry." Danny walked out and Faye raised her hands.

"Great."

When Detective Shims, me, and Deebo got to my parents' house, my mom was outside getting ready to go somewhere.

"Mrs. Jensen, may I have a word with you?" said the detective.

"Why are you here? Nobody told me you were coming, and I am on my way out."

"Yes, I am sorry for the last-minute notice, but it will only take a minute. It involves your husband," he added.

"Everything is my husband," she grumbled. "Okay, yes, I only have a few minutes."

When we got into the house, she led us to the sitting room.

"Mom, Mr. Shims has questions for you: where are you going?"

"I am putting my things down in the kitchen. What is it now, Detective?" Her face twisted with anger.

"You said your husband was lying on the floor the morning you called the ambulance. Is that correct?" he asked, holding a pad and pen.

"Yes, that is right. Is that all?"

"Mom, why are you acting like this?" I turned red. I was embarrassed that my mom acted like she hated my father. I left the room and went back outside to the front of the house. I needed some fresh air. Deebo followed right behind me. My mom started gathering her things and headed to the front door again.

"Excuse me, ma'am, I'm not finished asking you questions," Detective Shims scolded as he was walking fast behind her.

"I answered your question."

"Yes, I know that, but the medical examiner found a lethal substance in your husband's stomach. Do you have any idea how that got there? Did you see him drinking in front of you by any chance before he went to bed.?" His voice was stern.

My mom did everything to avoid the question, and she was going crazy looking for documents in the kitchen area, pulling out draws. I think whatever she was looking for was not there because then she went over to Dad's office.

"Mrs. Jensen. Mrs. Jensen," he called while walking behind her.

"I am looking for something. Will you give me a minute?" she spat.

"Tell me what you're looking for—perhaps I can help you find it." Detective Shims walked over to my dad's office. Then suddenly, my mom stopped tossing papers around.

"Silly me, I was looking for some papers, but I just remembered that I already have them."

"Do you mind if I look around? There is something that can explain any trouble your husband was in."

"Yes, he did mention that he was having some issues," she responded.

"What kind of issues? Was it with his business or someone in particular?" he asked.

"Well, I am not sure, but the day before he died, he mentioned to me that he was having some issues with clients about money he owed but he did not go into detail because he was not willing to share everything with me about the business."

"I thought the two of you owned the business together?"

"That is true—well, he took me off the company without me knowing, and that's why I am trying to gather all the documents to give to my lawyer," she added.

"Why did he remove you from the business?" he asked while writing down information.

"I don't know, maybe to have me replaced by his new bitch," she responded.

"Was your husband seeing someone else? Where is this lady and how can I find her?"

"Her number is over there by his business cards."

"Okay, I need to get my hands on those documents that you have because it is still an investigation, and everything having to do with your husband from here on in is evidence," he demanded.

"Of course, I am happy to help. Whatever you need, Detective," she said sarcastically. Detective Shims took most of the papers that were on my dad's desk. Deebo and I walked back outside. My mom tapped her foot while we were leaving. I did not even say good-bye to my mom, and she did not say it to me. I did not want it to end like this, so I went back into the house to say good-bye. She was gathering her things again to head out of the house. I walked up to her, but she kept her head down packing her purse.

She went through his things again. Then she saw a file with legal documents in it. She opened the file and started pulling out documents, one by one. I saw one with Dad's name as the full owner and saw there was a blank area for a co-owner. She then dug around in his desk and pulled out a pen. She signed the name of another owner. The whole time I was standing there just watching her. I kept quiet. She smiled and quickly put the documents back into the folder and put it in her bag and headed out the door. She did not bother to let the detective become aware of them. She ignored me. I waited for her so that we could walk out together. She walked past me without turning around. She got into her Mercedes Benz.

"Did she tell you anything else?" he asked. The detective pointed in the direction she drove off.

"No, she did not. I walked in to tell her bye, but she was busy looking for additional documents. I let her be and waited till she left," I commented.

The detective walked to his car and started the engine but stopped the car. He went through his pockets and glove compartment. He then checked the floor of his car. He finally pulled out a piece of paper with a number on it. I stayed to listen to the conversation.

"Hello, I am looking to speak with Mr. Jensen's girlfriend. I am Detective Shims investigating Mr. Jensen's death," he said on the phone. He watched me standing there and put the phone on speaker.

"Ugh, yes, I'm Michelle," said the voice.

"Are you Mr. Jensen's girlfriend?" Michelle's voice was weak. She was more emotional than my mom was.

"Yes, I am. Do you know who tried to kill him?" she asked.

"What makes you think he was murdered?"

"Doesn't the whole case sound weird to you?"

"That is what I am trying to find out. Can you text me your address so that we can talk in person?" said the detective. "Also, I am going to need to look around your place if that is okay with you."

"Of course, yes, I will text my address as soon as you hang up."

She sounded like she wanted to help in every way she could. Moments later, we got back to my house.

"Hey, what did you guys find out about your dad?" Kelly asked.

"It was a shit show. My mom ignored us for a good fifteen minutes before she treated us like guests," I responded.

"Wow, she's acting like she's suspicious of something," Faye said with one eyebrow up and one down.

"My mom was arguing with Mr. Shims and was not being cooperative, so we just went outside until he was finished," Deebo chimed in.

"Why is your mom arguing with the detective? Isn't he there to help find who killed her husband?" Kelly asked.

"Yeah, I do not understand it, but I am going to find the underlying cause of it. I just need to figure out what she is up to," I said softly.

"I don't blame you because even though your mom is acting like she didn't care about him, I'm pretty sure she didn't want him dead," said Faye.

"I don't know what to think anymore, Faye." That night we went our separate ways early that night. The detective ordered us not to attend school for fear of anything happening to any one of us. He figured whoever killed my dad was still out there, so he wanted us to be safe.

The detective arrived at my dad's girlfriend Michelle's house. He pulled up, and once he got out of the car, he started looking around the house doing his normal search. He allowed me and Deebo to come along. I was incredibly pleased about that. He located Michelle's car at the side of the house. He put his face through every window looking for anything suspicious. From the outside I looked inside the house, and our eyes met. I quickly moved my face from the window. She watched the detective look in her car. Eventually, she came outside to greet him. I guess she had enough of his Columbo moves.

"Hello, I'm Michelle."

"I am Detective Shims managing the murder investigation of Mr. Jensen." He extended his hand. "We spoke on the phone," he said.

"Yes, I know who you are."

"What are you looking for in my car?" she asked.

"For anything—a body or perhaps something that might be evidence of some sort," he said with boldness and authority. Michelle grinned at the detective. We followed her into her house from the back entrance.

"That's fine; I want to help. Feel free to look around," she said confidently. The detective took that advice and went ahead into the house searching for anything that could link Michelle to my dad's murder.

"How long were you seeing Mr. Jensen?" he asked as he prepared to write down the information.

"I have been seeing Mr. Jensen for two years now. He was still living at home with his wife, and that was something that did not bother me in the beginning, but recently I told him that I wanted him to move out."

"Why did you change your mind about the arrangements you once agreed upon?"

"He kept telling me that she was arguing all the time and going in his stuff searching his office. I did not want him to have to keep dealing with that constantly." The detective continued to jot down information as she answered his questions.

"Did he ever tell you what his wife was looking for in his office?"

"No, I told him to clear out his things because he removed her as a co-partner, and I know she was upset about that." The detective's eyes narrowed. "Have you ever met his wife in person?"

"No, not at all. In the beginning he suggested we meet, but when I saw how she was treating him, I decided not to meet with her."

"Okay, I have one more question for you. Why did Mr. Jensen remove his wife as co-owner of the business they both once owned together?"

"That is the million-dollar question everybody wants to know. I did not find out that he removed her until the day before he died. I called him that day and he was upset," she said.

"Why was he upset?"

"He said that he found out his wife was at his office snooping around looking for something to incriminate him with. I told him to go to bed and start moving out his things the next day. I remember that night he said he was making himself a drink and then went to bed."

"Do you know what he drank?"

"Oh yes, he drinks gin straight. He loves gin."

"Are you sure of everything you discussed with me tonight?"

"I wished he would have listened to me and gotten out of there earlier." She frowned and wiped the corner of her eye with the tissue in her hand. The detective rose and took a deep breath. "I do not have to tell you how I was feeling," she concluded.

He stood up and extended his hand. "Thank you for your assistance in this investigation. I will be in touch."

We walked out of the house, and me and Deebo left the detective to go back to our house. When the detective went back to his office, it was well past midnight, and he was gathering all the evidence that he collected to solve my dad's murder. He had his suspicions about what he thought happened, but he had to be sure.

After yesterday's mess, I called my mother, but her phone kept ringing so I decided to leave a voicemail for her to call me back ASAP. The word around town was that my mom was already on a private plane going to an undisclosed location. She was very secretive and did not call me to let her own daughter know what she was up to or where she was going. To top it all off, dad's funeral was this weekend, and leaving before the funeral was giving a bad message.

Detective Shims finally got the news that he was looking for and headed over to my parent's house to find my mom. When he pulled up to the house, he was accompanied by a police officer who arrived at the same time.

"Ring the bell and I will head to the back. This is an excessively big house, so make sure you search everywhere," he said.

"Got it, but why didn't you just call for additional backup?" the police officer asked.

"It is just one person we are looking for. I think we can manage her."

Before the detective got inside from the back, the police officer came back out running into the front to find the detective.

"Shims! Shims!" The detective heard his name being called and came back to the front.

"Hey, she is gone. There is no one here. I went upstairs and noticed everything was empty. She took everything," the police officer said.

"I was afraid of that. She is the missing piece of the puzzle," Detective Shims said.

"What are you talking about?" asked the police officer.

"It means Mrs. Jensen killed Mr. Jensen, her husband."

CHAPTER 11.
TO CATCH A KILLER

The evidence from my dad's murder pointed to my mom since she was the last person that saw him. He was poisoned from the same gin bottle that he was drinking out of the night he died. My mom's fingerprint was on the gin bottle, along with a small container filled with a toxic substance. That same substance was found at the crime scene.

Some documents show a change of ownership of one of the businesses that he owned, and it looked like it was recently added. I did not want to believe it, but it look like my mom killed dad, and she did it because he no longer wanted to be married to her. She tried to sabotage his business by forging signatures and changing dollar amounts in his accounts without his consent. That is why she wanted Chris, the cute guy, to help her look for documents in his office. That is why she tried to get all his papers when the detective came over to the house to speak with her, which explained why she just took off.

My mind produced all these assumptions. The news was already reporting the latest news about my dad's murder. My mom's picture was posted on television. It was embarrassing. I did not think my mother could do such a terrible act. I had to think that she was guilty, because she picked up and left. No one knew where she was, but law enforcement was searching up and down for her.

The rumor around town was that she might have flown somewhere overseas. Everyone knew that my parents had several houses in Mexico and figured she might be over there hiding. Detective Shims was already putting the pieces to the puzzle together.

He was supposed to tell me as soon as he found out the truth. He waited until the entire world found out and I had to see it on TV.

I was at home, doing nothing, when my doorbell rang. We have had visitors every day since the news broke about my twisted family. I assume that more relatives wanted to show up. I peeked through the windows. Detective Shims was walking up front. I opened the door and it hit the wall.

"How long did you know that my mom killed my dad?" I asked. I backed up into the hallway with my hands folded. My breathing was interrupted by my emotions. Detective Shims avoided looking into my eyes.

"I fucking asked you a question!" He stepped up to hug me, but I backed away from him.

"I am so sorry, Kayla. The evidence pointed to your mom exceedingly early on, but I had to be sure before I made assumptions," he said.

I quickly dropped my arms. "Get out!" I yelled.

"Look, Kayla, I know that you are upset."

"Get the fuck out"! The veins in my neck popped out. He paused for a quick second and my friends ran out to the front. He felt piercing eyes. He glanced at them and nodded.

"Okay I can respect your wishes, and I am sorry for your loss. If you need anything, you know where to find me." He turned around and walked back to his car. I walked back into the house after the detective left. *I must talk to my mother, and I wonder if I am too late*, I thought to myself.

My mom is hiding in Holbox, Mexico, to be exact. She loved visiting the city, and I had a funny feeling she was over there. It is a city a couple of hours away from Cancun, once a secluded vacation sanctuary, but now a place that people go to instead of Cabo. She was hiding out in a beautiful Airbnb and acting like she was not a widow. She had attendants waiting on her left and right like she was a princess of some sort. That was what the tabloids said.

Unfortunately, the Airbnb that she was staying at was not listed anywhere on the app because she removed the listing. So, it was exceedingly difficult for law enforcement to find her without knowing she even owned the place. I was calling her every day, and the detective kept leaving serious voicemails about her turning herself in and that he just wanted to help her. I was trying not to believe that my mom killed my father, but all the signs pointed to it. I decided that I wanted to get more information from Chris since he was the one who was collaborating closely with my parents.

My friends resumed normal activities at school and stayed occupied during the week. Danny and Deebo played sports at Forney High, and Faye and Kelly did whatever I wanted them to do to help in the murder case. After school, I texted Chris to come over so that we could talk. When the doorbell rang, Kelly ran to the front door to answer it.

"Hi Chris, let me get Kayla for you. Please wait here," she said and pointed to the sitting area.

"I got it, thanks, Kelly," I quickly intervened.

"Sure, I'll be upstairs if you need anything." For some reason, that comment seemed like it meant something, but I could not figure it out.

"Thanks."

I met Chris at the front of the house when he pulled up. He was better-looking than before.

"Come with me; let's go in the back room so we can talk," I authorized. He followed me but I could smell his cologne.

"So how have you been?" he asked, slowly sitting down on the ottoman.

"Well, finding out that your mom killed your dad over money or whatever is depressing. I was not close to them, but I did not think that my mother could do such a thing. She is rude, insensitive, and half the time emotionless, but I never saw that coming."

"Are you thinking she might be innocent?" His eyebrows raised. I shrugged my shoulders.

"Look, none of us did. I was collaborating closely with your parents, and I was not aware of their toxic relationship." He seemed calm. "You're going to get through this, and I will help the detective with whatever information you need from your parents' business."

"I think he has everything he needs, but if you know where she might have escaped to, please let me know," I said.

"Wait a minute—I know she had some documents that displayed the vacation houses your parents have. I can go by my house and get it if you want." He stood up.

"Of course I do, but why is my dad's stuff at your house?" I asked.

"Your mom asked me to take some of the business papers over to my house so I can work at home if I need to. Remember I am in school, and I get busy doing papers."

"Right. I forget that you are not my age."

"Well, let me hit the road and get you those papers and I will meet you back here then."

"Wait a minute, I will come with you if you don't mind." I got up slowly from the couch.

"Yes, of course, come on."

I walked halfway up the staircase. "Hey Kelly, I'm going to Chris's house for some paperwork; I will be right back," I yelled.

"Okay sure," she responded.

She sounded like she was unsure of me going to Chris's house. I let it go. If I am not home and Deebo asks where I am, the answer might not dwell with him too nicely.

Chris's apartment was neatly tucked away on the campus of a small college on the Dallas side. His living room looked like an office that had been hit by a train. There were files and books everywhere, on the office desk and on the kitchen counter.

"Sorry for the mess, but I keep your parents' documents in this folder right here." He pushed away piles of files. He handed me one of the files. I looked through them to find any clues as to where my mom would be. I started feeling very warm and uneasy.

"I am not seeing anything. She has additional papers with the properties on it." I put the file down. He continued to search and search. He paused. He came across a magazine with a list of properties that had a circle around them. His eyes widened.

"I found it. Your mother went to Mexico."

"Well, we knew that much. Does it say exactly what part?" I leaned in.

"Yup, she is in Holbox."

"I had a feeling she went there because that used to be our family vacation spot."

"Okay, well, I must call Shims and let him know so that they can go over there and bring her back."

I took a deep breath. "Listen, thank you for bringing me here and helping. I appreciate the fact that you kept all the mushy stuff for another time." Chris walked up to me close.

"You're welcome, but I am not done with taking you away from your bully boyfriend yet. When this is all over, with your permission of course, I will make love to you repeatedly until you agree with me that we belong together," he proclaimed. After he told me those words he walked out of his apartment. "Let's go find the detective."

I froze. Did he think that I was going to let what he said just go over my head? How does one respond to something like that? I shrugged my shoulders and walked out behind him.

Chris and I got to the police station to talk to Detective Shims, but when we entered his office, he was not there. I got on my phone immediately.

"Shims here," he answered.

"Hey, Detective—ugh, listen, sorry about earlier, but I have information about my mom's whereabouts."

"Where is she?"

"She is in Mexico, in Holbox. I have an address; I will text it to you."

"Are you sure this is where she is?"

"Well, I guess so; we found notes that she flew there."

"It is still not over for your mom just yet. Stay positive," Chris whispered.

What is he talking about? My mom was the only one with my dad the night he died. They say, "innocent until proven guilty," and I need to have that attitude, but she made it impossible to believe anything she said. The rest of the world was against my mom, and it was tough to see, and I was starting to agree with everyone.

We got back to my house, and we just sat in the car. "So, I know this is off subject, but did you mean what you said at your apartment about you and me?" My heartbeat sped up. I swallowed a rock.

"I thought you did not want to go there right now with everything going on with your mom and all." His eyes darted at mine.

"I know. I just can't stop thinking about it." He held my hands.

"You know I can repeat what I said if you like." Chills ran up my spine. Every time he touched me, I melted inside like ice cream.

"Yes, I meant it," he said. "You feel the same way about me as I do for you, but you must be honest with yourself before we can see each other."

"I think I'm in love with you, Chris." What? What did I just say? His eyes ripped my clothes off. He made me feel uncomfortable. Then he stared at the windshield.

"Did I say something wrong?" I said frantically. Did I make a huge mistake telling this college man that I am in love with him? What was I thinking?

"No," he answered. His index finger touched my face and started rubbing my arms. "I never had anyone tell me that before. I mean, I was in love before, but this is different."

I wanted to hide. I might have made a mistake telling Chris I was in love with him.

"Are you crazy? Hearing you say this makes me feel like I am not the fool who is in love with someone who does not feel the same way. I fell for you the first time I met you. I told you this before. I have not been able to stop thinking about you."

"I've been in love with you from the very beginning," I confessed.

"I would kiss you right now, but I am not trying to get you in trouble or anything," he said as he looked at the house. "When are you going to have that talk with Deebo? I am not rushing you, but at the same time I want the world to know you are my girl," he said as he flexed his arms in pride.

"I want you to kiss me too and yes, I will tell him right away. I just need a little time to get my thoughts in place. It is not like I did not have feelings for him. We were now getting to the place we wanted to be before I met you," I said.

"No. I understand that. Take your time. You have been through enough, and it is not right for me to want you to forget your life just to jump into mine to meet my feelings."

"You're thoughtful and kind. I love that about you."

"Just a little more mature than the guys you're used to seeing," he said with a smirk. "I'm just kidding, I'm just kidding." I softly punched him on his arm. We laughed and continued to talk for the next hour.

We ended our time together. I went into the house and waved good-bye. I watched him drive away before entering the house. I thought about how Chris is good for me. He was smart and very good-looking, and he was in college. He was mature, and thoughtful, and expressed how he felt about me on numerous occasions without hesitation. He was ready to let the world know that I was his girl.

Deebo, on the other hand, has been in my life for an exceptionally long time, ever since we met at the shelter. He is also fine, with a hot body because he works out every day. All the girls in Forney want him. Deebo always had a thing for me, but he was never open about it. He was always with other girls and changing them like he changed his socks. I have a thing for him, but I never said anything. I just accepted his boyish ways. We have chemistry and heat for one another, and when Deebo made love to me, I was in heaven. When he touched my body, I was in fire mode. He made me feel sexy and hot.

I now know it is just lust between Deebo and me. With Chris, when he kissed me that second time in my room, I was shy, but my heart was beating fast, and I could not control how I was feeling. I had butterflies with Chris, and even though we never slept together, I knew that it was a feeling I had never experienced. There was something more than physical attraction between us. I must talk with Deebo. The question was when.

I went back and forth over who was the better guy for me, and I could not make that decision as fast enough. It seemed like both men were good, but they both had different qualities. Naturally, I could not be with the two guys at the same time, because that would not be right. As I kept going on and on in my head, I heard movement. It was Deebo, entering the kitchen.

"Hey, how did it go with the detective? Did they find your mother?" He was putting his things down on the counter and reaching into the fridge.

"Ugh, yeah, my mom is in Mexico."

"Is it true?"

"Yup, it is. My mother killed my father. Ha, there is a delightful book for you to read."

"Look, I know you feel like shit right now and this is a big embarrassing mess, but you will get through this, and we all are here to help. What do you need for the funeral?"

I started wiping some crumbs into the sink. "Honestly Deebo, I do not even know if I want to go. I am so upset that my mom has not called me yet after all the voicemails and texts I sent her. She did not even feel the nerve to dismiss the accusations against her. I just do not want to hear relatives asking me stupid questions about the case."

"Yeah, but you still must go to your dad's funeral. I mean, it will look a little weird, especially since your mom will not be there."

I turned to look at Deebo like he was dumb. "Did you forget my parents did not care about me? I met you at the shelter because I had to go there. My parents kicked me out of the house with nothing because they thought I was on drugs. I do not care about how it is going to look. None of my relatives offered to take me in except for my uncle. I left that privileged life for a reason." I started to walk away from him.

"Where are you going? I thought we were talking here." He had one hand up.

"I will be in my room so we can talk later." I got annoyed. He shook his head, gathered his things, and went into his room. I made him angry, but I could not act like my parents were there for me and my sister Genoveve when they were not.

The next morning, I stayed in my room. I was the only one who did not go to school. It was also prom night, and I was not feeling it but decided that I would go to take my mind off things. Kelly sent me pics of flowers that were left in my locker. We texted all day in our group chat between us.

"Did you text Kayla, today?" asked Kelly.

"No, she was a little upset that I told her to go to her dad's funeral," Deebo replied.

"She's considering not going? That's weird," said Faye.

"Yea, which is what I said. She stormed off and went into her room."

"What did you do after that?" Curiosity consumed Faye.

"I went into my room," Deebo said. "I am not trying to be the bad guy, especially with that chump hanging around every chance he gets." They chatted like I was not able to see what they were saying.

"Hello. I can see you talking about me."

"Well, anyway, enough about funeral talk; it is too depressing. Do we have clothes ready for tonight? It's prom night, and we got the party bus to take us to the hotel. Please tell me you booked the hotel already," asked Faye.

"Yes Kayla, and I have our dresses and we booked the one night," Kelly added. They continued to have this chat conversation like I was not included in the group.

Eventually, I just came off the group chat. So here I was sitting at the pool getting some sun. The doorbell rang. I got up and walked over to the sliding glass doors that view the front of the house. I saw Detective Shims through the door windowpane. I quickly opened the door but then realized I was half naked.

"Hi, how are you?" he asked with his hands covering his eyes. "Do you want to put something on before we talk?"

"Yeah, sure." I ran to the next room to grab an oversized T-shirt. "I am surprised." He peeked through his fingers to see if I was decent.

"Why?" he asked.

"Well, most men your age are perverts."

"I believe I asked you a question," he repeated and looked at me like he was my father.

"I could not be better. I watch my mom's face on the television every night about her being the killer who murdered my dad. Um, let me see. I am doing great," I responded.

"I'm sorry I guess that was a dumb question," he said with his eyebrows raised. I walked him over to the sitting room so we could talk.

"Okay, what do you got for me?" I asked like I was ready to hear something new. He stood up as if he had to make an announcement. I raised my head at him waiting for more sad news since that was the way my life was going.

"We found your mother, and she is on her way to the States. I wish the circumstances were different. I wish I could arrest someone else for this," he said sternly.

"I still can't believe that this is happening, but it is what it is. Well, what do you need from me?"

He got up and walked to the front door, looking at the decor of the house as he passed pictures on the wall. Then he stopped walking. He turned around.

"There is nothing for you to do currently. Later, I will give you the date and time for the trial, but right now just enjoy your life, Kayla. You went through a lot, from working at the bar and witnessing a murder, to being kidnapped, and saving your friend from abduction. I would say you had enough to deal with for a teenager. Go ahead and be a kid." He raised his eyebrows. "Don't you kids have a prom tonight?" he added.

"Umm, I don't think I'm going." I walked behind him as he stepped outside. He then walked back up the steps. He got close to my face.

"Go to the prom." He stepped back down and walked to his parked car that was in front. I watched his car drive away. I thought about what he said. It is a clever idea to go to the prom, even though I am not up for it.

The school day was over quickly. My friends had hair appointments and malls to go to get ready for prom night. Danny and Deebo went to their barber to get a haircut, and Kelly and Faye headed straight to their hair salon. Luckily for them, they already had their outfits thanks to Faye staying on them to make sure of that. I was the only one who was able to style my hair without the help of a professional. I was in my room taking out the dress from the closet but keeping the garment cover over it to avoid getting anything on it. I laid my dress on the bed and took out some heels and accessories. My cellphone rang. It was Chris. I smiled from ear to ear.

"Hi, I just wanted to hear your voice. Can you talk?"

"Yeah, hold on, let me put you on speaker." Suddenly, I felt jumpy.

"Wait, why?" he said hesitantly.

"Well, that's the only way I can talk to you and get ready for the prom at the same time."

"Makes sense. I guess I must call my sister to see if she needs me for anything," he said kindly.

"Wow, such a nice brother. Your sister is incredibly lucky."

"Yes, she is. Is your room door closed now?" he asked suspiciously.

I stopped abruptly at what I was doing and looked at my phone. "Why did you ask me that?" My eyes squinched.

"You have me on speaker and if I want to talk dirty, I don't want your friends to hear what I'm saying to you. Are you alone?"

"Ugh yes, I'm alone," I said as I started walking toward the front of the house. Something was telling me that he was here at my house. I peeked into the door window and did not see his car outside. I smiled. I took another peek at the door window.

"Come on, let me in. I know you know I am here because you are not saying anything." He hung up. I did not see his car. He was smart to park on the side of the house to make it look like it was the neighbor's car. He peeked into the window and saw me peeking back.

"Open the door so I can make love to you," he said boldly. I turned away from the door window and started breathing heavily. I opened the door very slowly. Chris walked in and locked the door by turning the latch. He walked up to my face and planted a slow kiss on me. I melted. He picked me up while kissing me. He carried me up the stairs and to my bedroom. He then laid me down on the bed.

"This is the time where you tell me to stop or slow it down." I looked at him and felt like crying, but I was just so happy to see him.

"I don't want you to stop." I gazed into his brown eyes.

"Just tell me what you want me to do right now," he asked.

"What do you think?"

He got up from the bed and walked to the door. He closed it. He then walked back to the bed and started kissing me softly. I was in a whole other world, with nothing on my mind but me and Chris and what he was doing to me. He took off his shirt and helped me remove mine. He threw it on the floor. He held me tight as he was on top of me, and he cherished every part of my body like it was the most precious gem. He started to whisper in my ear.

"I want to be sure that you want me right now like I want you, but I don't want to do this if you're not ready," he whispered.

"I nodded. I am ready," I said softly. I was not sure what I was doing because I was supposed to be with Deebo. How was I going to explain to him that I slept with Chris? I knew that I was in a tough situation, but I was willing to risk it all for Chris.

He reached over to his pants that were on the chair by my desk and took out a condom. He ripped the paper with his teeth. His soft warm lips touched every area of my body. His eyes met back with mine. Then he entered me slowly. He wanted me to know that this was not a quick hit in the sack and that he absolutely loved me and wanted me forever. Okay, maybe that is all in my head. However, he loved me passionately. I could not believe that Chris was making love to me in my bed. His hands were sandwiched into mine as we held hands tight, but then I heard a noise coming from downstairs. Oh my gosh. The front door.

"Shit, oh my gosh, somebody's home. You must leave or hide or something," I said nervously. Chris stopped what he was doing and looked confused.

"Do I have to?" he gasped.

"Yes, please go in my closet." I slid from underneath him. Chris got up and grabbed his clothes and went into the closet. I threw on my clothes as fast as I could. I heard Kelly and Faye's voices from downstairs.

Faye yelled out to me, "I know you're not sleeping, because we have to get ready soon." I heard the stomping up the stairs. Kelly walked up to my room and tried to open the door.

"Hey, let us in, girl, we want to show you, our hair," she urged insistently.

"I am coming guys, hold on." I quickly fixed the bed so that it did not look like I was in there with someone. I opened the door with clothes in my hand like I was straightening up.

"Hey, wow your hair is beautiful." I did not even look at her hair. Kelly turned around. She walked in with authority and headed to my closet.

"Ooh, girl, don't go in there; I'm still trying to clean that mess." I rushed over to block her. She looked at me like I was a weirdo.

"Okay, well I'm going to get ready, so once you're done cleaning up, come in my room to show me your dress." she instructed.

"Yeah, sure, girl, go get ready and I'll do the same." I wanted her out of my room as quickly as possible. As soon as she left my room, I opened the closet door. Chris was fully dressed.

"I'm so sorry, but I don't want them to know that we are seeing each other just yet," I confessed.

"I do not understand why not. I thought you were going to let everybody know about us." His nostrils flared.

"I know, I just have not done that yet. Please do not be mad at me, okay?" I walked up to him and put my hands on his face. He removed my hands.

"I'm not." He walked to my room door, but I heard Deebo and Danny from downstairs. I heard Deebo rushing right in my direction.

"Please go back in the closet! Deebo is home!" I pleaded. Chris's face twisted. He went back into my bedroom closet and slammed the door. It made me jump.

"Hey, beautiful." Deebo came into my room and embraced me like he had not seen me in a long time. I hugged him back but released him quickly. I had a few cracks on my closet door, and I knew Chris was watching.

"I was thinking we should take a quick shower together before we get ready to go to the prom." Deebo was moving on me like he had not seen me for days. He started by kissing my neck. I tried to distract his plans to be intimate.

"Don't you have to get ready and help out Danny?" I pushed him away softly.

"Go help Danny? Danny is a grown-ass man!" He grabbed my arms. "I can help *you* if you want."

I stepped back. "No, let's go to your room and get your stuff together. I want to take some pictures. I need you to look good for the camera."

"We have time to fool around, and I can be quick," he assured me.

"No, we will not have time, and you know that." I pushed him toward the door.

"Okay, can I get a kiss first?" he pleaded.

"No, let's do that later."

"No, I want a kiss right now." I knew that if I did not kiss him at once, he would persist. I gave in. I was sickened that Chris would have to painfully stand in the closet and watch. He lifted my chin and kissed me softly. I tried to resist but I fell into the abyss. I forgot that Chris was watching. Deebo caressed me, put his hand in my shirt, and caressed my breast. He pushed me against the closet door.

"Okay, hot guy. Let us end this train ride before we derail it," I said anxiously. Deebo's phone started ringing. I got saved by the bell. He stopped his love train. He pulled his phone out of his pants pocket.

"This is my homeboy calling me about this party bus for the prom. We will continue this later," he said with a kiss on my head.

Shakily, I opened the closet door. Chris stormed out. He walked right past me. He stuck his head out the hallway and then walked toward the back door.

"Whose car is that on the side of the house?" Kelly asked. I ran out of my room.

"Is he still out there? Some guy was delivering something and had the wrong address." I lied my ass off.

By the time no one else went to look, Chris was already gone. I sighed. I blew things with Chris this time, and I did not know how I was going to fix the mess between us. After everything that happened, it was time to get ready for the prom. I went back into my room to go take a shower. My phone started buzzing. I picked it up and read Chris's text.

"You better have that talk tonight and no later. If I find out that you did not, I will tell him myself," he texted. I started to text back but then I threw my phone on the bed.

The last thing I wanted to do was hurt Deebo, and I did not plan to do it at tonight's prom. I thought of the humiliation if word got out that I dumped him for a college man. I was not going to be the bad guy. Everyone will hate me for it. I would not be able to forgive myself.

It was prom time, and all the students from Forney High were arriving at the Regency Hotel in Dallas for prom. One by one, luxury cars were pulling up to the valet section. The valet attendants were opening doors and helping students come out of the cars. We arrived on the party bus. The atmosphere looked glamorous. It looked like a scene at an awards show, the way everybody was dressed. Everybody stood outside to see who was coming out of it. Danny and Deebo stepped out of the bus. Danny had on a shiny suit. It was burgundy with a silver thread trim. Deebo wore all black. He was sexy. The girls were screaming at them like they were celebrities. Kelly wore a beautiful embellished gray gown. Faye mesmerized us in her off-white diamond gown. Then I came out. I wore a see-through tan gown. We all looked stunning. We headed into the lobby area, and the room was packed. We booked a few rooms just in case we got too tired to drive home. In the lobby, Mrs. Schaffer spotted us. She rushed over in our direction.

"Hello, everyone, you look amazing. I am happy you were able to come out, Kayla. We really want you to have fun tonight." She smiled.

"Thank you, Mrs. Schaffer, I'm glad that I did."

"We also let the hotel know not to let any news people or anyone from the media attend the prom. This is not the time to harass you and your friends or ask you questions about your mom," she promised.

I nodded. "I really appreciate that. Well, we better go in and get seated." I was ready to get the night started.

As the students entered the ballroom, the banquet staff came out with bread for each table. Then one by one the food items came out as the students settled. After dinner, students walked around mingling with one another and taking selfies. The school hired professional photographers and they were all around the ballroom. Me and Deebo were taking our own pictures with a camera we brought from home. A lot of the kids were doing the same thing and enjoying themselves. A few girls walked over to our table where we were sitting.

"Did they find your mother? We heard she was hiding in Mexico," said a random girl. Before I could answer the two girls, Deebo slammed his hand on the table.

"Hey, why don't you go to the bathroom and fix your face." The two girls looked flushed. One of them grabbed their mirrors to look at themselves.

He turned to me. "You okay?"

"I'm okay. I can't hide from people asking me about my mom and the murder of my father. I just must deal with it." I was holding the empty glass that was on the table.

"No, you do not. They need to mind their business, if you ask me," he said firmly. Moments later, the DJ started playing the music and students got up to dance.

"Do you want to go up to the room?" Deebo asked me unexpectedly. I thought about it.

"Yeah but I want to go alone for a little while if you do not mind." I put my hand on his. "You go ahead and have fun." I stood up.

"You are sure? Because I can come up with you," he added.

"No, I'll be fine." I walked to where the elevators were. I pressed the call button and looked up at the indicator. I had so much on my mind. Chris gave me an ultimatum. I did not want to break Deebo's heart tonight, and I was afraid that if I did not do it, Chris would be done with me. I got to my room door. I pulled out the card key and inserted it into the slot. I took off my earrings and shoes. I sat down on the bed. I put my earrings on the nightstand. I was about to rinse my face off when my phone started buzzing. I had it silent all evening. I pulled it out of my purse. It was my mom.

"Kayla! I need a favor from you." I could not believe she was calling me now.

"Mom! Where are you? I thought you were wanted by the police," I said quickly.

"Yes, I am calling you from this hell hole. I get a phone call or two. Now listen to me. I need you to get a hold of my lawyer. He has some papers to give me, and I have not gotten them yet. I do not know where he is, and I am about to fire his ass. Also where is Chris? He has been ignoring my calls and texts." Her voice was rude. She was still a bully. My mom said all that without a pause, and I was shocked that she did not say anything else regarding the case and of what she was accused.

"Mom, are you serious? I have not heard from you since dad died, and all you care about is some files for your lawyer. Are you kidding me?" Tears were building up in my eyes. I was trembling.

"Bitch, you better listen to me. You do not know shit about anything I care about. I do not have time to waste on you, so if you cannot help me, get Chris to call me," she added. I wiped my eyes with my hands.

"I am not getting Chris to call you or anyone for that matter. Mom, you are in prison for killing my father, your husband. What part of that is normal to you?" I looked down at my phone. She was silent.

"Mom, are you there? I asked you a question."

"Are you fucking Chris?" she asked with pleasure in her voice. A rock was in my throat. I could not believe she asked me that and called me a bitch.

"Yeah, well it figures. He has been in your ass from the first day he saw you. I bet you told him your side of the story too. You are a waste of my time." She was harsh. She ended the call.

My tears fell. I could not wipe them fast enough. I threw my phone against the nightstand. I took off the lights and went to bed.

CHAPTER 12.
MAKE A CHOICE

The next day after the prom, we checked out. Me and the girls carried overnight bags to the car. I put our bags in the trunk. My phone started to ring. I pulled it out of my pocket. Detective Shim's name spread across my screen.

"Hey, I hope you had a good time at the prom. I got news for you about your mom," he said firmly.

"I did have an enjoyable time. Thank you for advising me to go," I said kindly. "So, what is the news? My mom called me and ordered me to contact her lawyer for some documents she wanted. You know she never denied that she killed my father or any of the accusations against her," I confessed to the detective.

"Your mom is trying to appeal her case. It is too late for her, but she is trying. If all the evidence that we have on her sticks, she will get life without the possibility of parole." I started to feel sick. Even though my mom and I were not on good terms, to hear that she was getting locked up felt sickening.

"I am texting you her court date and the times. Make sure you are there. We may need you to testify."

I could not swallow. "Testify! I thought this was going to be quick and simple. You catch the bad guy that killed my father which happens to be my mom and she goes to jail, and I do not have to see her or talk to her again," I murmured.

"I wish it were that simple Kayla. Look I must get back to work; if you need anything give me a call." My heart sank.

"Thanks, Detective." I hit the end call button. I was up to my head with things to deal with, and testifying against my mom was the last thing I wanted to participate in.

A couple of hours later, Kelly and Faye were looking at the pictures and videos we took from the prom. Danny and Deebo were getting ready to go to the gym.

"So, what are you guys up to this Saturday?" Danny asked while stuffing his gear in his gym bag.

"Well, I am not going anywhere but to hang out at the pool all day and sip on some cocktails. I am exhausted and need some time to chill," Faye says in a deep voice accompanied by a yawn.

"What about you Kayla?" He turned to me.

"I think I will have to piggyback with what Faye said. Laying by the pool sounds like a plan for me too. The detective said I may have to testify against my mom in court, and I am not liking that plan at all."

"Ooh that's got to suck. This is the most bizarre thing that has happened to us by far. Es una locura." He only speaks Spanish if the situation is intense or when he is talking to a pretty girl.

Deebo walks in the kitchen where everyone was but kept silent. "Hey buddy, are you ready?" Danny asks as he gets his car keys out.

"Yup." Deebo nods. The two guys leave. At that moment you could feel the ice in the room. Deebo did not even look at me.

"Wow, that was cold. What is going on between you two?" Kelly asks for tea.

"Yeah, you guys need to fix whatever is going on between the two of you," Faye adds.

"I do not know. He is upset with me, and I must talk to him." I was putting on sunscreen to avoid looking at the girls.

"I think I know why," Faye intervenes. Kelly and I looked at Faye for the answer.

"Well, do not stop there. Spill it. Tell me what I am feeling?" I replied.

"You want me to spill it right here and now?" We followed Faye outside by the pool to hear this tea about me.

"You're sleeping with Chris. Basically, banging both guys and neither one knows what is going on but you," she says angrily. I got sick. I did not expect her to put me out there like that.

"I did not plan it, okay? I wanted to talk to Deebo about Chris, but I just did not know how not to hurt him," I cried.

"Girl, you what! This is not you. Deebo loves you. Why would you do this to him?" Kelly's mouth widened.

"I do not know. One-minute Deebo and I got to the place we wanted to be. The next minute, Chris comes into my life."

Kelly frowned. She shook her head. She rested her head on the lounge chair like she was done with me. The sun was bright, and it was a beautiful day. However, I felt like crap. After Faye embarrassed me with her assessment of my behavior, she put her sunglasses on. It was confirmation that the tea she gave was worth it.

"You better let Deebo know you're sleeping with Chris, because if he finds out beforehand, it's going to be ugly." Kelly raises her sunglasses just a little to peek at me.

"I am fully aware of that, Kelly. Did you forget that my mom is in prison because she murdered my dad?" I could not believe that they were forgetting that my family is in shambles.

"I know that Deebo is not as charming as Chris, but you really do not know him that well. Deebo, on the other hand, has been in your life since we lived in the shelter." Kelly continued to make me feel like a lonely gum wrapper on the pavement.

"Now that is true. I forgot that bit," Faye added.

"This Chris guy just comes into your life and suddenly and you become a slave. Don't you think it is weird that he was always at your mom's house?"

I was quiet . . . I did not think that it was strange that Chris was at my mom's house when I met him. He was working for them. He is in college. It made perfect sense to me, and I did not know what Kelly was getting at.

"Deebo knew how I felt for him for a while, and he just made that known. I am not making excuses, but he was not sure about me being his girl for a while. Chris is different. He does not hide from his feelings and wants the world to know how he feels about me. Believe me, I feel like shit sleeping with them both, and I know this must stop," I confessed. I hated how I prolonged the events between the two guys, and having the girls know about it made me feel worse. I got up and left the pool to go back into the house. Kelly looked at Faye, and they both sipped their cocktails.

Later that day, the boys came home and I stepped out of the house to sit outside. Kelly and Faye came in from the pool to talk to the guys.

"What did you girls do all day?" Deebo asks.

"Lay by the pool," Faye responds with her eyebrows raised.

"Well, what are we doing for dinner?" Danny rubs his stomach.

"I say we head out tonight. We have been hiding inside to avoid going outside because of the paparazzi," Faye whines.

"No one was outside when we came in, so I think the news about Kayla's parents is old news, no offense to Kayla," Danny mumbles.

"Where are we going? Never mind," he smiles. We laughed. Our favorite spot was on the agenda.

Later that evening, we enjoyed tasty food and drinks at our favorite restaurant in Dallas. Me and Deebo spoke a few words here and there, but it was different between us. When the detective spoke to me earlier that day, he mentioned that he had to get back to work. He was still working on my dad's case, and there were still a few things that he had to address. My mom was still sitting in a prison cell waiting for her day in court, and she was not trying to go down for it.

The next day, my mom was sitting in the visitor's booth waiting for her guest to come speak to her. I was not visiting her. It was my dad's girlfriend. She picked up the phone and waited for her to pick up the phone in the end. The detective has been monitoring her visitors and found out that my dad's girlfriend and my mom were friendly to each other. He had their conservations recorded as evidence. He allowed me to secretly listen in. He threatened me not to let anyone know. Unfortunately, my mom found out and had her attorneys stop the recording.

"Well, it took you long enough. I thought I was going to hire the police squad to find you," said my mom.

"You promised me that all I had to do was answer any questions that the detective asked of me. I did that. So why am I here?" said Michelle. Michelle was my dad's girlfriend. He was seeing her while he was married to my mom. I do not know the story about them because I was kicked out before that. She did not look like my dad's type. She was younger, and she looked like she belonged to a rock band. Her hair was blonde with pink streaks. However, she was slim and pretty.

Michelle and my mom speaking on good terms was not a good sign. Michelle spoke negatively about my mom to the detective, and she acted like she was against her. Were the two of them working together? Was this planned all along? A big secret that no one knew the answer to. The detective cleared Michelle of being involved in my dad's murder. She was free to do whatever she wanted.

"I called you here because my lawyer for some reason disappeared, and I need some paperwork that he has that can get me off. I have a court date coming up, and I will be granted bail until then. I need that paperwork," My mom demands.

"So why is this my problem? You are rich and can get anything you want," Michelle argues.

"You can have some of my money too if you do what you're told."

"I thought you sent me my money to help you with the detective. I am not doing another thing until I get my money."

"Stop your whining; you should have a check coming to your house today if it hasn't arrived already." My mom chuckled. Michelle smacked her gum.

"Your money is in your mailbox. A million dollars. Did I get the amount right?" My mom flashed who she was even in prison.

"I will get your stupid papers, and my money better be at my house. If it is not there when I get home, I will come back and kill you myself. Believe that, bitch." There was a sound of a spatter. It sounded like Michelle spit the gum at my mom.

"You know you can get caught saying that." Michelle slammed the phone. I could not believe that my mom planned this murder with this strange lady. This lady lied to the detective that she never met my mom, and here she is visiting her and talking like old friends.

Detective Shims was at his office looking through a new case when he got an envelope from one of the police officers. "Hey, what is this"? he asked.

"I don't know, I was told I had to deliver it to you in person," said the police officer. It was a letter from Mrs. Jensen's lawyer stating that Mrs.

Jensen was granted bail and that she was being released sometime today. He slammed the letter onto his desk. "Damn it!"

Meanwhile, my friends and I were at Film Alley in Terrell, a movie theater with a bowling alley and an arcade. We finally have been doing normal things that teens do. But the good times were about to end once again. My stomach always starts to hurt when my cellphone rings.

"Wait a minute, hold on, I believe it's our turn," I respond to the crew. I took out my phone after trying to ignore it.

"Hello Kayla, we have a problem." It was the detective once again.

"What's going on? What is it?" I felt nervous.

"Your mom is out of prison. She is on her way home," he said with assurance. I dropped my phone. The others noticed and ran over to see what happened.

"What happened? You look like you heard some shocking news," Kelly asks. I picked up my phone. I saw Chris's name flash across my screen. I put the phone in my pocket. I faced my friends.

"You're not going to believe what Detective Shims just told me." I had my hands on my head.

"Well, spill the beans—we want to know what could possibly be worse than what already happened," Danny persuades.

"Give me a minute. I'm going to the bathroom, and I will be right back." I rushed to the bathroom to talk to Chris. I walked into one of the stalls.

"Your mother is out on bail. Not sure if you heard about that, but I just found out. Call me when you get this so we can talk," texted Chris.

I called him immediately. "Hi, I am glad you texted me. I was worried you did not want to talk to me from the last time we saw each other," I said softly.

"I know you have a lot on your plate, and I am not trying to add to it. At the same time, I do not want to be played by a high school girl that I am in love with," he confessed.

"I have been in love with you too Chris ever since I met you at my mom's house. I want you to know that. I am not wasting your time at all." I threw myself at him with my words.

"Okay, well, what are you going to do about your mom? The police are saying that she might be cleared in the murder case."

"I do not know how that is possible since Detective Shims said they had evidence that my mom killed my father. I hope she is innocent, but if not, it is what it is," I replied.

"We will soon know enough," he said. "I miss you."

"I miss you too," I responded back.

"Come over to my house right now if you can," he demanded. I paused for a quick second. I wondered how I was going to leave my friends to head over to Chris's house without it looking suspicious. I thought I would have to say that I am going to see my mom, since she is out of jail, as an excuse. Hopefully, they will buy it. I came out of the bathroom. I took a couple of deep breaths.

"Hey guys, you are not going to believe this, but my mom is out. She just called me wanting me to see her. I guess I will meet you later at the house."

"Wow, not sure if that is a good thing or not, but do you want us to take you there?" Faye asks with an unsure tone.

"Oh no, my mom is sending her driver to get me from here. You go ahead, and I will catch up with you later." Deebo walked up to me and gave me a hug and kiss as if he knew I was lying.

"I will see you later when you get back. We need to talk."

"I will call you when I'm on my way back." I kissed him back. Knowing I was lying to Deebo again made me sick to my stomach, but what choices did

I have? It was as if the air displayed my lies all over and we were all breathing into the mess. Then again, I could have told the truth, and then everything would have been ruined.

My friends left the alley. I watched them get in the car. Afterwards, I slowly walked over to the front. I quickly texted Chris. "Hey, can you come and pick me up? I am at Film Alley. How long will it take you?" I asked anxiously.

"It is going to take me too long. I am going to have my friend that lives over there pick you up and bring you to me." His tone was firm. I waited in the front area for my ride that Chris was sending. About fifteen minutes later, the car pulled up and I jumped in. I pulled my phone out again to text him.

I got to Chris's apartment. He was already in the lobby area waiting. He grabbed me and kissed me when I walked into the building.

"I miss you so much." He was all over me.

"Maybe I need to be away from you more often. I love the treatment," I said with a smile. When we got into his apartment, he pulled me into the living room and moved me to the couch. Then he picked me up and took me to the bedroom, laid me down gently, and slowly unbuttoned my pants. He then took his shirt off and I unbuttoned his pants. He reached for a condom in his drawer. We made love until we got tired and fell asleep.

Three hours went by, and I got up and got dressed to get back home. I pulled my phone out to see if Deebo texted. My heart began thumping. No text. Chris was asleep. I tore up a piece of paper he had on his desk to write him a note. Instead of going home, I got an Uber to take me to my mom's house. I figured that if I still went to see my mom, it would not be a total lie. When I pulled up to the house, my heartbeat fast. It was like I was a stranger visiting my mother for the first time. I got out of the car and walked up the steps. My fingers trembled. I paused. It took me a few seconds to ring the doorbell. I did not know what to expect with my mom accused of murder and all. I pressed the button.

"Well, look who decided to come home to see their mother during the late hours." She was in this silk robe with hair and makeup done. Her nails were red, and she was smoking a cigarette. I walked into the house and entered the sitting room. "If you're going to be here you might as well speak."

I got up and went into the kitchen. I grabbed a wine glass from the cabinet and took a bottle from the wine room that was near the pantry. My mom put out her cigarette in the ashtray on the counter and headed into her bedroom. I followed her.

"Where are you going?" My mom kept doing things to avoid me. I hit the corner wall by her bedroom. She started removing her makeup in the bathroom.

"The question is, where I *went*. I was with my lawyer today managing some important stuff," she responded.

"I thought you couldn't find him?" I started to ask the million-dollar question but could not get the words out. She walked out of the bathroom with a bare face. She looked at me.

"I know that there were a lot of rumors and evidence that pointed in my direction. I hated your father's guts. I am not going to lie about that. When I found out that he was seeing someone else, I knew our marriage was over. When he took me off the business, we both owned together, I knew it was officially over between us. But there's new evidence out there that will clear me of this horrible crime that you think I did." She sounded convincing. My head got frazzled. I stood up and looked at her, trying to figure out what she just confessed to. I put the wine glass down on her dresser.

"I do not understand—if you say you are innocent and you did not kill my dad, then who did? Why didn't you mention this new evidence to Detective Shims?"

"Kayla, you were supposed to help with this. I asked you to get my lawyer to help me. Remember? I saw some things that your dad's girlfriend was doing, and I tried to find the underlying cause of it, but it was too late. That woman that your dad was dating killed your father. I know she did it because she was jealous of me," she said as if she was the popular girl at school.

I shook my head. How can I tell if she is telling me the truth? The information was too much for me to bear. *I must get a hold of Detective Shims*, I thought to myself.

"Look, Mom, I know you and I are not close, but I do not want you to go to prison for something you did not do. We must clear your name if what you are saying is true. I will find the underlying cause of this. I will make sure of it." I nodded. I was convincing myself that my mom is innocent. Unfortunately, my gut said otherwise.

"You're only seventeen. You cannot help with this. Leave it to the detectives to manage."

"I am going home, and I will call you if I hear anything," I said and started walking to the front door.

"Do you need to borrow a car? I have six of them here," she yelled.

"No, I'm calling Deebo to come get me." I pulled out my phone to text Deebo. As I waited for Deebo to come pick me up from my mom's house, I dialed Detective Shim's number.

"Shims, it is Kayla—please call me, it is urgent. My mom is innocent," I recorded. Deebo finally pulled up. I waved to my mom. I entered Deebo's car.

"Hey, are you okay? I tried calling you last night."

"I'm sorry, I think I had it on vibrate," I lied. I know, I suck like lemons. I was not happy with myself either.

"Who were you on the phone with?" he asked.

"I was leaving a voicemail for Shims."

"So, what is up with your mom? What is the news?"

"My mom told me she was innocent. She said she was trying to figure out who killed my father and that she thinks his girlfriend had something to do with it."

"What? No shit. Are you serious, Kayla?" He leaned in like I was telling him the answers to a whodunit.

"I mean, I do not know. The last time I spoke to the detective, he said there was new evidence, and my mom believes this new evidence can clear her name."

"Your mom was acting guilty, and she was not cooperating with the police and then she ran to Mexico. Why would she run if she is innocent?" Deebo had a point. Some things just did not make any sense. Things did not add up.

My mom's prints were on the same gin bottle that my dad drank out of that had the toxic substance. So how was it that it magically was not there anymore? Then she flees to Mexico without telling anyone, including her daughter, where she was going. How can I believe anything my mother says about that? Deebo and I got back to the house, and it was extremely late. Everyone was asleep. I was far from sleepy because of the news I heard today about my mom being innocent.

"Do you need anything?" he asked kindly.

"Um, no, thank you for coming to pick me up," I replied.

"Sure. I know you are tired, so I will talk to you tomorrow." Deebo walked away. I was surprised because I thought he would want to stay the night in my room. It was a good thing that he went to his room. I just could not deal with any love issues right now.

The next morning was the start of a new week for us. Me, Deebo, Danny, and Faye were in the kitchen getting breakfast. Kelly was still upstairs trying to get herself together. "Does anyone feel like shit?" Faye says.

"My head hurts so bad I could barely hear myself think," Danny says and rubs his head.

"Which fast girl was it this time that got you wasted?" Faye looks at Danny with a grin. Danny reached for the orange juice. He looked at Faye.

"You might do better with coffee since you have a head banger," Kelly says, walking into the kitchen. Laughter filled the room. Danny's eyes were fire red. He sat there with his lines on his forehead and squinched eyes. "Well, hook me up instead of laughing at me. Pour me some coffee Por favor, gracias," he begged.

"I'm sure you guys found out about my mom." I started the conversation with a hint of embarrassment.

"Yeah, when you told me I couldn't believe it," Deebo said and turned to me.

"We saw it on the news, Kayla, and everybody has been calling asking questions," Kelly commented.

"I do not know why. I do not have the answers to any of them. I am still waiting for Detective Shims to call me back." I sighed.

"Who did your mom say that did it then if it was not her?" Danny asks with his eyes widened.

"She said she thinks my dad's girlfriend has something to do with it." I shrugged.

"This is so bizarre; it's like one of those shows on the Discovery Channel." Faye and her comparison.

"Ha, which one? They got so many," Danny jokes.

"Hey now, we are talking about Kayla's mom here; let us have a little respect. If she is innocent, then we need to cut her some slack with the jokes," Deebo says angrily.

"It is fine. It has become a family mockery anyway, so have fun with it."

The next morning, we got ready for school. When we pulled up to the school, my phone buzzed. I pulled out my phone and saw Detective Shim's number flashing on the screen. I hit the answer button immediately.

"Kayla, I got your message," his voice jumped out of the speaker.

"Are you managing assignments overseas now?" I asked.

"No, I have been busy. I could not call you back right away."

"Okay, so what chance does my mom have of getting off?"

"Your mom has a good chance. When her lawyer sent me those documents and I went through them, it looked like someone was trying to make some last-minute changes," he confirmed.

"So, what does that mean?"

"I still do not have everything I need to answer that, but it is safe to say that your mom might be in the clear. I must pay Michelle, your dad's girlfriend, another visit. She was visiting your mom in prison, and something was wrong with that picture.

"I'm going with you," I demanded.

"Oh no, you are not. You are a kid, and you have already done enough help with law enforcement. I can get fired for getting you involved. I will call you when I have more information but, in the meantime, stay out of my way," he threatened. He hung up. I was not going to obey Detective Shims, especially since I helped him solve the last two cases. We were a good team, and I was going to help with this case because it involved my mom.

The school day went by amazingly fast. It was because all I could think about was my mom and my dad's murder. At the end of the day, we met up outside in the parking lot like we always do.

"So, what do you want us to do now?" Danny starts the conversation.

"We are going to solve this case and clear my mom's name," I said like I was one of the attorneys.

"Okay, well, it looks like we are back on our old shit again. Who do I need to call to help?" Danny pulls out his phone.

"Calm down, Danny. The first thing we are going to do is follow Michelle around. See where she goes during the day and night."

"Who is Michelle? If you do not mind me asking," Kelly asks.

"That is Kayla's dad's girlfriend, the supposed killer," Faye replies. Everybody stares at her.

"What, I listened to the news. I am following the case closely." She folds her hands and rolls her eyes.

"Yeah, don't hurt yourself," Kelly laughs.

"When are we doing this?" asked Danny.

"How about right now? I will text you the address, and when it is time to go, we will head over there. Detective Shims does not need to know what we are doing, so keep it quiet," I added.

"What? I thought he knew we were going over there, Kayla!" Kelly raises her hand. Her eyes were staring at me.

"No, he doesn't, but this never stopped us before when it came down to helping someone," I commented.

"Look, let's forget about that right now. This is Kayla's mom we are talking about, and it does not matter who helps," Deebo exclaimed.

This was not the first time that we got together to solve a crime. This time I had to find out what was going on. Was my mother telling the truth about being innocent of the accusations that she killed her own husband? Is it another lie, and she is just trying to get off and trick everybody? Or she was framing Michelle for the murder? I had these thoughts rolling around in my head.

Just as we started driving away from my house, I could feel my phone buzzing. It was the detective. Did he know we were going over to my dad's girlfriend's house to look around?

"Kayla, it is Shims. I am heading over to Michelle's house right now. I need you to keep an ear out for your mother and stay home," he demanded.

"I will meet you there," I said nervously.

"Kayla, you listen to me, I am ordering you to stay home. You are not a police officer, and you need to stay out of the investigation." I ended the call.

"You're not going to stop me, Detective," I whispered.

We pulled up to the house in my car. I had a 2014 black Mercedes Benz. I knew that the detective would spot my car immediately if he came here. I parked a block away to avoid getting caught.

"Remember, please let me do the talking and do not be rude. I do not want to chase her out of here." I sounded like I was leading a team. As we walked up to the house, I looked in the window. I did not see Michelle.

"Hey, looks like your girl has already left. I will check the back." Deebo goes around to the back of the house. I went to open the front door with the girls behind me. Surprisingly, the door was unlocked. We walked inside. The house was clean. Everything was in its place. The magazines were skillfully placed on the living room table. I walked into the bedroom, and everything looked untouched. The bed was made. There were three decor pillows skillfully placed on the bed. The gray comforter and the pillows matched perfectly. We walked back to the kitchen. There were some dishes in the sink. A few things were left around to look like someone would return, but I was not sure.

"Well, she might be coming back," said Danny as he started touching things.

"Do not touch anything! Remember you do not want your prints on anything," I instructed. Moments later, we heard another car pulling up.

"Oh no! The detective is here." Someone stomped up the steps. The door opened. Danny and Deebo were snooping around the house.

"I thought I told you kids to stay the fuck home. What part did not you understand about that?" the detective yelled. He walked around to see what else was being done without his permission. Danny and Deebo ran back outside to the front of the house, avoiding confrontation. Me and the girls were upstairs searching for something to help with the case.

"Kayla, come on down here right now," he screamed.

"Let's go, she's definitely gone," I predicted.

"How can you tell?" Faye gives the bedroom a last glance. "Looks to me like she will be back," she said with her eyes squinched.

"She arranged her house to make it look like that, but she's gone and probably not coming back." I walked downstairs ahead of the girls. We jumped when we saw the detective walking up. His nostrils flared. His face twisted.

"I need to see you outside right now!" he yelled. I shook as I walked outside. Danny and Deebo ran back into the car. I do not think we wanted to get the wrath of the detective for not following his orders. Faye started to walk out front, but Kelly pulled on her arms and shook her head no. Faye shrugged her shoulders and sat down and picked up a note that was on the desk with flight information.

"I told you not to come here. Did I not?" He charged toward me as if he were going to spank me for being bad.

"I know but this is my mom, and I was not going to just sit here and do nothing." My voice cracked and I could feel the tears starting to form.

"You can't keep putting yourself in danger because I have to explain to my boss if something happens to you," he replied.

"Okay, I'm sorry, but I just want to help," I added. He took out a cigarette box from his trench coat pocket. He pulled out one of the cigarettes and placed it in his mouth. He lit it and he looked at me. He had one eyebrow up and one down. He had the expression when you know someone is pissed at you. He sighed.

"I understand you want to help, but you must listen to me first. Do not forget how you were kidnapped not too long ago. He took a few puffs of his cigarette and threw it on the floor and stepped on it. "Since I know that you got to the house before me, did you find anything?"

"Not a damn thing. It was a waste of time." I was beginning to feel helpless.

"You see, that is why you should not be poking your nose in things you know nothing of. To you there is nothing to see in there, but for me there is a load of evidence laying around in there." He shook his head. Faye and Kelly quickly came out of the house.

"There is nothing in there; we searched the whole place." Kelly put her hands up. She sounded so sure.

"Looks like I will have to be the judge of that. You did enough damage by putting your fingerprints on evidence." He looked around. "Please go home, for the millionth time," he commented.

"Trust me, you don't have to tell us more than once," Faye assures.

"Ha, well, tell that to your friend Kayla." He walked out front. As we walked toward the cars that were parked down the block, Faye stopped walking.

"I have to go back to see the detective," she said anxiously.

"Why, did you see something?" I asked.

"Um, not . . . well yes, I need to give him this note. It was on the desk inside." The detective walked to his car.

"Detective Shims! Detective Shims!" Faye yelled at him.

"Go home now, you two!"

"No wait, hold up. I think you might want to see this. I saw this on the desk inside." Faye ran to Detective Shims' car.

"What is this?" he demanded.

"I do not know, but I thought it might help." She handed him the note through his car window. "Now we are leaving. Bye." He snatched the note and drove off swiftly. You could hear the screeching sounds of his tire.

CHAPTER 13.
LIAR, LIAR

We got back home after failing to be detectives on our own. We did not find anything that could help my mom's case, and it was a waste of time. I went into my room and fell onto the bed on my back. I looked up at the ceiling as if all the answers were floating around up there. As I lay there, I heard a text notification from my phone. What could it be now? I got up and picked up my phone. I read the text from the detective.

"Michelle escaped from prison! We know she is in Mexico." The note that Faye gave him indicated that she was on a flight to Mexico and that she was meeting up with someone. What she did not know is that Detective Shims bugged her phone when he interrogated her a few weeks back. He was able to hear all her conservations, no matter where she was.

"You got here quickly. How are you?" says a mysterious woman.

"Hi Jessica, I am doing great. Thanks for your generosity." Michelle, my dad's girlfriend, went to visit someone in Mexico.

"Well yes, I have been off the radar for a while now. So, what made you visit me after all this time?"

"I was told that I should come out here when I need smoke to clear."

"Ah, I see. What was this thing you had to take care of, if you did not mind me asking?"

"Believe me, the less you know the better, trust me."

"How can I collaborate with you on our project if I do not know what I am dealing with?"

"Look, I helped this lady kill her husband, all right? You do not need to know anything more," Michelle insisted.

The detective sent me an audio clip of Michelle's conversations. I listened to them and was more confused. I looked for the detective's number on my phone and hit the green phone icon.

"Now that you have her location, when are you going to arrest her? She admits to killing my dad."

"Hello Kayla." I clenched my teeth. "I will fill you in when we get her back. I need you to stay put and not leave your house. Make sure you and your friends follow my orders, or I will arrest you this time." His voice was deeper than usual.

I sighed. I took a deep breath and released the tension from my body. "Fine. Good-bye." I hit the end call button.

Chris was on my mind because I missed him, and I had not heard from him in days. Me and Deebo have not been intimate in a while, and I thought that I did not have to lie anymore about sleeping with Chris. Deebo was a little distant, but he was only staying away because I was giving him that vibe.

"Hey guys, I'm going to see my mom. I'll be back in a couple of hours," I yelled out. You could hear a pin drop. No one cared to respond to me. I was happy about that because I did not want to feel the guilt if I had to face Deebo. My house was a ghost town.

I got in my car and hit Chris's name on my phone. The phone just rang, and he did not answer. I drove over to Chris's. When I pulled up to his apartment, I saw his car was there, so that made me happy that he was home. I walked up to his apartment door. I knocked on it.

Chris came to the door and his eyes popped out of his head. He was not expecting me since we had not talked in a while.

"Hey, what a surprise. I have not heard from you or got a text."

"I was saying the same thing about you. Come on, let me in." I was fidgety. He stood by the door like he was a guard, but then gave in. I had a big smile on my face until I saw another girl at the desk with books and papers. Our eyes met.

"Hi," I said, and my smile turned into a frown.

"This is my friend. She was helping me study. We have a big exam coming up, and she is the only one that gets an A in the class." I proceeded to go to the door.

He pulled on my arm. "Hey, where are you going? I need a break anyway and I am glad you are here."

"Hey Chris, I am done anyway—if I try to squeeze any more information in my head, I am going to explode. Nice meeting you," his friend said kindly. I watched her pick up her bag and books. She smiled at me as she walked out of the apartment. I inhaled and exhaled. I realized nothing was going on.

"I am sorry for barging in like this. I was lonely and I wanted to see you," I confessed.

"Don't tell me you thought I was doing something with that girl," he smirked.

"Yeah, I thought that for a quick second."

"That makes me feel good. Does that mean that you and Deebo are over?" I put my head down. The tension had returned. I turned my head away from him. Just as I did, my phone buzzed.

"This better be good, Shims," I whispered. I hit the accept button and put the phone on speaker.

"We got her. Michelle is on her way to the station. We are arresting her for falsifying documents and her involvement with your dad's murder." I felt calm.

"So, what happens now. I mean, when is the trial?"

"I will confirm and let you know. Thank your friend for the tip since she is the one that found out where Michelle's whereabouts were."

"I will talk to you soon." I hit the end call button. I was ready to get back to Chris. I pulled him into his bedroom.

"I know you are not going to leave me hanging. What did the detective say?" He raised his hands up.

"They got Michelle. She is my dad's girlfriend, and it looks like she might be guilty of killing my dad." I sighed.

"Damn, this case is getting more serious by the minute. I hope they can get this wrapped up so you can get your life back." He moved a few strands of my hair away from my eye.

"My life is fine with you in it. Let us get comfortable now please," I begged. He gave in. He picked me up and took me to his bedroom.

Meanwhile Detective Shims was at the police station interrogating Michelle. He was texting me everything that was going on with her at the station. She was sitting in the room and was not a happy camper. She did not want to cooperate.

"Why are you harassing me? I answered all your questions," said Michelle.

"Yeah, let us get down to business. Why did you flee to Mexico if you did not do anything?" he said.

"It is a free country. I thought I could travel anytime I wanted. I did not know I needed permission."

"Well, that's true, you were free to go, but usually if you're in the middle of a murder investigation, the smart thing to do is to stay put and not leave the country." Detective Shims pulled out a file with papers in it. He pulled out one of them that had Michelle's name on it as the owner of the company that was owned by my dad.

"Explain to me how your name got on this document stating that you are the new owner of your deceased boyfriend's business." He slammed his hands on the desk.

"What?" Michelle picked up the paper and looked at it. "I do not know anything about this. Where did you find this, and who gave you this?" she demanded.

"Cut the shit, Michelle. They found your prints on the same gin bottle that Mr. Jensen was drinking out of. Also, there's evidence that you went to see Mrs. Jensen to talk to her about some money. Were you extorting her?" His eyes squinched. Michelle got up and slammed the paper on the desk. Her first ballad.

"I am not telling you another damn thing. Get me the fuck out of here so I can call my lawyer." She faced the door and started banging on it.

"Okay, you don't want to talk to me, great—you will want too sooner or later." Detective Shims got up and knocked on the door with his hand. The police officer that was standing outside opened the door, and Michelle stormed out.

The following week was court day, and my mom and Michelle had to be in attendance. The two women were sitting with their attorneys. As the case went on, testimonies were given, and I had to testify just as Mr. Shims said. Almost eight months later, the verdict was finally in. The spectators were not happy with the verdict, and everyone was in shock. The evidence was clear as day, but money somehow has a way of getting you out of trouble. My mom was acquitted. The jury found her not guilty of the murder of my dad, due to lack of evidence. I was not happy about it because in the beginning the police report said that my mom's fingerprints were on the bottle with the poison.

After the verdict, I walked up to my mom and hugged her. She watched the police officers take Michelle away, who was screaming, "That bitch set me up." I looked back at Michelle when she yelled. What was she talking about when my mom set her up? I looked at my mom. She smiled. She got all the companies that my dad owned, and her name was back on the document as owner of the business they both owned together when they got married. Things were still unclear to me. It will be a matter of time when the truth comes out about her setting up Michelle, but by the time that comes out, people will have forgotten all about that case. She paid someone in court or in law enforcement to wipe away all the evidence that pointed to her.

A few months went by, and for the first time everything was back to normal. My friends and I tried to stay out of trouble. We were still financially well off from the diamonds we stole from our old boss at the nightclub. I demanded that we continue not to do any suspicious spending to avoid attracting attention. We were living in a big house that my aunt left for us to stay for as long as we wanted to. The world as we know it is now a perfect place. The only thing that needed to be fixed was the love triangle situation that I was wrapped up in. You know, the one between me, Deebo, and Chris. Things between Deebo and I were not going well, and it was a good thing, since all I had to do was break up with him so I could be with Chris.

It was Friday, the end of the week, and we were getting ready for school. With four weeks left for summer break, everyone was on their last thread. We could not even think about graduation, because we had so much going on with our lives outside school.

"Kayla, I'm glad you and your mom are in a better place now that she's been cleared of your dad's murder," said Faye.

"Yeah, maybe you can work things out with your mom and possibly have a relationship with her," said Danny.

"Guys, guys, I still must take baby steps with my mom. We still have a lot of things that she did to me that I am still waiting for an apology for. I had not talked to her in a year before all this happened, and she had not started calling me until now. So, what does that say about her?" I looked at my friends for the answers.

"It is going to take some time; do not rush it. It took me a while before I buried the hatchet with my family," said Kelly.

"You don't even talk with your parents, Kelly," Danny said with his eyebrows raised.

"Yea I know. I am just saying." We all laughed. My friends got ready for school except for me. I was staying in and wanted to take another day off from all the drama.

"Bye Kayla, see you later, girl," said Faye. Kelly, Faye, and Danny left for school. I went to my room to clean it up and do some laundry. A few minutes later, I heard some movement upstairs. I went toward the stairs to see who it was.

"Hello, who's up there?" Deebo came downstairs. I jumped when his appearance came into view.

"Why are you home? I thought you went to school." Deebo had clothes in his hand and took the clothes from my hand and went into the laundry room to drop them in the washing machine. I followed him.

"I wanted to take the day off. I am glad you are home too because we need to talk." I poured the detergent in the washing machine, and Deebo helped take out the clothes from the dryer.

"Yes, I am glad you feel the same way. I've been wanting to talk about our relationship," I confessed. "Let us talk in the living room." Deebo followed me into the room, and we sat down.

"Well, I know that you had so much going on with the loss of your dad. I know that I did not help by arguing with you about that chump your parents were working with. I owe you an apology. I am sorry for being an ass and not taking all, you were going through into consideration," he said.

"Yeah, it's been rough these past couple of weeks. Our relationship took a turn and I want to apologize for that. I wish we could have done a better job during this tough time," I commented. I was happy that he was about to break up with me and I did not have to do the dirty work.

"That is why I am glad that everything with your mom panned out okay. I want us to work on our relationship. I want you to be my girl, Kayla. I am in love with you, and I want us to be together." He got closer to me and touched my face.

I was stunned. *What? Get together? Oh no. He wants us to be together. I thought he wanted us to break up.* I felt the beginnings of a massive headache. I started rubbing my forehead. Suddenly I was blind. My sight disappeared.

I just sat there while Deebo confessed his love for me. *Finally, but why now?* I thought. I was thinking about how I was going to get out of this tonight and run into Chris's arms.

"What's wrong? Are you all right?" His eyes watered.

"Umm yes, I am just feeling a little tired. I am going to go lay down." I felt sick. I was food poisoning sick. That is how I felt.

"Is it something I said?" he asked nervously.

"No, no of course not." I was shaking. I was lying again.

"Do you feel the same way about me?" I was talking to myself in my mind and did not know what to do or how to answer. Am I still in love with Deebo? Why can't I just say I am not in love with him? I turned to face him. He walked up closer to me. He touched my face again.

"I am in love with you Deebo and I never stopped."

What? Shit, shit, shit, I thought. *What am I saying and why am I lying to myself? Well, I am still in love with him. Why can't I figure this out?* I asked myself. Deebo held me close and kissed me softly. Then he hugged me tightly against his body. I loved every minute of it and accepted his affection. He took me toward the bedroom and laid me down on my bed. He undressed me. I was so upset with myself that I was not able to let Deebo know that I was sleeping with Chris.

We made love repeatedly. Then I laid there on my bed while he got up to go work out. I had a lot on my mind and was trying to figure out how I was going to manage this situation. I was still in love with Deebo and did not want to continue to lie to him for my own selfish reasons. After school, I could hear Danny and the girls coming into the house. I was in the kitchen fixing something to eat.

"You should have been in school today. It was a wrestling match with these two girls and the teachers could not break it up," Faye said.

"Wow, I'm glad I missed it." I had my head down the whole time Faye spoke to me. I could not face her.

"Yeah, it was not a good sight. Anyway, what did you do? Deebo stayed in, so I hope you had that talk with him like you promised." Kelly made eye contact with me. I tried to avoid the conversation, but it would only make me more guilty.

"We talked and got some things out."

"Oh good. So does that mean no more lying to Deebo?" she asked.

I sat down with my hands on my forehead like I was preventing another massive headache.

"Looks like they talked, but the wrong things were being said." Faye gave me a sorry look.

"Kayla, you promised to fix things. What is wrong with you? If Deebo was playing you like this, you would not be tolerating it," said Kelly.

"I tried to end it between us. We were distant; we had not slept with each other in a while. I thought things were going in the breakup direction. Then he said he was in love with me. He started telling me how he really felt. For some reason, it made me feel for him even more," I explained.

"So, you slept with him?" asked Kelly.

"Yes, and I liked it and did not want it to stop. So, shoot me, okay. I am going to go take a walk." Kelly shook her head while she was putting back the juice carton in the fridge. I got up and went outside and slammed the door.

I was outside walking, and I got a text from Chris.

"Hey beautiful, can I come over? I miss you," he texted. I read it. I felt so good hearing from him.

"It's a full house right now, but why don't I come to you?" I responded back. Chris hesitated to respond but then texted me right back.

"I am guessing you did not talk to Deebo yet. Let me ask you a question. Are you sleeping with him?" My heart stopped, and I could not believe he was asking me that question. *Can he see me way over here?* I thought. I do not want to lie to him, and I do not want to hurt him either. I bit my lip and squinched my eyes.

"No, we hadn't done that in a couple months." I lied and it felt horrible, but I would rather lie than tell Chris the truth. At the same moment I saw the Detective's name flashing on my screen. I was happy to get off with Chris to get out of the hotseat.

"I got to go Chris; it is Detective Shims. We will talk about it later."

"Hey Kayla, I got some bad news, and I wanted you to hear it from me."

"Detective, you are scaring me. What is this about?"

"Michelle broke out of prison. We do not know where she is now," he said. I dropped onto the floor.

"What do you mean?"

"Listen to me, I need you to go to your mother's house right now. There is a possibility that Michelle may pay her a visit and try to hurt her," he said firmly.

My body was weak. "I have to warn my mother."

"I am sending a police car to your house right now to take you there. Tell everybody else to be on the lookout. She might send someone over to you too. We are not sure how she is going to play her cards, but better safe than sorry."

"How did she get out?"

"Kayla, I am afraid that is not the question you should be asking. The question is what your mother did for that woman to break out of prison."

The water behind my eyes fell on the cue. I quickly got up and went to my car. Detective Shims was still on the phone calling me. I heard the call drop. I then clicked on my mom's face on my phone, but no answer. An hour later, I got to my mother's house. The front door was open. I slowly walked in. My first view was of tossed clothes on the floor. I saw a red substance spread on the floor.

"Mom!" I yelled. I walked through the house, and I heard someone's car in the front. Knowing that Detective Shims was pulling up, I kept calling out for her.

"Mom!" My mom was nowhere to be found. I stepped on clothes, papers, and garbage that covered certain areas in her bedroom. I could hear the footsteps of someone rushing into the house.

"Get back in the car. Kayla, get back in the car; I will look for your mother. I stood there frozen. Get out of here." He pointed to the front door with one hand while the other held a gun. I ran back to my car feeling the tears in my eyes. The detective walked slowly through the house.

"Mrs. Jensen! Mrs. Jensen!" He kicked her clothes and papers out of his way. He entered her room and he called for her again. Blood was smeared on the carpet and had a trail into the bathroom.

The detective walked slowly to the bathroom, then dropped his hands. "Aww, man, Mrs. Jensen, who did this to you? Shit!" The detective pulled out his phone.

"She died from several gunshot wounds to the head." He walked back outside, and I got out of the car to meet him.

"Is she in there? Is she okay?" He raised his arm in front of me.

"I'm sorry. We were too late." He held me close.

"No, let me in. Let me in right now. Get off me, let me in. It is my mother," I cried. I fought with the detective. The ambulance came and the paramedics ran in. Minutes later they came out with her body covered. The neighbors ran over to see, and people in the street crowded the area. Detective Shims put me in one of the police cars. I watched as police officers and crime scene unit people rushed inside. Kelly, Faye, Deebo, and Danny came running to the scene. The detective directed them with his hands to come to the car, where I was.

Chris pulled up and ran out to me. I got back out of the car to meet him halfway. I hugged him hard. Deebo, Kelly, Faye, and Danny walked up to where I was. They bombarded me with hugs. Chris looked at Deebo and Deebo looked back. I turned my head to see Chris and Deebo having a staring match. Deebo walked back to me and grabbed my hand. I knew it was going to be ugly from here.

"Chris, please take Kayla to your house. I will meet you there later," Detective instructed. Chris nodded yes and signaled to me to come with his hands.

"No. We can take her home," Deebo responded.

"Your house is no longer safe for her, or for any of you, for that matter. I need all of you to go in my car and wait for me." Danny, Faye, and Kelly walked to the police cars. I started to walk in Chris's direction.

"Kayla, why are you going with him?" Deebo cried.

"You heard what the detective said—he wants me to take her home," Chris added.

"Kayla, don't do this right now, please," Kelly watched as she entered the police car. Deebo's face frowned and he balled his fist. I ignored Deebo with tears falling. I buried my face against Chris's chest.

"Kayla, please stay with me. I can take you somewhere safe, I love you." Chris continued to walk with me and put me in his car. I turned back to Deebo and whispered that I was sorry.

"Don't do this to us, Kayla, please come home with me." He continued to yell at me like I was going to change my mind. I was a piece of shit to do this to Deebo, without hesitation. Kelly quickly got out of the car. She turned him away from our direction. Chris got onto the driver's side. We drove off and I did not even look back. I knew I hurt Deebo, in the worst way, and there was no coming back from that. At that moment, I knew I had lost one of the most important loves of my life.

Kelly, Faye, and Danny waited in the car. The detective got back to the car. "I must take you to an undisclosed location. Do not worry about your belongings. I already have someone meeting us there with your stuff."

The secret is out. I chose Chris over Deebo, and I knew he was the better man for me, because I loved him more. I lost both of my parents and one true best friend. The loss I experienced was something I was going to have to fight to get through. I kept playing the scene over and over in my head. I walked away from Deebo and did not say a word. I could not at that moment. It was like I was hypnotized or something. I knew that I lost Deebo forever because there was no way he was going to forgive me for what I did to him in front of everyone. Sometimes love is not that strong to overcome hurt like that. He will hate me forever.

We got to Chris's apartment, and he put me to bed. He brought in some tea and kissed me on my forehead and left the room. I must have been sleeping for a long time because when I woke up Chris was still not in bed with me. I was feeling so empty. I look around in the bedroom I was in. It was lonely. How was I going to live without my parents? We were not close, but at least if they were living, I had that opportunity to visit them if I wanted to. I was ashamed that I did not make things work out between us. I let some petty situations make decisions for me. I needed them more than ever, and I realized how important that was at that moment. I snapped out of it and started thinking about Chris. It was a little strange that he was not with me right now hugging me and consoling me. I decided to get up to see what he was doing in the living room.

He was sitting on the couch texting. I could not see who he was texting, but I was able to see who was texting him back. His bedroom was behind the living room and the couch was facing the back. So, I was able to sneak up on his back to see what he was doing without him knowing. When he got the response back, it said, "You should see the envelope in the folder in your school bag."

Immediately I was concerned. I wanted to know what envelope this person was talking about. I watched him walk over to his school bag and take out a folder, and inside was an envelope. He opened it. It looked like a check from my point of view. Then for some reason, I must have made too much noise trying to get a clear view, so I hopped back in the bed. He turned around and came back into the room. I pretended to be asleep, and he was looking for a place to hide the check. Fortunately, for me I had one eye squinting, and I saw exactly where he put the check. It was in a Gucci tote that he had between his bookshelf and mirror. It was slim enough to fit in between. He put the check inside the tote. I had a funny feeling, and it was making me sick to my stomach. I had to find out who wrote the check, and I decided to pretend I was waking up. I started to toss and turn, and he looked at me with a fake smile. At that moment I knew I had a problem that I was not going to be able to fix.

"Can you get me some soup? I am feeling so sick right now and cold." He looked at me, caressed my face, and kissed me on my forehead.

"Of course, I will. Anything for you. What else can I get for you, my love?" he asked lovingly. Suddenly, I was starting to feel like he was an evil soul. I was getting angry without even knowing what was going on.

"Nothing else. I am not feeling well right now," I added.

"Babe, you just found out that your mom was murdered. Really both of your parents were murdered. This is an exceedingly tough time for you, and I am going to make sure that I take diligent care of you from here on in. Get some sleep and I will be back with your soup. I may even bring you back something special." I heard the door close. I jumped back up and went straight to the tote bag to get the check. My heart stopped on sight. Tears came falling on my face like a small waterfall. I had recognized the check and who it was from.

It was a check for one million dollars, and the check was made out to Chris from my mom's checkbook. I swallowed a ball of spit that felt like a marble. I could not even talk or cry or do anything. I was in a frozen state. I belted out a cry that sounded like it was a mouse wheezing from being caught in a trap.

I was in complete horror, because it was at once that I realized Chris planned a scheme to set up my dad's girlfriend so that she would think my mother planned the whole thing to get her arrested for my dad's murder. He knew that she would seek revenge and come after my mom to later wipe her off the face of the earth.

I could not feel my hands. I finally knew the truth. Chris was the mastermind of this whole mess with my parents. He knew that he could get my parents' money. He had access to their accounts and important documents. He pretended to fall in love with me the whole time, but he was the liar. I had never felt so low and hurt like this before. I was sickened by the whole thing because I was making love to this person. I thought about all the crimes and lives that I helped to solve and save with the detective. Here I was with one. I was thinking that he would return soon from the store.

It was unfortunate that I was able to save the families of Forney, but not mine. This was not the end for me. The tension in my bones released. I wiped my tears with my hands. I rushed back to bed. I wiped my face again and counted to ten to calm my nerves. My heart fell back to its normal rate. There was some noise at the front door. He returned from the store. I heard him opening the cabinet in the kitchen. A few seconds later he came in with a tray and a bowl on top of it.

"Wake up, babe. I have your soup." I opened my eyes and displayed the best smile I could create. I needed him to continue to think that he got away with murdering my parents.

The next morning, I woke up. I got out of bed. I walked into the living room. I was alone. Chris's apartment was small enough for me to see if someone was at home or not. I walked back to his bedroom. I walked over to the chair with my clothes on it. I got dressed. I looked for my phone and keys.

"Got it." I opened his door and peeked out. Then I walked out and closed his door. As I came out of the elevator I bumped into the detective.

"Shims! Oh, my goodness."

"Hey, I need to talk to you and Chris." I pulled the detective back into the elevator.

"No, we have to get out of here before Chris gets back."

The detective shook his head. "What is going on Kayla?"

"Please, I will tell you when we get out of here." I was jumpy and shaking. "Where did you park? Let us go in your car." I said timidly. He led the way to his car.

"Okay, get in." We got in his car. I hit the lock button.

"What is wrong with you?" The tension in his voice increased. I sighed. I had my head down. I continued to inhale and exhale slowly. The detective remained patient. Suddenly, I was weak. The tears ran down my cheeks.

"Chris is the murderer." I could not get the words out of my mouth. My body trembled.

"Okay, calm down. I know what you are trying to tell me." He put his arms around me. "I have never seen you like this before."

"Did Chris have something to do with your parents' murder?" He was right on target. He is a smart man. I nodded. I was still unable to move my lips. I could not pry them apart. He looked at me.

"Do you have any proof? I need proof, Kayla, to defend what you are saying about Chris." I nodded again. I was helpless. I did not imagine that I would be numb like this.

Come on. Come on. You can do this, I said to myself. My brain was having a party. I had too many things circling in there.

"All right, we are going to wait here until he gets back, and I will have a talk with him."

My lips moved. "No. Please. I would rather you search his apartment first. He has a check for a million dollars that my mom wrote to him. He has documents and text messages from strange individuals." I took a deep breath after disclosing information. The detective wore a blank face. He faced the windshield and then looked over to Chris's apartment.

"I am so sorry Kayla."

I looked back at him. "Sorry for what? You did not do anything."

He leaned over to me. He put his arms back around me. "I am sorry that I put your life in danger. I made you go home with him." I pushed back and removed his arms.

"No, you did not know. I did not know."

I tried to reassure the detective that he was innocent in all this. We were all fooled by his good looks and his sexy charm—at least I was. The detective gathered his gun. Then I saw Chris walking right in front of the car.

"Shit! He is right there." I pointed. My voice cracked and I trembled at the sight of him.

"Stay in the car, Kayla. I will be right back. Lock the door." The detective opened the car door. He signaled me to hide.

"Hey, I wanted to check on you. How is Kayla doing?" The detective met up with Chris and they walked together.

"Oh, she is good. She has me running to the store for her already." I watched them as they walked back to Chris's apartment building. I watched them until they were out of my sight. I could not stay still. I held my hands together. I tried placing them on my thighs, and on the window. I looked around the car. My body was dripping with sweat. I was too afraid to remain in the car, so I opened the passenger side and walked out. I walked in the direction of Chris's apartment.

By the time I caught up, they were already in the elevator. I pressed the call button. I had shaky fingers. I looked around my surroundings. I jumped in the elevator. I got to Chris's floor and stepped out slowly. The hallways were lonely. I walked up to the door, and it was ajar. I peeked in. I heard the men talking.

"Kayla, do you know where the envelope is?" The detective's voice startled me.

"How did you know?"

"You do not listen. I knew you were going to come up here eventually. Get the check you told me about." Chris tried to move, but the detective pulled out his gun.

"No, not you. I need you to stay put." Chris smirked in anger. I walked into his bedroom and pulled the envelope out from his bookshelf. I walked back to the living room and handed the detective the check.

"He has text messages that may have more information of his involvement," I commented. The detective pulled Chris's hands together and handcuffed him.

"Yup, I have his phone already. Let's get out of here." We walked back to the elevator. When we got to the lobby, several police officers were already there. They took Chris.

"I went through his phone. He was involved. I am arresting him for his participation in all of this. We have enough evidence to nail him." I sat down on the chair in the lobby. I had both of my hands holding my head. The detective sat down next to me.

I watched the police officers walk back and forth to Chris's apartment with his stuff. They took a lot of his things as evidence.

"Once again, you helped solve another case. I am sad that it had to be close to home for you."

I sighed. "I made a big mistake, Shims. I hurt someone that I love. I picked the wrong boy. What does that say about me?" I turned to him.

"Kayla, you did not know. That is what you said to me. Chris fooled me too. I thought he was a nice guy. You cannot beat yourself up for things you do not have control of." He got up and extended his hand. "Let me take you home. I am quite sure your friends are worried about you." I grabbed his hand. We walked outside the building, and everybody was running all over the place.

"What happened here?" A police officer ran up to us.

"I am sorry, boss. He got away," he explained.

"What? What do you mean, he got away?"

"Chris escaped. We put him in the car, and somehow, he was able to run without us knowing."

"Damn it! Kayla, stay with me. I always need you in my sight." I became glued next to the detective. I stood up under his arm.

"Get the squad out. Tell them who we are looking for." He looked down at me.

"He will not get far, Kayla. Do not worry. He will not get far. I promise." Tears poured out of my eyes as I stood there knowing the person that got my parents killed was running loose. He was free.

CHAPTER 14.
CATCH ME IF YOU CAN

The detective and the police could not find Chris. Detective Shims believed that he had already fled the country and that it was going to take a miracle to find him anytime soon, especially with the amount of money he had on him. The detective thought it would be best to put me back in an undisclosed location just in case Chris wanted to take me out for revenge. He put me in this one-bedroom apartment in Dallas Fort Worth. The building looked like a safe house. It was old and beaten down. It did not look much, but the detective reassured me that I would be safe here because they usually have undercover detectives staying here for cover. He said if I needed anything, all I had to do was call him and someone from this building would come to help me. I was instructed to call every few hours to let him know that I was okay and if I needed anything to let him know. I was not allowed to go anywhere and talk to anyone. That was okay with me. My friends were notified about Chris. I was told that they were the only ones that could come to visit me.

So here I was waiting for Deebo, Kelly, Danny, and Faye to come and give me the "told you so" speech. I was not ready for it. As soon as I told myself that, the doorbell rang. I walked over to the broken window that had a shade with a rip in the middle. I peeked through the rip and saw Deebo's car parking in front. I watched Danny and Kelly get out of the car. I did not see Faye. I opened the door to look for Faye.

"Where is Faye?" Kelly and Danny walked in quietly. Deebo walked in afterwards. He looked at me and did not speak. I closed the door to brace myself for the guilt and blame that I deserved from my friends. They walked in and sat down in the living room. I walked up to them to face them.

"Before you start tearing me apart, I want to know where Faye is."

"She is okay. She is with her boyfriend." Kelly walked up and started looking around the place.

"Well, the outside looks like crap. However, the inside looks amazing. I like this place." She nodded her head as she admired my secure location.

"I'm glad she is okay." I could not take the silent treatment from them. I understood the reason. I walked over to my ripped window shade.

"Hey Kayla, we are a little taken back by what happened with you and Chris. We all know that you did not know what he was up to. I know you had feelings for him." Danny walked up to me from behind. He put his hand on my shoulder.

"Just give us some time to get over everything that he did." I touched his hand. I turned around to face him.

"Thank you. I know that I messed up. I will make it up to all of you. I promise. I will help the detective find him, and we will make him pay for what he did to my parents." I glanced at Deebo. He had his face down. He had his hands together like he was going to pray. He continued to keep his eyes away from me.

"You must give him some time. He is hurt. You chose another man over him," Danny whispered as he glanced over at Deebo. My tears fell right on cue. My heart sank. I thought about the hurt I did to Deebo the day I found out that my mom was murdered. I went home with a stranger instead of staying with my friends whom I had known way before Chris. Chris was a stranger that I let into my life, and he ruined my life forever.

I ordered food so that we could have dinner together. Everybody spoke except for Deebo. After a few bites of my food, my throat was closing in. My stomach turned.

"Deebo, please talk to me. I would rather you curse me out instead of this cold shoulder."

Deebo got up and threw his plate into the sink. It cracked into two pieces. He looked at me for a quick second and went into the bathroom and closed the door. I got up and walked over to the bathroom. I looked back at Danny and Kelly to see if they were going to stop me. Kelly stared at me and frowned. Danny started cleaning up. I faced the door and put my hand on it.

"I am so sorry, Deebo. I hurt you and that is on me. I must live with that for the rest of my life. I love you. My feelings for you have never changed. I was in love with both of you. I did not know that was possible until I was in that position. I do not want to lose you. I will fight for you for as long as I must." I turned around and walked back to the kitchen. My phone started ringing. I did not care. My phone was placed on the counter.

"Do you want me to answer it, Kayla?" Kelly held my phone in her hand.

"Sure, why not." She picked it up and hit the green phone icon. She had the phone to her ear.

"This is Kelly, Kayla's friend. Can I help you?"

"Hello Kelly, this is Detective Shims. I am afraid I have sad news. I need to speak to Kayla."

"Okay, let me see if she wants to talk." Kelly looked up at me. She extended her arm with my phone in her hand. I shook my head no.

"I am sorry, Detective; she does not want to talk right now."

"Let her know that she must come down to the office. Her sister Genoveve is missing." Kelly's face changed. She dropped my phone. My body had a sick sensation that came over me immediately.

"What happened?" I walked over to Kelly slowly. She could not face me.

"What happened, Kelly?" She looked up at me. Her eyes were filled with sorrow. I did not know what was said to her, but I started gasping for air.

"Your sister is missing. Your aunt said she went out last night. She thought she was in bed sleeping. She went into her bedroom this morning and saw she was not there."

I had nothing else to feel. "Danny, please take me to see the detective," I said to the bathroom door. Danny came out of the bathroom.

"What is going on?"

"Genoveve is missing. We are going to the detective now to help find her," Kelly responded. Deebo ran outside.

"Kayla!" I turned around. He walked up to me. His arms felt like a warm blanket.

"Where is your sister?" he asked.

"I do not know. Chris may have abducted her. The detective just called."

"I'm coming." We walked to the car. He opened the passenger side. I got in. He walked back over to the driver's side. When we got to Detective Shims' office, he was waiting outside for us. His arms opened wide for me to come to them.

"I am sorry, Kayla. I cannot imagine how you are feeling now." He led us to an empty room. It was a classroom set up. "We have everybody on this. We are hunting down friends, relatives, and kids from her school as we speak."

They had pictures of Genoveve plastered on a whiteboard. They had Chris picture up there next to her.

"Do you think that Chris took her?"

"We cannot rule anything out. It is possible he may be holding her for leverage. We must consider all possibilities."

He killed my parents, and who knows who else. There was no way I was going to let him take the only family I had left. Police officers and men in suits were walking into the room we were in. The detective stood in front of the crowd.

"Everybody, please pay attention. We are dealing with a very smart individual. He was able to fool the Jensen's," he pointed to me, "Kayla's parents. This individual pretended to be a student at one of the universities here in Dallas. Kelly and Danny's heads raised. My eyes popped out of my head. All this time this fool was pretending to be a college student.

"Who was he? Is his name even Chris?" I asked. The detective looked at me.

"He is a felon. He has several aliases he goes by. His real name is Ron Tech. He was arrested several times for identity theft, money laundering, kidnapping, and a few home break-ins. He is twenty-eight but he looks incredibly young. We believe him posing as a college student got him inside a lot of places where he could hide on school grounds to trick everybody in his path."

My mouth dropped. I leaned back in my seat. Danny leaned in for a closer look. His eyes were fixated on the rap sheet. Deebo and Kelly went through the papers like they were looking at a monster. The detective read all his crimes like an introduction to the hall of fame. I shook my head. I was defrauded and used.

"I want to help. I brought this man into my life and my friends' lives. I am the reason that we are in a mess. I owe it to everybody to help," I confessed.

Danny stood up. "Me too."

Deebo stood up. "Count me in."

Kelly stood up. "Me too."

I turned around and looked at my friends. I nodded.

"You're not alone, Kayla. We are going to help these guys do whatever they need us to do to catch him," Deebo added. My friends made me feel loved. I was starting to believe that Deebo forgave me for everything that I put him through. Then again maybe that is pushing it. He gave me the look that he did.

After the meeting, the detective wanted us to come back into his office. We walked in and waited for him to meet us there. When he walked in, he closed the door behind him. He went to his desk and sat down. He only had two other chairs in there. Danny pulled out one of them for Kelly to sit and Deebo pulled out the other one for me. The detective went through some of his files.

"What about my sister? She is still missing," I proclaimed.

"That is why I had you all come in here. I wanted to discuss your sister privately. We have our men searching for her right now. We are talking to anyone who has been in contact with her during the last twenty hours. Do you know of any place she might have gone to?"

"I wish I knew."

"Does she have a boyfriend perhaps?" he asked. I was helpless.

"I wish I had answers as to where she is. I left my home too soon. I did not get a chance to meet her friends or see her crushes. Who her best friend is." Deebo rubbed my arms.

"Let us not waste any more time. I have a few addresses that I want you to go to and check out. Let us see what we can pull up. Meet me back here in a few hours if you get something," he instructed.

"Thank you. I wish I knew more." I got up and walked out of the office. Danny and Kelly followed. We walked out of the office, and I stopped at the bathroom. I went into one of the stalls and sat down on the toilet. I heard my phone buzzing in my pocket.

Hold on. Let me pee first, I said to myself. After I finished doing my business, I walked over to the sink. I pressed the soap pump into my palms. When I dried my hands, I pulled the phone out to see who was calling me.

"You got to be freaking kidding me." I looked down and saw Chris was calling. I took a deep breath. My hands were shaky. My veins boiled up underneath my skin.

"How are you, dear? I had you. Do you still love me?" He laughed devilishly.

"Where is my sister?" I screamed.

"All I wanted you to know is that I have your little sister. She is so cute. I will not harm her, but I need you to tell your detective friend not to pursue me and to let all his dogs stay back. If I sense that you did not relay the message, I will start pulling out the exceptionally fine hairs on her head one by one until she is bald. Byeeeeee." He ended the call.

My face turned red. My heart sank to the lowest part. The door swung wide open. "Kayla, are you okay? The detective wants to wrap things up. Kayla what happened?"

"Chris has my sister."

"Oh no. We must tell Detective Shims right now." She tugged on my arm, and we walked back to the detective's office.

"What's wrong?" Deebo looked at me with sad eyes.

"Detective! Chris called Kayla. He has Genoveve."

The detective dropped his pen. "Give me your phone!" Kelly handed my phone to the detective. He rushed back to his computer in his office.

"Change of plans. I want all of you to come with me." He went into his drawer and grabbed his gun. He slammed it back and walked out the door.

"Let's go find this son of a bitch," he demanded. Deebo held my hands as we followed the detective. When we walked with the detective, we passed his peers in the hallway.

"I need you and you to come with us." He pointed to a couple of officers.

"Chris has Kayla's sister. He is going to call us back. I want to be ready for when he does." We looked like a SWAT team the way we walked in rhythm. Danny, Deebo, Kelly, and I drove with Detective Shims. The other police officers jumped in a police van.

We got to Chris's apartment. I thought it was his apartment off campus, but he was never a student. I wondered if that girl that I saw when I visited him was in it.

"Okay, guys, I want you to look through everything in here. We are looking for anything that can tell us where he might be with Kayla's sister. Turn everything upside down if you must." You could see the tension on the detective's face. He stomped around throwing things around and he did not care if he broke Chris's items.

I looked around at everyone. Danny stomped on papers that were on the floor. Deebo tossed boxes and garbage around like he was angry at how messy the place looked. We all were angry that Chris took my sister. I did not know where she was or where he might have taken her. We tore up the place and we still did not find anything.

"Hey Shims, there is nothing here. We are going to head back to the office. I will let you know if we hear anything," said the police officer.

"Kayla, we will find her. I will do everything in my power to find your sister." The detective touched my arms. His eyes spoke to me. I nodded.

"Thank you, I know you will. Thank you to all of you. I love you and appreciate you," I added. We went back outside. As we walked out, Faye was outside coming in.

"Hey guys, I think you're going to want to see this," Faye says.

"Faye, how did you know where we were?" asked Kelly.

"I called the station, and they told me that you were at Chris's place."

"What do you have Faye?" the detective demanded.

She took out her cellphone. "So, I got a text from Genevieve's phone. I lunged at Faye's phone.

"Let me see this."

"What does it say, Kayla?" the detective yelled.

"Oh my gosh. Genevieve tried to text me. She says she is at a mall with Chris. She remembered him from when he collaborated with mom and dad."

The detective hurried to his car. "I want all of you to meet me back at the station. I will have my assistant track her phone."

We rushed over to Deebo's car. When we got back to the station, we were in a race to track Genoveve's phone. The detective took the phone to another guy in a suit. He took it and brought it to some other guy who had a bunch of computers and equipment. We kept quiet and watched them work.

"So, this will tell us their location and if they move." We watched the tracker like our lives depended on it. It did. My sister's life. It only took a few minutes.

"We got it!" The guy gave us back the phone.

"They are at the NorthPark Mall."

"Let's go. Kayla, you and your friends will drive with me. I want the rest of you in the other car." Everybody obeyed him like he was our boss.

An hour later we got to the NorthPark Mall. We parked in the garage. I opened the passenger side of the back seat, and the detective got out and closed it back.

"I need you to stay in the car."

"Wait a minute. No, I must go with you," I yelled.

"I need you to stay here just in case you see your sister with Chris. We need eyes inside and outside," he added.

"Okay, I will wait outside." I understood the assignment. What he said made sense to me. If Chris comes out of the mall, I will be able to see him. I sat down in the car with Danny, Deebo, and Kelly.

"If you see him, call me immediately." I nodded. The detective and the other police officers rushed into the mall entrance from the garage. I remained in the car sitting in the back seat while I did nothing to save my sister. Danny and Deebo sat up front.

"I do not know how you can just sit so calmly. I am itchy and fidgety." The restlessness I felt was beginning to drive me insane.

"Come on Kayla, we must do what Shims says. We cannot interfere with the investigation. We are not the police officers," Deebo explained.

"I know that. I just feel like we could be doing something while we wait," I added.

"We can. Do you know if Chris has social media? One of the main reasons criminals get caught is because they cannot stop bragging on the Internet about the things they do," Faye explained.

"You are right. I can check to see if he has an Instagram or Snapchat." I pulled out my phone and started searching. Then I realized something.

"I forgot his real name. Remember, Shims said his name is not Chris." I sat back in the seat. My head got flooded with zero ideas to help. I turned my head to the window and stared at the stores in my view. I saw a guy with a girl walking. She walked away from the guy. She looked unhappy. As I continued to watch this couple, I noticed a familiarity.

"Oh my gosh. That is them." I pointed. A weird sensation ran through my body.

"What are you talking about?" Danny turned to me in the car. I watched the couple get closer in view.

"It is them," I whispered. My sister looked ragged and worn.

"Call the detective now!" Deebo yelled. I hit the detective's name on my phone.

"Detective!"

"Do you see them?"

"Yes, we do. They are walking toward us." I kept my eyes on them like a radar. I could hear the detective calling my name. I stopped talking to him because I did not want to lose focus.

Chris and Genevieve were standing on the curb like they were waiting for something. I knew staying in the car was no longer an option and that I had to do something now. I slowly opened the back door and walked out.

"Kayla! Kayla! Shit! Come on, man, we must follow her," Deebo yelled at Danny. I hid behind a building so that my sister would not see me. I did not want my sister to see me because then she would yell my name. I stayed hidden until I could not. I jumped out from behind the building.

"Chris! Please let her go." His face turned white.

"How did you find me?" He looked at my sister.

"Don't look at me—I am just as curious as to how she found us. I am glad though." My sister was fine. She was still able to be humorous after everything.

"The police are here. They know everything that you did. Just let her go. You can take me instead." My sister looked at me with worried eyes.

"Wow. I like your offer. I might take you up on that. What do you think? Do you think I should take your sister instead?" He smirked. My sister held her head down.

"Let her go. She has nothing to do with whatever you want or are after. I do not know what you want, but I can be more helpful to you than she can." I stared at him as the tension built up in me.

"All right. Let's do it. Walk toward me slowly and we can do the swap."

"Kayla, what are you doing?" exclaimed Deebo as he watched.

"Kayla, this is ridiculous!" Danny echoed. I walked until I was face close to Chris.

"Come over here Genoveve, it is okay." Deebo called my sister to run to him. I sighed and took a deep breath. I was relieved.

"Please take her to the police officers," I demanded. Deebo nodded and took my sister to safety. Danny did not move. His eyes pierced Chris's.

"Okay, well, let's go, Kayla. A deal is a deal." I began to walk to him.

"Chris! I cannot let you go with Kayla. We have this mall surrounded. You will not get far. Give it up." The detective popped up out of nowhere. Chris smiled.

"Detective, how nice of you to come. Kayla made a deal with me. She must come with me now. I will let you know when we get to where we need to get to safely. I promise." Chris pulled out a gun and pointed it at my head. He grabbed my hand. "Let's go, hon."

The detective brought his barrier down. I followed Chris to a car that pulled up. We got in the car.

"I want all my units to follow this piece of shit. Get the plates and run them. He thinks he is disappearing, but he is not." Detective Shims turned around and walked back to his car where Genoveve and Deebo were standing. I watched my sister and my friends from the window.

I sat on the passenger side. Chris was on his phone, and then it hit me that he had put the gun down. I did not want to touch it, so I had another idea in mind.

"Give me a few seconds, dear, and we will be on our way," he whispered.

"Where are we going?" I asked.

"That is none of your business, but if you must know, we will be going to a beautiful, warm location. You will love it."

I shook my head. I thought about just talking to him to distract him so I could make my move. Then he got off the phone and started the car.

Do something, I said to myself. I turned slowly and touched the door handle and grabbed it. I turned the handle and realized it was unlocked. I ran out of the car and ran as fast as I could.

"Shit. You bitch! I will find you!"

As I ran for my life, I heard the car start and the sound of the car driving got louder in my direction. I tried to pull my phone from my pocket, but I could not grasp it while I was running. His car got up to me and I wasted time and in every direction I could to prevent him from running me down. The sound of the car shook the hell out of me, and I knew I had to run into a store or something. The car got closer and closer until the headlights shined right through my body.

I stopped running. I ran out of gas. I bent down with my hands on my knees. I breathed in and out for several seconds. When I got back my strength, it was too late. The car stood right in front of me. He revved the gas pedal. The tears fell like a waterfall. I was facing death. My body weakened with fear as I watched my life end in this scary situation. He drove the car slowly toward me. I backed up with my arms shielding my eyes from the headlights. I backed into the wall. Then he came forward with the car closer to me. My heart stopped beating.

This is it, I thought. *I am going to die.* When the car touched my stomach area, another car came out of nowhere heading in next to Chris's car. A man ran out of the car and ran up to Chris's car. The detective got to Chris's at the driver's side and pulled out a gun. He sprayed the driver's side until he saw Chris's head drop. The blood splattered on the window like a paint job. The car revved up and the car came at me at full speed. As I saw my death happening, a huge sweep and my body was lifted and thrown against the ground. It was Deebo. He grabbed me at the last minute. The car crashed into the wall. The detective ran up to me.

"Are you okay?" I laid on the floor on top of Deebo. He was bruised. He had smoke soot all over him. I covered his body with all of mine.

"Yes, I am okay." I had trouble getting up and walking.

"I saved your life. Do not forget that," Deebo said softly. His body was buried with all the broken concrete from the crash.

"I am sorry. I stopped you from breathing," I said with a laugh. I heard footsteps running toward me.

"Kayla! Wow, you were on top of Deebo." I sat up with a heavy head. She bent her body down to hug me.

"I'm glad you're safe," Genoveve commented. I smiled. The detective drove me and Deebo to the hospital to make sure we did not have any broken bones. When Deebo grabbed me, his body slammed hard onto the pavement. The nurse put me in a bed and took me to a room. Deebo was right next to me in another bed. Kelly, Faye, Danny, Genoveve, and Detective Shims stared at us.

"The nurse is going to make sure the both of you are okay."

"I should arrest you." The detective's eyes pierced into my head.

"Come on, Shims, she was trying to save her sister. Anyone would do the same," Deebo added, lifting his head from the pillow.

"Well, then you deal with her. One of these days she is going to get all of you killed. If it were not for your trade offer, your sister would not have made it out alive." The detective raised his eyebrows. "You saved your sister's life." Genoveve smiled and hugged me.

"I can't believe I missed all of this action," Faye said.

"Yeah, where were you?" I asked.

"I was told by this guy here to stay at the station. She pointed to the detective.

"Kayla, you are a ninja girl. Eres una ninja." The room filled with laughter. The nurse came in because we were having too much fun.

"Okay, we must break this up. These two need to get some rest. We will take some tests to make sure you are okay. When the results come in, you can leave if it shows you are in good health."

"Get some rest, kids." I waved bye.

"See you later?" Deebo waved.

After everybody left, two hours passed, and the nurse came in with a trolley. She carried two trays filled with food.

"Steak and potatoes are not bad," Deebo commented.

"You have to eat to get your strength up." I sat up and pulled the tray close to me to pick up my food. The aroma of the steak went straight to my nostrils. I poked into it. The half-red, half-brown texture was tempting. The potatoes were firmly cooked and sauteed with onions and paired with vegetables. The food was great, but I could not eat. Deebo on the other hand ate like it was Christmas dinner.

"Why are you not eating?" he asked. I looked over at him.

"For some reason I do not have an appetite. Deebo, I am so sorry for choosing a stranger over you." I looked at him.

"It's okay, Kayla. He was a con artist. He played you." He took one more bite of his steak and pushed the tray to the side.

"You can have mine if you want." I picked up my tray and handed it to him.

"Now I've lost my appetite," he added. He took the tray and put it on top of his.

I am not angry with you anymore, Kayla that was in the beginning. After I realized what we were dealing with, I knew it was not your fault. You thought this guy was in love with you. He showed you things that I did not. That was my fault. He draws you near to him with his lies. I am not going to punish you for it," he confessed. I took a deep breath. I was happy. The nurse came in.

"Well, only one of you was hungry. Who was it?" Deebo raised his hand. "Did you try?" I shook my head.

"I will take these and come back in the morning with breakfast. You will have better luck then. Good-night! She walked out into the hallway with the tray of food. I got up to use the bathroom. I took a shower. When I got back, Deebo was not in the room. I sat on my bed putting lotion on. My cellphone rang. I saw my sister's face on my screen.

"Hey you. How are you feeling?" I asked.

"I should be asking you that. Have you eaten yet?" I sighed. She sounded like herself. I cannot wait to get out of here.

"I did not have an appetite, but the nurse will be bringing in breakfast tomorrow."

"Oh good. Thank you for saving my life. I love you very much. You are the best sister."

I smiled. "I love you too. I want you to live with me in Rockwall." She made a humming sound.

"Okay, I would love to. When do I move in?"

"Whenever you want. I do not want to boss you around. I just want you to have the life that you deserve. We are all we got now. We must protect each other."

"Can I move at the end of the month? I have a lot of things that I need to do first," she added.

"Sure. I love you back, kiddo." She gave me a little laugh. Her smile shone through the phone. I hit the end call button. My heart was beginning to feel happy again.

I got back in the bed and pulled the covers over my legs. I grabbed the remote to put on the television. Deebo walked in.

"Where did you go?" I asked.

"I went to the gym and then showered."

"There is a gym in here?" I pointed.

"Yea. It is for people in rehab. Do you need the light?" he asked.

"No, you can take it off." He hit the switch that was by his bedside.

"I want to ask you a question." He took off his shirt and laid it on the bed. He sat on his bed, putting on another shirt. I waited for him to get emotional. I sat up. He lay on his bed with one hand behind his head, looking up at the ceiling.

"How do you feel about me?" I did not see that coming. He wants to know how I feel. Ouch. I put my body in the same position. I looked up at the ceiling. I took a deep breath.

"I have feelings for you. I like you a lot," I confessed. He turned toward me. He got off the bed and came over to my bed.

"Move over," he said softly. The two of us lay on one bed. It was a twin bed, so the space was tight. I did not mind at all. I was still hot for Deebo. My heart never beats faster. He turned to me, so we were face to face.

"I never stopped loving you, Kayla. I always wanted you, but I did not want to put my feelings on the table. We were young when we met."

My eyes widened. "Are you saying what you are saying?"

He turned back to the ceiling. "Yes. I fell in deep the first day I met you at the shelter. I had to keep it to myself because you were a mean bitch."

I looked at him with a grin. "What! I am not mean. I was a little. I was new at the time. I was fresh off leaving my home," I added.

"Even though we slept together a few times, I did tell you how I felt. I did it my way. I know you wanted me to show you more like Chris did." I raised my eyebrows. Deebo is finally opening to me. I did not know how to feel now. His hand intertwined with mine. After our discussion, we closed our eyes.

The next morning the nurse came in with breakfast. The smell of eggs, bacon, and pancakes soothed my senses. "Good morning. I hope you had a good rest. It looks like you had company," she said with a smirk, looking over at Deebo's side.

"Thank you. I feel very hungry today." I took my tray and put it over on my side. I went into the bathroom to brush my teeth. Deebo came into the room while the nurse was leaving with the empty trolley.

"Where were you?" she asked.

"At the gym if you must know." He grinned.

"Hey. How did you sleep?" He poked his head in the bathroom. I had a great sleep. I spit some of the toothpaste out of my mouth. I washed it out with water and dried my mouth and hands with the hand towel that was hanging up on the rack.

"I'm hungry." I sat down in front of the tray. After we ate breakfast, Danny, Kelly, and Faye entered our room.

"How was last night?" Danny asked, looking at the two of us like we were guilty of something.

"Sorry but doing it in the hospital is not my idea of romance," Deebo responded.

"I can't disagree with you on that one." I got up and went back into the bathroom with my clothes.

"What happens now?" Faye yelled through the door. I came out to answer her. I zipped up my jeans.

"We go back home and try to live our lives. Where is my sister, by the way?"

"Shims dropped her off at your aunt's house. She has school," Faye commented.

"Good. I need Genoveve to live her life with some form of normalcy. It breaks my heart that she no longer has parents to take care of her," I said sympathetically.

Kelly came over to me. "She has you. She always had you, and now you can be her legal guardian."

"Yes, you are right."

"I will get your results from the nurse so that you can get out of here," Kelly said.

Our test results declared us healthy. An hour later, me and Deebo were free to go. When we got home, I called the housekeeper to come clean our house. It was a mess. Later, that day we spent time together in the movie room.

"What do we want to watch? I do not want to see anything in the horror genre." Faye was going through the streaming services with the remote. We were stretched out on our gray L-shaped sectional. We had popcorn and sodas all over the room. Our movie room mirrored the movie theaters we go to. As we got settled, the doorbell rang. I called out for our housekeeper to get it. A few seconds later, Detective Shims walked in.

"Well, I see you guys are back to normal." He glanced at the room, nodding his head.

"I am glad the courts gave you your parents' assets. You deserve it you have been through it."

"Do you want to join us?" I asked. I was popping popcorn in my mouth with a few falling over my shirt.

"Thanks for the invite, but I have to get back to work."

"Detective, we got the bad guys. You can take a day off," Deebo chimed in.

"I must get back to work to keep you teens safe and out of trouble. Hopefully, you will do that." He walked out of the room.

"Bye," I yelled.

We watched movies until the early morning. I glanced at my friends. They fell asleep. I could not sleep. I thought about how they looked out for me and how we worked together to help each other. I helped save my friends from kidnapping. I helped the detective solve the murders of my boss and the landlord. I saved my sister from a sociopath, and I solved the murder of my parents. I thought that I was in love with two guys. The truth is that now I know that my heart belonged to Deebo.

Although I want to be with him, I owe it to myself to give myself time to think about us. I realized that I wanted to live my life the right way. No more crime. No more lying to the guy I love. I wanted us to do things honestly. Forney is now a safe place for the time being. I imagined it would not last long. There will be more bad guys to chase and more kidnappings to solve. More murders, and more bad intentions.